The Lasso

By Dave Bair

Chapter 1

Eureka, Montana, is the type of place that just barely shows up on a map. With a population of approximately 1,100, it's just about as small as a small town can get these days. Being located just nine miles from the Canadian border, it's a very picturesque place, with pine trees reaching up to the sky everywhere you look. The Rocky Mountains are in every direction, many of them snow-capped all year round. Eureka is surrounded by mountains, rivers, and a number of small lakes that provide an abundance of activities all year round.

It is nestled right smack-dab in the middle of God's country. Absolute beauty is a great way to describe the landscape. Eureka happens to be located just to the west of Glacier National Park. People from all over the country roll through Eureka while taking in the sights during their summer vacation. Tourists bring in plenty of money during the summer months for businesses to stay afloat during the winter.

To most people, Eureka is a peaceful town. Not a lot of crime and everyone knows everyone for sure. Eureka has a little bit of everything. You won't find McDonald's or Burger King up there. You can forget about finding any franchise altogether. It's a town of privately owned businesses that harmonize together in the summer months and are a friendly sort of competitive in the winter months. What you will find in Eureka is a town filled with business owners who take pride in their businesses and shops of all sorts doing what they do.

Beeman's is the butcher shop, hands down the best place to get your meat in most of Montana. People come from all around to look over Beeman's vast selection and top-quality meat. Beef, poultry, and the native meats like deer, elk, and buffalo are the best you'll ever get. If you want a coffee or a latte, then you might stroll into Café Jax. Café Jax has everything a main-stream coffee franchise does at one-third the price and tastes better too!

If pizza is your thing, Valley Pizza isn't a bad choice. Valley Pizza boasts over one hundred different toppings available for your pizza, and they have a gargantuan mega twenty-four-inch pie with up to twenty-four toppings on a double crust. It's a pizza lover's haven! Just in need of a good watering hole? Of course, there are a couple of saloons in town to keep your whistle wet. Eureka has a couple of hotels, and a B and B called the Buck Stops Here. Hell, there's even a small casino.

That being said, a small town really doesn't need or even *want* any other businesses to appear, especially another saloon. Business owners in small towns are a bit territorial, you might say. Based on the law of averages, if you own the only donut shop in a small town and a second donut shop opens up, the amount of business you do just got cut in half. This is a free-enterprise country; no one is going to tell you that you can't open up a business, but in a small town, it might be tough to get it off the ground, especially if your customers are loyal to someone else.

None of the hurdles that lay ahead seemed to bother Jesse. With his faithful companion, Louie, riding shotgun, California was behind them and "Eureka or Bust" was his mindset. Nothing was going to stop him from living his dream.

Chapter 2

On the edge of Eureka there was a six-acre lot that had a wooden For Sale sign posted on it. The rusty barbed wire fencing was in shambles with most of the posts rotting off at ground level. There was an unidentifiable pile of rubbish a couple of hundred feet from the road that was once some sort of building. The only inhabitants now were rodents and termites, and it appears to have been that way for quite some time. Between the for-sale sign and rubble, you could barely make out the outline of what looked to have been a parking lot. The available land behind the building looked to be plenty big enough for future expansion. It was probably big enough to build a drive-in movie.

Right now, it was nothing more than a field and rubbish. However, if you put a business here, it would be the first place you saw as you came into town, and if you did it right, you could position a sign that would be visible from the highway. *This is the perfect spot*, Jesse thought to himself as he imagined his new business, *"The Lasso"* erected in the field.

The phone number on the for-sale sign was 406-555-7290. "Call Desi" was printed directly below the number. On the second ring, the phone was answered by a woman.

"Hello, this is Desi."

"Hi, Desi, my name is Jesse Buck, and I'd like to talk with you about the six-acre lot that's for sale here on…"

"Yes, Mr. Buck" The woman immediately interrupted. "I know the property you're talking about. When would you like to meet?"

Almost stunned with the aggressive response, Jesse didn't really know quite how to answer.

"Well, I'm at the property now," he started to reply. "Where is your—"

"Perfect!" Desi interrupted again. "I'll be there in less than ten minutes," she said in a hurry and hung up.

Pondering the conversation, he just had with Desi, Jesse leaned against the front of his rainforest green Chevrolet Silverado and waited. Jesse had no real plans for the day as he'd just arrived in town. Being in his early forties and needing a fresh start, it was time to live a quieter life; and he figured Eureka, Montana, was the place to do it. He literally woke up a few days ago, bought a new pickup, put his dog in the front seat, and hit the road. Being divorced and not having any children, it was pretty easy to up and leave. Being financially secure didn't hurt either.

True to her word in less than ten minutes, a black Dodge Durango Citadel pulled off the side of the road and stopped a few feet from where Jesse was leaning against his truck. A beautiful long blonde-haired woman stepped out and approached him. She was wearing a silk blouse that was untucked, a tight-fitting pair of designer jeans, and red boots. Her silk blouse accented her figure as she walked toward him. Her blue eyes sparkled, and her smile was amazing.

Jesse picked up on the massive diamond ring on her left hand and immediately knew she was off-limits. Jesse's father told him as a young boy, "Never mess with another man's woman," and he wasn't about to start. Messing with another man's woman is a great way to get yourself in trouble or even killed. Only an idiot would do something like that.

"Hi, Desi?" Jesse asked, reaching out to shake hands.

"You must be Mr. Buck," she replied with a smile and receiving handshake. "What can I tell you about the property? What do you want to do with it?" Before Jesse could say a word, out came the real question Desi was asking. "You're not from around here, are you?"

Jesse replied, almost laughing, "No, I'm not from around here. Just rolled into town. Is it that obvious?"

"I've just never seen you before. Eureka's not a very big place, and the California tags on your pickup are a dead giveaway."

Desi had a sparkle in her eyes that was as brilliant as the sparkle in her ring. Her husband was a lucky man, Jesse thought to himself as he admired God's creation.

"Three hundred sixty-nine thousand dollars buys you the lot, complete with a building permit. It's been for sale for so long that zoning has been lifted—you can basically do whatever you want, within reason." Desi talked more about how it could be a bed and breakfast or restaurant or any number of other businesses before she asked Jesse, "What were you thinking about doing with the property?"

"Well," Jesse started with a sigh, "I've always wanted a saloon and I figure this would make an ideal location. The lot is perfect!"

"A saloon?" Desi asked with deep question.

"Yea, a saloon," Jesse said sharply, looking straight into the realtor's eyes.

"Let me save you some time," Desi started. "There are already three saloons in town, we don't really need another one. Besides, the owner of the property isn't going to sell it to you if he knows you're planning on putting a saloon here."

"Why's that?" Jesse asked with the same sharp tone, crossing his arms across his chest. "Thought you said there was no zoning, and I could basically do whatever I wanted."

"Mr. Buck," Desi spoke softly as she stepped toward Jesse, "I'm not trying to piss you off here. Small towns are a little different from the big city in which you came from. I'm telling you, if the owner of the property doesn't want another saloon in town, there isn't going to be one. The property comes with building permits for *anything* other than a saloon or a bar. It is what it is."

"Desi, relax, you're not pissing me off. I'm just asking questions," Jesse assured her.

Jesse could tell that Desi knew what she was talking about but had a hard time with the whole "it is what it is" comment. His unspoken thought was he'd do whatever he wanted, this is America, but the little voice in his head convinced him to keep his mouth shut, at least for a moment. If he couldn't build his dream here, he needed to get back on the road. He didn't want to leave; this location was absolutely perfect. After a moment of pondering, he decided he was either not asking enough questions or, even more so, he was not asking the right questions.

"Desi," Jesse asked, looking out into the field, "I'm having a hard time connecting the dots here, and I'm hoping you can help me out. Who is the owner, and may I have a conversation with him?"

"The owner of the property is Jack Beaver, and he wishes to talk to no one," Desi answered, speaking with a calm voice.

"Can you tell me why the owner, Mr. Beaver, is so dead set against another saloon in this town?" Jesse fired off the question, with his blood boiling underneath; you'd never know it on the surface, but Jesse was breathing deeply trying not to lose his cool.

"Actually, Mr. Buck," Desi replied with confidence, "I can."

Now we're getting somewhere, Jesse thought to himself as words started to free-fall from Desi's lips. Jesse had asked the right question, or one of them at least. The owner of the other three saloons in town was a guy named Jack Beaver. Jack didn't want the land but didn't want another saloon in town because that would create competition for him. He currently has the monopoly on saloons in town, and he wanted to keep it that way—plain and simple. Desi went on and on about Jack Beaver; she even told Jesse what he looked like.

Jack Beaver was described as an arrogant fellow that stands six feet four inches tall and carried a belly that hung over his belt buckle. He had an unkempt beard that covered his mouth, and his eyes were dark and sunken into his weathered face. The dirty brown cowboy hat that he wore never left his head. It was old and worn, matching his dirty brown boots perfectly. His boots wore spurs that had the letters "JB" engraved on both sides, which also matched the "JB" engraved on his hidden belt buckle. He only ever dressed in red flannel shirts and dark-colored jeans. Jack looked a mess even on his best days, even on Sunday.

"Desi," Jesse finally interrupted, "back up a minute. Are you telling me I can't have a business here that serves alcohol?"

"No, Mr. Buck, not at all," Desi replied with the utmost sincerity. "You just can't have a saloon here."

Jesse continued questioning the realtor. "What about a restaurant, would that be okay? Can I build a restaurant that serves beer, wine, and liquor?"

"Sure Mr. Buck, that'd be just fine," Desi said with enthusiasm.

"Desi, let me ask you this. What's the difference between a saloon that serves food and a restaurant that serves alcohol?"

"Well, Mr. Buck, that's easy," Desi explained. "A saloon can have revenue of 100 percent alcohol sales—after all, it's a saloon. You don't have to serve food whereas a restaurant's alcohol sales can only be a maximum of 50 percent of your total revenue."

Nothing more than a technicality, Jesse thought to himself. He could live with that. He'd have to alter what he had in mind a little, but he could certainly work food into the overall scheme of his dream. In fact, maybe, just maybe, he could use it to his advantage. At this point in time, it was a hurdle, but certainly not one that couldn't be overcome.

It would take some additional planning and some reconfiguring, he thought to himself, but it could be done. Without a doubt, it could be done.

"Desi," Jesse asked, "just out of curiosity, what did this place used to be, and why is Jack selling it?"

"That's kind of a loaded question, Mr. Buck," Desi replied cautiously, almost as if she were trying to avoid answering at all.

"I've got time," Jesse insisted.

"C'mon then, walk with me." Desi nodded her head and started walking through the knee-high grass toward the pile of rubbish.

"Hang on, let me get a friend," Jesse told her as he turned around and headed back toward his truck.

Jesse went to the door of his truck and let his dog Louie out of the cab. Louie was a miniature Australian shepherd that had been with Jesse through a lot of tough times; he was the epitome of man's best friend. Louie was a small twenty-five-pound black tri, but he had a fifty-pound heart. He was smart, loyal, and alert. At twelve years old, he still had a lot of puppy left in him.

Louie launched himself out of the pickup and pounced into the knee-deep foliage like a gazelle. The only way you could see him was when his head popped over the top of the foliage or by the weeds and grass parting as he made his way through them. Jesse and Louie made their way to Desi, and the story began.

"Back in the early 1990s, when the economy was slow, Jack Beaver's uncle, Jude Beaver, died and left him a 2,800-acre cattle ranch. Jude owned the cattle ranch and sold his cattle at a cattle auction owned by a local man named Tim Johnson. This property was the cattle auction. The pile of rubbish over there was a barn that was used as the auction house."

Jesse listened very carefully to every word that Desi said. She pointed to the rubbish pile and talked about how the weeds weren't really weeds at all; it was native grass that had been here since before Columbus. The native grass was ideal for premium cattle to graze on while they waited to be bought and sold.

"Jack Beaver now had the cattle ranch and wanted to buy the auction from Tim. Tim didn't want to sell the auction to Jack—it just wasn't for sale. Being this is, or was, the only cattle auction around and that the two men, Jack and Tim, apparently couldn't work together, Jack Beaver decided to sell off his herd to a competitor under two conditions.

"The first condition was the rancher had to use a different auction to sell the cattle, and the second condition was that Jack had the right to buy back 20 percent of the cattle if done so within twenty-four months of the sale."

"Desi, stop a moment," Jesse interrupted. "So where does Jack sell his cattle now?" he asked in disbelief.

"Pay attention," Desi said, smiling as the story continued.

"Jude, now Jack was not only Tim's biggest customer, but one of only a few. With the alleged liquidation of the cattle ranch, the cattle auction went into foreclosure. Tim Johnson had pulled out equity on the auction to build a home down the road a piece and now couldn't pay the note. Now he couldn't pay the note on the cattle auction or the note on the new home.

"When the land was being auctioned off, Jack Beaver raised the price of the highest bidder, primarily to spite Tim Johnson, to prove to Tim that the cattle auction was indeed for sale and that he was going to buy it at all costs. You with me?" Desi asked.

"Yea, I think so," Jesse replied cautiously. "Where does Jack sell his cattle now?"

"I'm getting there," Desi said with a sigh. "Jack Beaver now had a cattle ranch and a cattle auction with no cattle. Because it took longer than twenty-four months, the cattle rancher who bought Jack's cattle wasn't obligated to sell any back. So, Jack Beaver turned the 2,800-acre cattle ranch into a 2,800-acre Christmas tree farm and let the cattle auction rot.

"This infuriated Tim Johnson. Tim Johnson had lost everything out of spite from another man. With no cattle auction and no house, no source of income, Tim had hit rock bottom. He bought the biggest bottle of booze he could find one night, drank the whole thing, broke into the abandoned cattle auction, and hung himself. It was weeks before they found him there. It was tragic." Desi had stopped talking and was waiting for some sort of response from her new client.

"That's wow, some story," Jesse said in disbelief. "Let me see if I have all this sorted out in my head correctly. So now that Jack has won the war, he has no need for the property, right? No one in town wants to buy it because Old Man Johnson hung himself in there, right?" Jesse asked for clarification. "Jack's ready to dump it, but he's asking more than it's worth, right?"

"Basically, that's about it," Desi agreed. "He just wants his money out of it. As long as it's not a saloon, whoever wants to pay for it can have it."

Jesse stood there and recapped the situation in his head one more time. *This story isn't over*, he thought to himself.

There is no way the story can possibly be over. A few long minutes of silence passed before Jesse made a decision.

"I'll take it at $369,000, with the building permit for a restaurant, must be able to obtain a liquor license or the deal is off. Please ask your client if cash is okay."

Desi couldn't believe her ears. They shook hands and started back to their vehicles.

"Hey, Desi," Jesse asked as they were walking through the grass.

"Yes, Mr. Buck?" Desi answered, almost giddy.

"Okay, you can call me Jesse, we're past the Mr. Buck thing." Desi nodded with an okay. "I'm going to need a place to call home. Can you help me with that too?"

"Actually, Mr. Buck, ah—Jesse, I most certainly can."

Chapter 3

Desi led the way back to her office. It was a small five-hundred square-foot office in the middle of town. Pictures of cabins with mountain views covered the walls. Custom homes on acreage with rivers running through them, sky from horizon to horizon—the photos were all amazing. There were also photos of Yellowstone and the Grand Tetons.

"My main office is in Kalispell," Desi said, finally breaking the silence while Jesse's eyes still wandered the walls. "This is just a satellite office for me. Mountain Country Cribs is the name of my company. You can have a seat here." She pointed to a rocking chair made out of deer and elk antlers. Jesse paused and stared at the chair.

"Is it safe?"

"Of course, it is," Desi replied, laughing lightly.

"It's comfy too."

"Let's keep this simple," Jesse started as he slowly sat down in the rather bizarre chair. "I'd like to find a few acres with some water and not many neighbors." Desi wasted no time jumping on the computer.

"What about house size? Beds? Baths? Budget?" Desi asked. After a brief conversation going over needs and wants, Desi had a list of thirteen different places to look at. Four of these places were crossed off the list right away for being too far from town, and two more places were just land. That left seven to check out.

"You're right," Jesse said. "It really is comfy." Referring to the chair he'd been occupying. "I'm actually surprised at how comfy it is," he said, admiring it more and more as he climbed to his feet.

"I can look at as many of these as you want to today," Desi said, getting back to business. "After that, it's going to be a couple of days before I can make it back up here. How does that sound?" Desi asked. Jesse stood there staring at the floor as if he never heard a thing. "Mr. Buck, are you okay?" Desi was not a very patient woman, and it seemed as if her client just locked up mentally.

"I have my fifth wheel set up at Blue Mountain," Jesse talked slowly in a soft voice, never looking up away from his focus on the floor. "They know I'll need to set up there for thirty to forty-five days until I find a place and get it closed. You do what you've got to do." Finally, in normal conversation, Jesse looked up at Desi. "I'd say let's look at two or three of these that are in the direction you're heading, and we can go from there."

"Let's go," Desi said, smiling and nodding her head. "You can follow me," she continued as they headed out the door.

Less than two hours passed as Desi drove the Montana hills with Jesse following. Some of the places the two stopped at Jesse didn't spend more than thirty seconds at and wanted to leave. In less than two hours, the list was exhausted. "Nope, not it," was the only feedback that Jesse could give. Desi was beyond frustrated. Her initial thought was to just call it quits for the day; however, she knew in her heart that when the right place was found, it'd be a quick sale and more than likely a cash sale! She kept driving, now backtracking toward town a bit. Jesse just followed her, wondering if she knew where she was going and what she was doing.

"Well, we can always sleep in the truck if we get lost, can't we, Louie!" Jesse said as he reached over and scratched Louie between the ears.

A few minutes later, Desi signaled with her blinker and turned onto a dirt road.

"Rock Creek Road," Jesse said softly to himself, talking out loud. "Don't remember this one in the list." The drive down the dirt road was slow as Jesse followed in the cloud of dust kicked up by Desi's Durango. They passed a small run-down horse barn on the right; there was a meadow followed by mountains to the left. The dirt road turned out to be a substantially long driveway instead of a road at all.

As the two cars approached the end of the driveway, a small log house appeared. Desi pulled up and stopped, not getting out of her car. Jesse pulled up next to her. He shut off the Silverado and stepped out, leaving the door open for Louie to follow. Mesmerized by the scenery, Jesse walked slowly and took it all in. Desi, now standing by the front of her Durango, just watched from afar to see how Jesse was going to take to the place.

There stood a small three-story house made of log. It couldn't have been more than 2,600 square feet or so if he had to guess. It had a green metal roof that looked to have been fairly new. Behind the house was a lake that glistened in the afternoon sun. To the left was a small rickety pier with two canoes lying on it. Up the shore from the pier was a log cabin that wore a covered porch, it also had a green metal roof.

Jesse walked slowly toward the back of the house to get a better look. On his way, he noted two large solar panels on a pole facing direct sunlight. *This house must be ecofriendly*, he thought to himself as he made his way to the back. There was a large deck that ran the entire length of the house and up the other side. The deck had expansive views of the surrounding area and water. With Louie by his side, Jesse stepped onto the deck and walked over to the railing.

The wood was painted dark red and was in great shape. The two-board railing was sturdy and didn't block any of the magnificent view. Jesse leaned on the middle of the railing and stared over the water. When he finally turned around to look at the back of the house, he saw a wall of glass that overlooked the deck and the lake.

There was a stone chimney protruding from the roof and a pair of French doors that would let in the night air. He saw himself fishing in the lake and walking around it with his faithful companion. Louie sat next to Jesse, and they both took in the sight. This place was amazing. Jesse didn't care what the price was; he knew at that very moment he had found his new home.

"Thank you, God, for blessing me with this amazing property," Jesse said softly, looking up to the sky.

"Come again?" Desi nearly yelled, stepping onto the deck from inside. She pushed the French doors open. As they swung out over the deck, she made a grand entrance with her arms in the air and smiling from ear to ear.

"Welcome to tranquility!" she said, sending an echo across the lake. "Was that a 'yes, I love it' or a 'nope, not it I heard you say?" Her boots echoed across the lake with every step as she crossed the deck. She stopped next to Jesse and crossed her arms as she looked over the water.

"It's pretty here, isn't it?"

"It's heaven," Jesse whispered back as he continued to take it all in.

Pines surrounded the lake. There was about thirty feet of lush green grassy area from the edge of the lake to the tree line, maybe up to fifty feet in some places. There wasn't another house in sight. Nothing—just land, grass, and lake. As a light breeze blew from the sky, you could hear the pines whispering to each other. A pair of loons swam together along the shoreline, never paying any mind to the strangers on the deck watching them.

A rustle in the distance caused everyone to look up and see a moose approaching for a drink on the shoreline across the lake from the deck. With zero hesitation, Louie launched himself off the deck and started to make his way around the lake to greet the unknown animal with his ferocious bark.

"There he goes, fast and fearless," Jesse said, watching his dog intently.

"He's a lot braver than I thought," Desi said with a laugh. "Should we be worried?" They watched Louie make awesome time running around the lake at full speed.

"I don't think so," Jesse said, watching with caution. Louie ran right up to the moose and barked at it a couple of times, not sure what to make of the enormous creature. The moose reared its mighty head and snorted at the Aussie. That was all it took for Louie to do an about-face and head back to the safety of his master at full speed.

"I guess that settles that," Jesse said. The two chuckled together as Louie had made his presence known and hurried back.

"So, tell me, Desi, what's the deal with this place?" Jesse asked with great question, never looking away from the water. "This seems a little too good to be true."

"C'mon," Desi said with her already infamous head nod. "Walk with me. You look, I'll talk." She stepped toward the door; Jesse followed. Desi talked as they walked through the inside of the home. Jesse tuned her out as he envisioned himself living at the lakefront house. Jesse didn't hear a word she said as she led the way through the home. The house boasted a clerestory in the main room and a loft above. A couple of bedrooms and a couple of bathrooms, it was a cute place that would work; a little remodeling to do, but it felt like home.

To Jesse, the house didn't matter; it was the land and the privacy that was the deal maker. This was close enough to town that he could get there in a hurry if he needed to and far enough away that no one would come looking for him. It was perfect.

"What's the asking price?" Jesse interrupted without even visiting the lower level yet.

"Four hundred thirty-nine thousand dollars," Desi replied, almost insulted that she hadn't finished her tour of the home.

"Done," Jesse said sharply. "I'll take it. This is the house, and I want the six acres at the edge of town. I'll be paying cash for both. When can we do the paperwork? Better yet, how fast can we close?"

Chapter 4

Jesse wasted no time getting things done. In less than two days, both properties were his with deeds in hand. In less than a week after that, construction crews went to work immediately building a custom garage near his home by the lake. Sixty-by-one-hundred foot with twenty-foot-high ceilings, temperature-controlled, the whole nine yards. A second contractor was frantically building the new restaurant on the edge of town, and yet a third contractor was "freshening up" the inside of the home. Jesse was in his element. Overseeing all three projects simultaneously, he didn't miss a beat. He had a mental timetable that needed to be met. A schedule for getting everything done that was tight against the clock with no margin for error or delay.

Some of Jesse's background is in construction and project management. He used to run three job sites at the same time—problem-free back in the early 2000s when the economy was booming. Jesse is the kind of guy that had a backup plan for the backup plan even if it was never needed. He is the kind of guy that is very resourceful and thinks outside the box. In Jesse's mind, problems don't really exist. There are only situations and resolutions. How you handle any situation, directly and indirectly, determines the outcome or, in this case, his own personal projects. The key is to come up with the best solution at the time for the given situation; however, the challenge is knowing what all of your possible options and potential outcomes are for every potential scenario.

Somewhere, someone has already had the same thing happen; the question becomes who was it and how did they resolve it. A good project manager will research this and be prepared if that situation ever happens to them. When you show up to the table prepared, the end result is positive.

Townspeople were talking about the new guy in town who seemed to be fairly nice and friendly yet 'to himself' at the same time. He wasn't one to talk about his past or boast about the projects going on at the present; Jesse was in "get it done" mode. All the small talk could wait until the projects were completed.

Jesse stands about five feet eleven inches tall. He has a stocky, athletic build—certainly not a bodybuilder build. Weighing in at 225 pounds, one wouldn't think he was fat at all, even if he did tend to be carrying a few extra pounds from the holidays. His calves and forearms were larger than most, hinting that he was a hard worker when it came to tending to the land.

His chest, although not cut with muscles, was definitely muscular. His hands were like vise grips. He once tested over 400-foot pounds of grip strength in each hand. His brown hair was just starting to show a hint of gray creeping in. His green eyes told you who he was. He has a good soul and a warm heart. Jesse is the guy that is always eager to help, but not one to be taken advantage of. When provoked, he could be very intimidating even if he never raised his voice.

Jesse has a warm genuine smile. With a gap between his front teeth that he always hated, he was sure to try to keep it hidden, but every now and again, it would show. The ladies never thought twice about his imperfect smile, but it always seemed to be the one thing he would change about himself if he could. In fact, Jesse never had a problem with the ladies at all. His wolfing days were over, and his desire to be in love with the right woman was overwhelming. At forty-three years old, he is divorced with no kids. No alimony, no child support, a fresh start on life. The Lord above had blessed Jesse with a "do over," and Eureka, Montana, is where he is making it happen.

Chapter 5

The Lasso looked to be massive in size from the street, and it was. A pair of single light swinging doors in the middle of the structure led you to the inside. A rustic-looking horseshoe-shaped bar was located in the center with wagon wheel tables peppered throughout the floor. To the left were a half-dozen poker tables up front with billiard tables in the rear. A dozen dartboards covered the wall between pictures of the Wild West. To the right was a thirty-by-thirty-foot dance floor with a stage that ran the length of it at the far end.

The stage was plenty for a DJ or a band with plenty of room for even the most animated entertainers. In the far right-hand corner was a Rock-Ola CD jukebox that was wired into Bose speakers hanging from the open timber roof some twenty feet above. Not far from the jukebox up against the wall was an eighteenth-century upright grand piano that looked like it had been through a few gunfights on the outside but was totally restored on the inside. Jesse himself pulled the wooden top off the piano and put a few bullet holes in it to give it the look of the old west. A bar rail and stools were wrapped around the perimeter in sections, maximizing seating but sure to not overcrowd.

On either end of the establishment were ten-foot-wide screens that retracted from the ceiling, both with their own HD projector. These were capable of displaying Blue-Ray DVDs or the signal from the satellite out back.

Barrels full of peanuts were strategically placed throughout the establishment. Customers would be encouraged to drop the peanut shells directly onto the floor where the oil from them would naturally seal the oak planks from the foot traffic—just like they did in the old west. Most of the floor was salvaged solid oak planks from the pile of rubbish that used to occupy the field where the Lasso now sat. The bathroom signs were originally labeled "Cows" and "Bulls" in light of the grounds' previous life as a cattle auction but were later changed to "Guys" and "Gals."

Behind the scenes was a kitchen that served typical bar munchies. Wings, fries, skins, and a few specialty items were on the menu along with some comfort foods— nothing too elaborate, but top-of-the-line taste. The brewery was also in the back where Jesse hired a guy named "Bill" (as in "Wild Bill's Wicked Ale," Wild Bill is a famous brew master from the 1980s and 1990s that eventually sold his empire to Anheuser-Busch) to brew a few of the beers that were going to be on tap.

The Lasso was ready for opening night. It was a cool place. It undoubtedly had the look of an authentic saloon with a hint of modern pizazz. The kind of place Doc Holiday and Wyatt Earp would set up in if they were around. It was perfect.

There was a second story to the Lasso, which from the street was designed to resemble a brothel but was really four two-bedroom apartments that were unfinished. A four-car garage was out back that could accommodate the future tenant's needs when the apartments were completed. Right now, the apartments were nothing more than an office and a crash pad for the nights when Jesse couldn't make it home from working too late. The walls were insulated and sheet-rocked, but that was about it. Running water and heat were there too. No doors, no floor coverings, no nothing other than a desk, a queen-size bed for Jesse, and a doggie bed for Louie.

Chapter 6

The Lasso is open for business from 2:00 p.m. to midnight, Monday through Thursday, and 2:00 p.m. to 2:00 a.m. Friday and Saturday. The Lasso is closed on Sunday. Thursday night was opening night. Jesse knew with the gossip in town he was going to do well on opening night, but way underestimated the outcome. There was a line to get in most of the night, and by the time last call was announced—it was a good thing because the town of Eureka drank almost every bottle of beer in the place! The floor was covered with peanut shells and the bar was nearly empty. The kitchen had completely run out of food and Jesse's voice was a little horse from saying "Welcome to the Lasso" all night long. Jesse didn't know if this was a blessing or a curse, but he did know that he had to act fast in order to be ready for the Friday crowd!

Not a minute to rest. After the last guest had left the Lasso, the cleaning crew that Jesse had hired went right to work. Jesse went upstairs and was working on the books while the cleaners were doing their thing down below. It's now two thirty-seven Friday morning. Outside, Jesse heard the unmistakable sound of a Chevrolet Corvette pull up. Jesse has had a number of Corvettes over the years. Corvette race cars, street cars, and project cars, he's had them all.

Among his favorites, which he uses frequently as a regular driver, is a 2004 Commemorative Edition Z06. Only 2,025 of these cars were made, and less than one-half were still around. It is a beautiful car. A deep LeMans Blue in color with racing stripes over the hood, roof, and deck lid. The polished aluminum wheels added the perfect touch. It has a carbon fiber hood from the factory and was some kind of wicked fast. He knew how they sounded and could pick one out of a crowded parking lot any day.

Piquing his curiosity, he went to the window to take a look. By the time he got there, the Corvette was pulling off. A full-throttle acceleration. *Chirp* went the tires as the driver shifted into second gear. *Chirp* again in third gear, and the car sped out of sight. He could tell by the taillights it was a fifth-generation Corvette, a C5 as the car world would know it.

Probably nothing, Jesse thought to himself as he went back to his previous task of counting money and receipts.

With only a couple of hours of sleep behind him, Jesse woke with the sun shining on his face. It's now daytime, Friday morning. He needed some deliveries for food and alcohol, and he *definitely* needed some staff. Last night's skeleton crew got the job done however it was pure chaos for them all. Tonight, was going to be a busy night and daylight was burning. Jesse sat up and got his bearings. His clothes were wrinkled from sleeping in them, and he had nothing to change into. Looking over his appearance in the bathroom mirror, he wanted to get a shower and change but didn't have time to run back to his house. *Screw it*, he thought to himself. *It's a ball cap and Listerine kind of day*.

Wasting not another minute, he headed downstairs, swishing mouthwash on the way. Jesse paused when he got to the bar and looked around. The Lasso looked perfect. He was absolutely amazed at how clean the place looked. The cleaning crew, consisting of four Native American college students that lived on a local reservation, deserved a raise. Even the kitchen was spotless. Not a peanut shell on the floor. Not a napkin in the trash. The place looked as if no one had ever been there. Jesse spat out the mouthwash in the kitchen sink and headed for the door. When Jesse got to the door, he stopped and turned around looking at the interior of the Lasso. He slowly panned from left to right, taking in everything that had been accomplished and the final result.

Bam, bam, bam, someone pounded on the door, startling Jesse as he jerked around to see who was there. He opened the door to find Desi standing there with another woman. "Jesse," Desi said immediately with a smile, "you hiring?" Before Jesse could tell her yes and that he really needed some help, Desi continued.

"This is my niece Erin who needs a job. She has a degree in restaurant management, she knows how to tend bar and has lots of waiting experience, and she can start today." Erin held out her hand to shake but didn't say a word. Jesse was rather stunned; while he needed help, this wasn't exactly what he had in mind.

Jesse looked Erin over. She was an above-average-looking woman with an above-average body. Like her aunt Desi, she had blonde hair and blue eyes and a fantastic smile. She had on black stretch pants, boots, and a flannel shirt that looked to be covering a bodysuit. Erin was certainly not hard on the eyes, and truthfully, seeing her made Jesse's heart race. Erin is gorgeous, and he instantly wanted her. Other than being half Jesse's age, Erin was the woman for him.

"Come on in, ladies," Jesse finally said, backing away from the door.

"Erin," Jesse said, taking a sigh, "I do need help. I don't know how much I can pay you. I don't really need a manager, but an assistant manager might be nice. I need to hire some waiters and get food and beverages ordered and delivered for tonight. I must go to the bank to make a deposit, get home, cleaned up, and back here to open by 2:00 p.m. It's already pushing eight o'clock, and I don't really have time to talk right now."

Erin stood there for a moment and thought about what was said.

"Mr. Buck," Erin replied. "I'll get everything ordered. I was here last night so I know what you need. I'll get some staff in here for tonight. I can call a few people. You go to the bank and do what you have to do. If you could be back here by 1:00 p.m. to go over the game plan with the new staff, that would be perfect, and you and I can work out our details later. How's that sound?"

"That sounds perfect to me!" Desi said, turning and walking toward the door. "Thanks, Jesse!" were the last two words Desi said as she closed the door behind her.

Erin and Desi are definitely related, Jesse thought to himself as he processed what Erin had just said.

"I don't have a better plan right now," Jesse said, looking Erin in the eye. "We'll try this out for a few days and see how it goes. If it's not working—"

"I've got this, Mr. Buck," Erin interrupted just like her aunt would. "Go, do what you need to do. I've got this." Erin started past Jesse and headed to the kitchen to take inventory. "Go! I've got this!" she yelled over her shoulder as she walked away.

"Erin!" Jesse fired abruptly, stopping her in her tracks. "It's Jesse," he said.

Turning around and locking eyes, Erin asked with sarcasm, "What?"

"It's Jesse, not Mr. Buck. Call me Jesse," he replied in a normal talking voice.

Without saying a word, she spun around and disappeared into the kitchen.

"Lord," Jesse said while looking up toward the ceiling, "don't leave me now!" With a half-smile on his face and a few butterflies in his stomach, Jesse walked out the door and headed toward his truck.

What a beautiful woman! What an incredible body! he thought to himself. *I can't wait until 1:00 p.m.*

Chapter 7

The trip to the bank was effortless, and soon Jesse was on his way home. When he rolled up in the driveway, he was greeted by his trusty companion Louie and a total stranger. Getting out of the truck, Jesse's welcome from Louie was happy and energetic.

"Hey there, boy!" Jesse said, petting him rapidly all over. "You want a treat?" Jesse said excitedly. "C'mon, let's go get a treat!" Louie knew what that meant and made a beeline toward the house. Jesse stood up and locked eyes with the stranger as he walked straight toward him.

Like everyone else in Eureka, the man wore jeans and cowboy boots. This particular fella was slender and wore a black Oakland Raiders sweatshirt, with a small logo on the right breast, and a well-worn Oakland A's baseball cap. Not at all intimidated by Jesse's coming home, he didn't flinch as Jesse walked up to him.

"You must be the man they call Jesse Buck," the stranger said, holding out his right hand to shake. "I'm Pastor Raines," the stranger continued. "I'm the minister down at the Christ Church, just a hint down the street from the Lasso." Reaching out and shaking hands, Jesse answered almost with a sigh of relief.

"Yea, I'm Jesse Buck. Nice to meet you, Pastor. You have a first name?"

Chuckling with a warm friendly laugh, the minister answered, "Pastor *is* my first name, Raines is my last name. My parents had it in for me right out of the gate".

"Nothing wrong with being unique."

"I see you have California tags on your pickup. You a Raider fan?"

"As a matter of fact, I am an Oakland Raider fan." Jesse answered hurriedly. "And an A's fan for that matter, but I'm sure you're not here to talk about sports. What brings you out this way, Pastor?" Jesse asked, heading toward the house where Louie was waiting patiently for his treat.

With Pastor following Jesse just a few feet behind as he walked to the house, he explained to Jesse the nature of his visit.

"You've made quite a stir in this little town since you've been here, Jesse. I figured, as the minister, I'd come see what you are all about. After all, I like to know all of the sheep in my flock."

"Well, Pastor," Jesse said, turning around and looking him straight in the eye, "I'm a very busy man today, but I'll give you a few minutes." Jesse nodded his head for Pastor to follow him inside. "I've got to get cleaned up and head back down to the restaurant," Jesse said, finally getting Louie a doggie treat from the pantry. "What do you want to know?"

"What brings you up here from California?" Pastor asked. "Why Eureka?"

Jesse took a sigh as he collected his thoughts. He respected a man of the cloth and felt he should show that respect.

"I'm California born, been around a bit, ended up here. Not much to tell, really."

Pastor looked around the house, admiring what Jesse had done with the place since he'd been there and listened without saying a word.

"When I was a kid, my father took my brother and me on a cross country trip. We stopped in Montana for a time, and I was taken in by it. Always wanted to come back. Always wanted a quiet little place by a lake to call home. Recently, I woke up, hooked up the trailer, and left. Never to return. I ended up here and loved it. There you go, Pastor," Jesse said. "That's the Reader's Digest version. I trust you'll keep that between us, right? No one else really needs to know all of that."

"Sure," Pastor replied, rolling his eyes. "No need in letting *that* cat out of the bag. What was it like, you know, being a SEAL?"

Jesse's eyes locked into a dead stare with the man that just asked the question.

"What makes you think I am or ever was a Navy SEAL?" Jesse asked very defensively.

"Look, Jesse," Pastor started. "I mean you no harm, no disrespect. I haven't always been a pastor. I know people looking to settle into small towns typically have a past that they are trying to leave behind them. Like I said, I like to know who's in my flock."

Mental note to self, Jesse thought. *Need to investigate Pastor Raines. What is this man's background?* However, it's not really that hard to find out who served in the military and what they did. Maybe this was nothing; however, Jesse decided to proceed with caution.

Jesse took a sigh and looked at the floor for a moment. "You know," Jesse started, refocusing on Pastor, looking him straight in the eyes and talking in a solemn voice, "I can't really talk about my time as a Navy SEAL Commander. It's classified—all of it. Every mission I was on was 'secret squirrel classified.' I will tell you this. I did a lot of things that saved a lot of lives. There were lives that got taken, lives that got sacrificed. It gets to the point where you are so disconnected from normality that you tell yourself that the life you just took was just a target. Eliminating your target saves American lives and lives of countless other citizens around the world.

"It got so bad on one mission that I promised God if he got me out of there alive, I'd go to seminary and learn his word and share it with others."

"You're a minister?" Pastor interrupted excitedly. Jesse held his hand up, signaling as to let him finish speaking his thought.

"God did bring me home, but I lost my entire SEAL team in the process. I and one other survived the ambush. PTSD set in deep on the other guy. Don't know what happened to him. He went home, wherever that was, some place in Texas. Allen, Lieutenant Allen is his name, we called him 'Recon' and I've never heard from him. I kept my word to God. I spent a couple of years reaching out to the families of my fallen brothers, and finally, it got to be too much. I didn't want to be reminded of the lives that I took or be reminded of the brothers that I buried. My hands, Pastor, are stained with the blood of others and believe you me, you don't want to live with that on your conscience."

Pastor stood there in silence. He knew there was much more to the events of Jesse's life, but no more words were going to be spoken now. Changing topic and moving forward, Pastor, with a cheery voice, changed the subject.

"Old man Johnson sure would be happy to see what you've done to this place. It looks amazing!"

"What was that?" Jesse asked with great question.

Pastor proceeded with caution and surprise in his voice.

"You didn't know? This was Tim Johnson's residence— he also owned the land you bought where your establishment now sits."

"No, Pastor, I didn't know this was old man Johnson's place," Jesse answered. "My realtor failed to mention that to me." Jesse said putting the pieces together in his head.

"Now, Jesse," Pastor added almost with a chuckle, knowing exactly what she had done. "Desi is a real fine woman, and it just probably slipped her mind. Doesn't matter now anyway. The place looks incredible, and Tim would be glad you have it. Really, he would."

What happened to full disclosure, was the only thought Jesse had going through his head. Knowing time was getting away from him, Jesse had to get back on track. Before he got another word out, Pastor started toward the door.

"Jesse, we all have a past. I haven't always been a minister."

"Yeah, you mentioned that earlier. Anything you care to share, Pastor?"

"We're brothers Jesse. You and I are brothers. Especially through the eyes of the Lord. You can come to me if you need anything." Jesse was relieved to hear those words; for some reason, they were comforting. Jesse seemed to get a good vibe from Pastor, a man he could trust.

"Let me walk you out," Jesse said as he walked toward the door.

The two gentlemen left the house to find a third standing in the driveway.

"Well, Jack Beaver!" Pastor shouted. "What brings you down to these parts?" He continued talking with a big booming voice, a voice that could certainly be heard in the back of the sanctuary on Sundays. Jack Beaver's appearance was exactly how Desi described him—exactly. Jesse just stood there with eyes locked on the man whom he knew didn't want him around.

"Came to do a little fishin'," Jack said, not taking his eyes off Jesse.

"Where's your pole?" Pastor questioned.

"Left 'er in the rig when I seen them cars. Didn't know this place was occupied." Jack spat on the ground as he chewed a wad of tobacco. He slowly turned and walked toward his pickup, not taking his eyes off Jesse until he had to.

"Behave yourself, Jack! See you in church Sunday!" Pastor yelled as he walked away.

"Don't count on it, Pastor—I don't need saving!" Jack yelled back, never stopping or turning around. Jack got into his pickup and backed down the drive, leaving nothing but a cloud of dust.

"Should I be concerned about that guy?" Jesse asked Pastor with a raised eyebrow.

"What? You're a Navy SEAL, what in the world have you got to be concerned about?" Pastor said jokingly. "That guy's a blowhard. Pay him no mind. A little competition in town might do him some good." Jesse watched Pastor leave down the drive. He knew he was running behind and hurried into the house to get cleaned up.

Chapter 8

Friday afternoon, 4:00 p.m.

Jesse was late getting back to the Lasso. Not knowing what to expect when he got back, all he could hope for was that it hadn't burned to the ground. He imagined pulling up to a pile of ashes and finding Erin sitting out front crying.

"Kill any intruders," he said to Louie as he gave him a pet and raced out the door. "I'll be home late tonight, old friend."

Jesse hauled the nail back to the Lasso. One would have thought he was qualifying for the Indianapolis 500 the way he was driving. When he rolled up to the parking lot, he looked around, astonished with what he saw. It was four thirty in the afternoon, and the parking lot was two thirds full. He parked in back and slipped in the back-door, stealth like. He wanted to see what was going on before he announced his presence to Erin.

His entrance was silent and unnoticed. He paused by the door to the kitchen and peeked through the window where he saw three people cooking. *The chili smells incredible*, he thought to himself as he closed his eyes and savored the aroma.

"There you are," spouted Erin, crashing the moment. "You, Jesse, are late. C'mon, let's go over a few things. I'm sitting at the table by the piano, I'll meet you over there in a minute." She pushed Jesse in the direction she wanted him to go.

Jesse couldn't believe his eyes. People were bustling about really enjoying themselves. There were about half a dozen servers meandering around tables taking orders and delivering food. People were playing darts and shooting pool. There was a group of fellas at one of the poker tables playing Texas hold'em, having a great time.

The barstools were almost full, and of all people, and to Jesse's utter amazement, Pastor was behind the bar tending it! *Not always a minister*, he thought to himself as he watched in disbelief. The jukebox played country music in the background and filled the air with the perfect volume of tunes from Toby Keith.

The Lasso was a dream come true.

"Thank you, God," Jesse said out loud, looking up.

"I could use a thank you too," Erin said, walking past him with a tray of food and drink. "C'mon, let's go."

Jesse sat at the table as instructed. Without saying a word, he watched Erin place some food sorts in front of him and then sit down. Folding her arms and leaning on the table, she looked at Jesse.

"I'll talk, you eat."

Just like her aunt, he thought as he looked at the food in front of him.

"This is part of your new menu," she started. "I found your recipe book in the back. Your chili recipe is award-winning, but I should tell you, we substituted the ground beef for Italian sausage, and now it's perfect. You should enter it in the chili contest at the rodeo, but we'll talk about that later."

Jesse was starving and dove into the food Erin had placed in front of him while she went over staff, hours, cooks, menus, and other things that he completely tuned out. The modified chili recipe was indeed perfect. The appetizers were the standard: mozzarella sticks, buffalo wings, southwestern egg rolls, and more. There were a few sandwiches, and a few dinner items, one of which included "TJ's Black Bourbon Steak," which sounded incredible. It was a New York–cut piece of beef marinated in bourbon BBQ sauce and then rolled in a buffet of seasonings and seared to perfection.

"Who's TJ, and why is this 'his' steak?"

"TJ is your head chef and it's *his* signature steak."

"How did you do all of this?" he asked.

"Try to keep up here, Buck, we're busy," Erin replied. "There is a small music group that plays country with a hint of attitude that will be here tonight from 8:00 to 11:00 p.m. Their name is the Hickory Sticks, and they are playing for free drinks. You'll like them."

"Erin, stop," Jesse said with a serious look on his face. "How did you do this?"

"Mr. Buck," Erin said, standing up from her chair and crossing her arms. "You hired me to do a job, and I'm doing it. I made a few phone calls. Are you displeased with my performance thus far?"

Jesse leaned back in his chair; he was speechless. With nothing to say, he merely shook his head no.

"Good," Erin said with a smile. "Don't dally, you are tending the bar with Pastor when you finish your dinner."

With that, Erin was off to continue a smooth operation of the Lasso.

"Tell your aunt I'm looking for her!" Jesse yelled as Erin walked away. He watched her leave. Her body, her curves. He wanted to ask Erin out terribly bad, but he knew she'd think of him as a dirty old man and put the thought out of his head. Her beauty, her take charge attitude, Erin was the perfect woman for him, but he knew he could never have her.

While finishing dinner, Jesse thought he saw something fly through the air out of the corner of his eye. When he looked up, he was stunned to see Pastor juggling liquor bottles behind the bar—and pouring shots at the same time! The crowd was going wild watching "the Minister" cut loose, placing bets that he'd drop a bottle—but he never did. Jesse waited for the performance to end before he wandered over. Putting on an apron, Jesse stepped behind the bar where Pastor was working.

"Just one of your many talents?"

"Like I told you," Pastor responded with deviance. "I haven't always been a minister." Winking an eye at Jesse and wearing a Cheshire cat-like smile, there was an untold story about the man in cloth and where he came from.

Jesse and Pastor worked the bar like long-lost teammates. Totally synchronized with each other, that is until Pastor tried to teach Jesse how to juggle. When the second full bottle shattered on the floor, the crowd deemed it to be alcohol abuse and begged them to stop. How could either of them argue? For the rest of the night, all bottle tossing would be in the hands of Pastor.

Then came 7:00 p.m. and Erin started charging a $10 cover charge to get in. This went against Jesse's idea of how the place should be run, but instead of questioning her, he decided to ride it out and see what was going to happen. After all, Erin had proven thus far to have control of the situation and had been a blessing, even if this was only day one for her. Jesse thought maybe he should watch her work. By seven fifteen, the Hickory Sticks were setting up onstage.

Maybe there was a method to Erin's madness, Jesse thought to himself and was glad he decided to watch from afar instead of questioning her actions.

The Hickory Sticks consisted of four young male musicians: the lead singer, who also played the banjo; an electric guitarist; a bassist; and a drummer. With a mediocre soundcheck, the group started playing at eight o'clock on the nose. With much amazement, they sounded good; they sounded really good.

For the next three hours, they divvied up their time with cover songs and originals. The crowd loved them, and what was really impressive, was when the banjo player spun his instrument behind his back and jammed out on the piano in the corner. There was a lot of talent here, and Jesse was already hoping that they would come back. For three hours, the foursome played music and drank beer. People danced and tapped their feet. Everyone was having a great time. The Lasso was so alive it seemed to have its own pulse.

Eleven p.m. came, and the band finished their last set. In less than thirty minutes, they had packed up everything and were huddled around a table eating and drinking, talking about how great it was to play here. They were most definitely interested in coming back, which was good news to Jesse's ears. Jesse told them that whatever they ate and drank was on the house and he'd have Erin contact them about a regular schedule if they were interested. Like a pack of wolves, these four guys devoured everything they ordered.

At 12:30 a.m., the crowd had diminished to six or eight tables, and the Rock-Ola had redeemed its place with background music. Pastor had since left, and most of the wait staff had gone. The kitchen was all but closed, and things were winding down. That's when she walked in. She was a very attractive woman. Couldn't be more than five feet two or five feet three. Shoulder-length blonde hair and stunning blue eyes. Jesse couldn't take her eyes off her as she made her way to the bar. Her petite body was in good shape and moved gracefully. Black cowboy boots covered her feet. A perfect-fitting pair of designer denim jeans covered her legs. She was wearing a cream-colored silk blouse, modestly buttoned, and a designer black leather jacket. This woman was not from around here. Maybe thirty years old. Certainly, no more than thirty-five for sure.

"Johnny Walker, black, on the rocks," was all she said as she sat down at the bar, away from anyone else. Shocked by her order, Jesse was on this drink, pouring a complimentary double for his new customer.

"Not many women can appreciate a blended scotch," he said, setting the drink down in front of her. Jesse caught a whiff of her perfume as he was placing her drink—and it smelled amazing. The woman, not looking up to acknowledge Jesse's comment, rolled her eyes and didn't say a word. Jesse was intrigued by this woman and wanted desperately to have a conversation with her. To start one with her at least.

"Rough day?" he asked softly.

"I just need some space right now, okay?" the woman finally replied, again never looking up to acknowledge Jesse. Jesse backed away and let her be. As much as Jesse was attracted to Erin and wanted her badly. Erin was a little young and Jesse had a policy of never, absolutely never dating anyone he worked with. The blonde that sat before him was more his age, so he figured, what the heck. Since he couldn't have Erin, this woman was on his radar.

Maybe she'll warm up a little if I give her some room, he thought to himself and proceeded to check on the customers at the other end of the bar.

Slam! opened the front door of the Lasso.

"I thought I told you never to come in here!" yelled a tall rough-looking character. This guy was every bit of six feet four or six feet five. Couldn't weigh in at a buck eighty. Tall and lanky, long greasy hair. Dirty jeans, dirty sneakers—and of course, like a lot of other men in Eureka, a flannel shirt. "I'm talking to you, woman!" he yelled at the top of his lungs.

By now, the whole restaurant was silent. Jesse watched with a sharp eye, ready to intervene if necessary. If one lesson was learned from being a SEAL, it was never get involved if you don't have to. Most situations defuse themselves before they ever get going. The only noise other than this fool yelling was the Rock-Ola. Jesse watched intently as this fella made his way to a table where three young women sat.

"Get outta here, you don't belong here!" the man yelled at a woman sitting at the table. "Let's go now!" The man grabbed the woman's arm. She yanked her arm out of his grasp, yelling back at him.

"You're my boyfriend Ned, not my boss! You can't tell me what to do!"

With that came a *smack!* A swift backhand right across the face from the man. It came so hard and so fast that it knocked the woman clean to the floor.

"The hell you disrespect me! Let's go now!" the lanky man continued to scream. Jesse deemed it was time to get involved.

Before Jesse could get his apron off, the little blonde-haired woman was off her stool and heading over to the scene. She held her hand up to Jesse as she walked away as if to say, *"Stay there, I've got this."* Still, Jesse reached under the bar and grabbed a Colt .45 that he now tucked into the back of his jeans, under his shirt - just in case things got any worse.

This ought to be interesting, Jesse thought to himself as he watched what was about to unfold. The blonde-haired woman, now in the middle of things, knelt to the woman on the floor.

"C'mon, get up. Go into the ladies' room and get yourself cleaned up."

"Hey, blondie! This don't concern you! Get outta here!" the man yelled.

The blonde-haired woman, ignoring the man at this point, helped the girl off the floor.

"Go get yourself together," she said and pushed her toward the sign on the wall that read 'Gals'. The girl scurried off and disappeared into the ladies' room without saying a word.

The tall lanky man, "Ned" as his name appeared to be, spun the blonde around by the arm and reared up to backhand her just like he did his assumed girlfriend.

"I'll teach you to butt into my business!" he yelled as his hand came around. The blonde-haired woman leaned back just enough for his hand to miss her and with spring-loaded legs jumped up. Spinning around, the blonde woman landed a roundhouse right on the man's temple, sending him across the room into an empty table. The crowd watched in amazement, and this certainly had Jesse's attention. Some of the guys at the bar chuckled at Ned as this so-called tough guy just got taught a lesson by some woman half his size. The blonde-haired woman landed, planting her feet firmly, not taking her eyes off the threat. As Ned got his bearings, he climbed to his knees. While kneeling on the floor, he reached into his boot and without a flinch hurled a knife at the woman.

With lightning-fast reflexes, the woman caught the knife and sent it right back to him, burying the blade deep into Ned's left shoulder. The woman threw the knife so hard that the blade completely penetrated his shoulder with the tip coming out the back! At that moment, the woman turned and headed for the door, not saying a word.

"Hey!" Ned yelled in great pain. "Hey, woman! I'm talking to you!" He yelled holding his left shoulder with his right hand, the knife still buried deep.

"Who do you think you are, woman! Get back here! Let's finish this!" Ned yelled in screaming pain. "I will find you!" Ned was now back on his feet. At that moment, the blonde-haired woman stopped. She paused for a moment, turned around slowly, and marched back to Ned.

Ned tried to grab her with his right hand, but before he had an inkling with what was really happening, the blonde-haired woman kicked his feet right out from underneath him, bringing him to the floor. With one knee on his chest, she grabbed him by the throat with her left hand and grabbed the knife with her right.

"This *is* over," she said with a chilling, almost sinister voice. "This is over now." Her face was steel cold as she spoke, and the look in her eye was unmistakable—this gal meant business.

"Listen to me very carefully," the blonde continued. "If you ever strike another woman, you'll be over too. Do you hear me?"

"I'll find you," Ned said with as much attitude as he could muster trying to overcome the pain he felt from his left shoulder. The blonde started twisting the knife counterclockwise, pushing it in deep and twisting slowly. Ned screamed in pain.

"Do you hear me?" the blonde whispered. "Do you understand me?"

"I'll find you." Ned barely got out before he screamed again. The woman squeezed his throat a little tighter and twisted the knife a little further and asked again.

"Do you understand me, Ned?"

"Yes! Yes!" Ned gasped with what little air he could breathe in, and tears coming from his eyes. "I under . . . stand, yes," he muttered.

The blonde-haired woman stood up, ripping the knife out of his shoulder. Ned rolled around on the floor, coughing and yelling in severe pain from the knife wound; gasping for breath as his throat was freed of the woman's grip. The woman turned and headed for the door once more.

"Hey, woman!" Ned yelled from the floor. "Who do you think you are, woman!" The woman stopped and slowly turned around, just like she did the first time, but this time she walked slowly toward Ned who was still lying on the floor. Ned tried scooting away from her as she got closer, a true coward.

"Karma," the blonde-haired woman said, just a few feet from Ned. She stopped moving toward him, and looking him straight in the eye, this woman had a stone-cold stance, and she was undoubtedly serious.

"You can call me, 'Karma'," she said with gusto.

She took two steps backward, spun around, and walked calmly toward the door. Right before she left, she dropped the knife from her hand. Just like that, "Karma" was gone. The crowd immediately started chuckling and clapping, cheering on the mystery woman and chanting her name as Ned lay on the floor in shame.

Jesse couldn't believe what had just happened. He was impressed with this guest "Karma" and hoped she would return soon. Nonetheless, Jesse figured he should wander over to this guy on the floor and see if there was something he could do.

"Hey, buddy, you need some help?" he asked, extending his hand.

"Get away from me, boy!" Ned yelled. "You're going down!" Ned staggered to his feet, holding his bleeding shoulder. "You know who I am? You're done! Do you hear me! You're done! You're all done!" Ned yelled, pointing to everybody in the place. Ned stormed past Jesse and headed toward the door.

"Screw you, Ned!" someone in the background yelled, and the rest of the crowd burst into laughter. Ned was gone.

"Ned, wait!" the woman whom he'd struck said, running after him. "I'm sorry, Ned, wait!" Just like that, the episode was over.

Jesse stood there for a brief moment and wondered if every night was going to be like this.

"Last call in thirty minutes!" Jesse shouted out to the remainders as he straightened up the table and chairs from the excitement. Jesse glanced toward the door and noticed that the bloody knife was still lying on the floor. He went over and picked it up, then he made his way back behind the bar. As Jesse was about to fold the blood-covered blade back into the handle, he noticed the manufacturer's name engraved on it. Spyderco.

"Interesting," he thought to himself. *"A professional throwing knife. Homeboy thinks he's a tough guy."* He folded the knife up in the apron he was wearing earlier and stashed it under the bar with his .45. Looking around, no one was the wiser.

Jesse then noticed sitting on the bar was the drink he had poured for Karma that only had a sip or two missing. Rather than waste the alcohol, Jesse decided to finish it himself—after all, it didn't look like she was going to.

Jesse stood behind the bar and took everything in while he sipped Karma's scotch. It was like nothing had ever happened. There wasn't even any blood on the floor. Not a drop. The only evidence was the knife rolled up in the apron, which Jesse had decided to get rid of in a means other than the trash at the restaurant. The last tables were winding down, and no one was talking about what had happened earlier. It was already history.

Chapter 9

It was late. The last guest had gone. Jesse sat at a table by the piano while he worked the books. That night, Jesse was acting completely out of the norm and sat with a bottle of Johnny Walker Black and a glass of ice. The scotch he had earlier tasted so good he figured he'd sip some more while he sat and did his accounting. What the hell, right?

Deep into his train of thought, he paused. Jesse suddenly felt as if he weren't alone. As if he were being watched. He stopped writing and slowly looked up from the table toward the door. He was right. He was being watched. Nearly startled by the surprise, he started to get up when he recognized the figure, then the hair.

"Karma," he said loud enough for the blonde-haired woman to hear, "right? Why don't you get a glass and some ice from behind the bar and join me for a drink?" Jesse held up the bottle of scotch. *For the second time*, Jesse thought to himself as he watched "Karma" move across the floor, *the night just got a little more interesting*. The blonde-haired woman did exactly what she was told. First a glass, then some ice, and then made her way to where Jesse was sitting.

"Sit down," Jesse said in a very warm and inviting fashion.

"I just came back to finish my drink," the woman said, standing next to the table, setting her glass down for Jesse to pour. "I'm guessing since you told me to fetch my own glass you threw my other drink out?" The woman spoke with a certain attitude that was playful, witty, and cautious all at the same time. Jesse chuckled as he replied.

"No, no, no, Ms. Karma—I drank your scotch. I poured you a double so I couldn't toss it and please sit with me." Jesse pointed to the chair across from him.

"Please sit, toast with me," Jesse said, holding up his drink. "To our new friendship." Karma picked her scotch up off the table and clinked glasses with Jesse.

"To something," she added, and they both sipped their drinks, solidifying the toast.

Jesse leaned back in his chair with a smile and a raised eyebrow and asked, "Ms. Karma, what really brought you back here tonight?"

"I told you," Karma replied, pulling out the chair and finally sitting down. "I came back to finish my drink. I'm surprised you're closed."

"It's not exactly Chicago up here. If you knew I was closed, why did you stop?"

"I told you, to finish my drink." This was apparently Karma's story, and she was sticking to it. "The light was on, and the door was open, so I poked my head in. I poked my head in to find out that you finished my drink for me."

"Ha!" Jesse laughed. "I call shenanigans!"

It didn't take long for Karma to sip right through her first drink. She pushed her glass across the table in Jesse's direction.

"Please pour me," she said, lifting her hands up to her head. "I've got to take this wig off." Jesse watched the scotch pour with one eye and watched Karma with the other. Just like that, it was magic. Karma transformed herself from a beautiful blonde-haired woman to a jaw-dropping woman with raven-black hair. She teased her hair a bit and looked up. Her deep blue eyes contrasted her black hair with supermodel beauty.

"Different, huh?" Karma asked, reaching for her fresh drink. "You prefer blondes?" Karma asked after Jesse sat without saying a word.

"I'm sorry," Jesse finally replied. "You, are beautiful."

"You're drunk," Karma fired back immediately.

"No, seriously. I very much like the black hair over the blonde," Jesse went on, "and I'm also very glad you stopped by to finish your drink." Jesse finished with a smile and a wink.

"You're a mess!" Karma said in reply, also with a sip and a wink back.

"So, tell me, Ms. Karma," Jesse asked with great curiosity, "where you from? What brings you up here to Eureka, or better yet, who are you running from?"

Karma leaned back in her chair and crossed her arms, eyeballing Jesse. The silence went on for about fifteen seconds. Jesse finally realized that maybe, just maybe, that was too deep a question for the first night.

"Ah!" Jesse broke the silence. "A better question—are you hungry?"

"Yes," Karma replied, laughing. "That is a better question and yes, actually I'm very hungry. You got anything good in this joint?"

"Got something good?" Jesse responded and jumped out of his chair excitedly. "Baby, you're gonna love this!" he said, running out to the kitchen.

Karma put her hands to her mouth and yelled, "I'm not your baby!"

"What?" Jesse yelled back, laughing. Karma stood up and again with her hands around her mouth yelled: "Don't call me baby!"

While Jesse was in the back, Karma rolled up her blonde-haired wig and stuffed it into a pocket of her jacket then took her jacket off and hung it over the chair. She sipped her scotch and looked around the Lasso. *This really is a cool place*, she thought to herself.

"I wonder what the scoop is on this guy, the bartender that seems so hospitable."

In what seemed to be only seconds, Jesse returned with two of everything—two bowls of chili, two sets of silverware wrapped in beige-colored cloth napkins, two glasses of ice water, and a bowl of Fritos brand corn chips. He served his guest first and then himself and sat down to eat.

"Sure does smell good!" Karma said with a smile. "Your recipe?"

"Yes," Jesse responded. "It's a secret recipe so don't ask."

"Hahaha." Karma chuckled to herself as she dug right in. Following Jesse's lead, Karma tossed a handful of corn chips over the top, followed by a quick stir.

"Wow. This has awesome flavor!" Karma told him, being very impressed with her host's cooking ability. "I love it. It has just the right amount of zing without being too hot to taste. Very impressive. This is how chili should be made!" Karma was blowing through this bowl of chili like it had been a while since her last meal. She had perfect table manners but ate as if she were on a mission.

"I'm glad you like it!" Jesse said while watching his beautiful companion eat for a moment.

Karma paused, putting her spoon down and wiping her mouth.

"Hey, bartender," she spouted out, "what's your name anyway? How rude of me to not ask before now." Jesse wiped his mouth and got up from the table and walked the two feet over to where Karma was sitting.

"Ms. Karma," he said, offering his right hand to shake.

"Jesse Buck is my name and it's a pleasure to meet you. How rude of me to not offer it until now." They shook hands, and Karma chuckled again.

"You know, Jesse, Karma isn't my real name."

"So, what is your real name?" Jesse asked since Karma didn't offer it.

"My name is Rachael"

"Is there a last name?"

"Rachael's good for now."

"Well, Ms. Rachael, after seeing what I saw earlier tonight, 'Karma' suits you just fine," Jesse said chuckling, continuing with his bowl of chili.

"Nice." Rachael replied with a smile.

Chapter 10

"Knock, knock, sheriff's department here," broke the silence.

"Sheriff Rodney here. Anyone home? Doors unlocked."

Jesse and Karma locked eyes for a moment before Jesse got up to answer.

"Come on in, Sheriff. Something I can help you with?"

Jesse walked toward the sheriff. They met in the middle of the floor shaking hands.

"Jesse Buck, owner, how may I help you?"

"Well, Mr. Buck, I don't really know," Sheriff Rodney started. "Seems like I'm getting conflicting reports of an incident that happened here tonight. Anything you want to share with me?"

"Sheriff," Jesse replied while heading over to the table where Karma was sitting, "Why don't you head over to that table by the piano and have a seat. Let me get you a bowl of chili, and we can talk about anything you want." Before the sheriff could say no, Jesse had gone to the kitchen. Before Sheriff Rodney could make his way to Karma, Jesse was returning with a bowl of chili.

"Sheriff," Jesse continued, "this is my good friend Rachael. Please have a seat and join us."

"Thank you, Mr. Buck, don't mind if I do. This chili smells mighty fine," the sheriff said, sitting down. "Ma'am," he said, tilting his hat toward Karma.

"So, what kind of incident are we talking about here tonight, Sheriff?" Jesse asked as if he knew nothing.

"This chili *is* mighty fine!" Sheriff Rodney answered. "This chili would be a serious contender at the chili cook-off this summer at the annual rodeo. I think you should consider entering." The sheriff managed to finish chewing and set down his spoon without taking a breath of air. He removed a little black spiral notepad from his pocket and flipped to a page of notes.

"Well, Mr. Buck, let's see here," Sheriff Rodney went on. "Don't have my glasses so it might take a moment for them pupils to get their vision." He moved his head to get some focus.

Sheriff Rodney Sampson was written on the badge that the sheriff wore. He was probably about the same age as Jesse, possibly a bit older, a little heavyset with a big deep voice. Salt-and-pepper hair and mustache. He had a belly that just barely hung over his belt. The sheriff may have talked slow, but Jesse gathered that this was a calculating man, meaning, he didn't miss anything. *I'll bet this guy is a lot sharper than he makes out to be*, Jesse thought to himself while the sheriff was trying to focus.

"Well hell," Sheriff Rodney finally said, "let me just tell you what I got since I can't seem to read right now." The sheriff shoveled another couple spoonful's of chili into his mouth before he went on.

"Seems like I got conflicting stories 'bout an incident here with a feller named Ned, Ned Beaver," Sheriff Rodney explained. "One story is he fell on a piece of rod iron and put it through his shoulder. Another story I got from a local drunk that stumbled into jail to lie down was that Ol' Ned got beat up by a little girl. I personally would have liked to see that myself and like that story the best,"

Sheriff Rodney said. "Little blonde girl. Hell, I'd like to shake her hand." He chuckled. "When I heard Ned was in the hospital getting stitches, I figured I'd check it out. He tells me that he was jumped by three Mexicans out in your parking lot. Took his wallet, money, and everything."

Sheriff Rodney paused a moment to look Karma and Jesse in the eyes. There was no emotion from either of them, just two people listening to a story.

"Funny thing is," Sheriff Rodney went on, "ain't no one said nuthin' 'bout the knife hole in Ned's shoulder but Georgia-Jean, the ER nurse at the hospital that stitched him up." The sheriff paused again to look at his audience. Still, there was no response, just two people listening. The sheriff proceeded. "Nurse said she had to stitch up both sides. Either of y'all see a knife fight here tonight?" Sheriff Rodney asked, looking at Jesse then at Karma.

Karma shook her head no as Jesse answered.

"You know, Sheriff, I'm not sure what to make of all that. It was pretty busy being the crowd we had. I don't recall any sort of ruckus like that while I was tending bar. If there aren't any gunshots being fired, I tend to not get involved," Jesse said with a laugh.

"I sure do hear that," The sheriff replied with a chuckle. "Well, I tell you what." Sheriff Rodney said while he got up from the table. "I'll close this report out as Ol' Ned getting a licking from these three mystery Mexicans. If y'all hear som'thin' different, give me a holler." Sheriff Rodney tossed his card on the table and tilted his hat toward Karma, saying, "Evening, ma'am." Jesse stood up and shook hands with the sheriff.

"Will do, Sheriff, let me walk you out."

Jesse and the sheriff walked at the sheriff's pace to the door. "That's a mighty good bowl of chili you done put together, Mr. Buck. I'm serious 'bout you entering it into the contest this July. It's a contender," Sheriff Rodney reiterated.

"Thank you, Sheriff, I'll give it its due diligence,"

"Mr. Buck," Sheriff Rodney said, stopping at the door, "Ned Beaver can be a handful. Him and his father both. They ain't all together, if you know what I mean," the sheriff chuckled.

"I've got you, Sheriff," Jesse said, holding out his hand to shake one more time. Jesse and the sheriff shook hands, and the sheriff was gone. This time, Jesse locked the door so there wouldn't be any more "walk-ins" and made his way back to where Karma was still sitting.

"Sounds like 'Ol' Ned' took a lickin' by three Mexicans leaving here tonight, doesn't it?" Jesse asked with a big smile as he sat down across from Karma.

"Sure does," Karma replied back with a smile, holding up her empty scotch glass. "Something we should drink to."

Chapter 11

Huh! Where am I? Karma thought to herself as she jerked awake from a dead sleep. She sat up in bed abruptly. She looked around to get her bearings.

"Where am I?" she said to herself softly. She was fully dressed; even her boots were still on. She wiggled her fingers and toes—they were all there. Yup, all accounted for. She felt around her body— there were no injuries. No headache, no dizziness, no pain at all.

"Am I at Buck's house?" she said softly to herself. She looked out the window to see a dog running out to greet an unknown man. Getting closer to the window, she could see her black Corvette outside. She looked around the room again to see her purse and keys on a dresser made of pine wood and her leather jacket hanging on the back of the door.

On the other side of the room was a private bathroom. Karma went in to check herself out. "No makeup or anything, and you still look great, well almost!" she said to herself, looking in the mirror. She splashed some water on her face and combed her hair with a brush out of her purse. "This is as good as it's gonna get right now," she said to herself, walking to the door. Karma reached to open the bedroom door. Pushing down on the lever, she realized it was locked from the inside. She unlocked the door and slowly opened it. She listened carefully. Tiptoeing through the house, looking around sharply, she could hear voices coming from the back porch. One of the voices was Jesse, the other one unknown. Tiptoeing to the back, she carefully peeked outside.

Not knowing the other man at all, nor recognizing his voice, she deemed it safe to proceed. She slowly opened the French door and entered the patio.

"Well, sleeping beauty!" Jesse said with a big grin on his face, getting up to greet her. "Good morning, sunshine. Rachael, this is Pastor, Pastor Raines, our local, well, pastor. He just came by to ask me why I wasn't in church this morning. Pastor, I'd like to introduce you to my good friend Rachael," Jesse said, bringing the two close enough to shake hands.

"Well, I'll be," Pastor replied. "I guess now I know why you weren't in church this morning."

"Haha," Karma chimed right in, "that's not the reason." She smiled. "What are you talking about anyway, you folks go to church up here on Saturday?" Karma asked.

"Rachael," Jesse said, pouring her a glass of orange juice from the table on the patio. "Have a seat, love. It's actually Sunday, about 2:00 p.m. You've been asleep for, wow, over thirty hours now."

"That's impossible," Rachel said, looking around a little stressed. "Why didn't you wake me up?" She asked with concern.

"Rachael, I have a business to run. I figured you needed the rest, you were safe, not to mention you locked me out!"

"And for good reason!" Pastor interrupted with a laugh. "I would've locked you out too!"

"I just let you sleep," Jesse continued with a soft genuine voice, soothing to hear. "Louie was here to keep an eye on things." Jesse said this with the biggest of hearts, pointing to his loyal companion, Louie. Louie, hearing his name, perked up and looked around.

"There's a note on the kitchen counter I left for you when you woke up, but you were out cold, so I let you sleep."

"Looks like you two kids have some catching up to do," Pastor interrupted. "I'll find my way out." Pastor headed to the end of the deck to walk around the house. Before stepping off the deck, he stopped and turned around. Looking at Karma, he asked, "Ms. Rachael, is that your black Corvette I see parked out front here?"

Karma wondered if that was really the question he wanted to ask so she replied with, "Yes, Pastor, it is, why do you ask?"

"Well, ma'am," Pastor started, slowly walking toward her, "what's a pretty little thing like you driving around in a Z06 Corvette for? Isn't that, well, a little outta place?"

Jesse burst out into laughter. "You're gonna love this!" he yelled from the table.

"Well, Pastor," Karma started, "that is a 2010 Corvette Z06. It gets thirty miles per gallon on the highway when I'm just cruising. Here's the thing. I like a car to do exactly what I tell it to." Rachel started into her dissertation as to why she was driving such a high-performance sports car as if Pastor *really* wanted to know. Putting her arm through his, she walked him toward the driveway while she continued to answer his question.

"It has a 7.0L V8, a six-speed manual transmission, and will go zero to sixty in about 3.7 seconds. Top speed on that car is nearly two hundred miles per hour. That car, Pastor, does exactly what I tell it to do. See, I'm a performance girl. I need a car that, well, gets it done. You can spend more on a Porsche, Ferrari, or others, but at the end of the day, there aren't many cars that are going to go toe-to-toe with a Corvette. Especially with me driving it! Good enough?" Karma asked, looking Pastor in the eye with the most innocent of looks.

"Good enough," Pastor replied, chuckling, now standing next to his pickup. "Jesse said you were a handful." Pastor reached out to shake Karma's hand.

"Did he now?" she said, shaking back and looking over her shoulder toward the house. "It was a pleasure to meet you," Rachel finished and turned to walk away.

Pastor Raines watched Karma walk away until she disappeared around the corner of the house.

"That's a mighty fine creation you've got there!" he said softly, looking up toward the sky. "Mighty fine." Pastor got in his pickup and was gone.

Karma returned to the table on the patio where Jesse was still sitting and sat down.

"Buck," she started with a sigh, "is it really Sunday?" There was great concern in Karma's voice.

"Karma, I'd never lie to you. It's really Sunday. Almost three o'clock now," Jesse said again in a soothing, sincere voice. "What's the matter? Are you okay? Talk to me." Karma had this look of concern on her face that was borderline panic.

"Do you not feel safe?" Jesse asked.

"No, that's part of the problem," Karma replied, finally finding her voice. "I do feel safe here, I feel safe with you."

Dave Bair

"Look around," Jesse said with a chuckle. "We're the only house out here on the lake, you are safe. Nothing's going to happen to you on my shift."

"You don't understand," Karma replied. "I've never . . . I've never slept for that long before, ever."

"You were warm and cozy, you were safe," Jesse said, brushing it off. Jesse got up from the table, leaned over the railing on the deck, looking over the lake. "You obviously needed the rest," he said, talking to Karma with his back turned to her.

"Buck," Karma said with a sharp certainty in her voice. "Thank you *very* much for your hospitality, but I've got to get out of here. I have something that I need to take care of." Jesse turned around and watched her leave the table and head inside. He wanted so much to ask her not to go, but he couldn't. Something was up with this woman, and he really didn't want to get involved. Seconds later, Jesse heard Karma's Corvette Z06 fire up, and he ran around the house to meet her before she left. Running up to her car door, he tapped on the driver's side window. She put the window down to see what it was that he wanted to tell her.

"Karma," Jesse said, looking into her beautiful blue eyes, "come back safely, okay?"

"Who says I'm coming back?" she replied sharply.

"You'll be back," Jesse said just loud enough for her to hear over the growl of the engine. "You feel safe here, remember?" With that, the window rolled up, and Karma sped off without saying a word.

In a high-speed cloud of dust, Karma was gone. Jesse didn't know where she was going or how long she'd be gone, but he knew in his heart she'd be back; at least he hoped she would. Jesse's heart sank as he stood there in the drive, hoping she'd be back in a moment, and when she didn't return, he felt sad. He stood there until the cloud of dust was gone, watching, wishing for Karma to come back. She didn't. A woman he barely knew sped off in a black Corvette Z06 with Nevada tags, leaving him feeling a little melancholy in the dirt driveway.

Bark, bark, bark! The sound of Louie barking like a rabid dog could be heard from the back of the house. *What on earth is he barking about?* Jesse thought to himself as he headed toward the back to check things out. *Probably another moose.*

Chapter 12

"You idiot! Who cares about that little bimbo you're dating, huh?" Jack screamed at his son Ned while they stood in the middle of their Christmas tree farm. "We lost a day of production because you got beat up by a little girl, are you kidding me?" Jack yelled with ferocity. "Do you not know what we're doing here? Do you not know what a lost day causes us? We bring in ten Mexicans a day to dig thirty tree holes."

Ned just stood there like a frightened lamb while his father unleashed on him, fearing he would be slaughtered with one of them. *Smack!* Jack landed a hard backhand across Ned's face, knocking him clean off his feet. "Get up! Get up and be a man!" Jack yelled at the top of his lungs.

Ned picked himself up off the ground and stood before his old man, hoping there wouldn't be any more violence. Jack could see fear in Ned's eyes.

"You're a wussy, getting beat up by a girl half your size," Jack said to his son, looking him in the eye. "You're your mommy's boy. You're a disgrace. You'll never be a man! Say something!" Jack yelled at Ned. Ned just stood there, speechless, trembling with fear and anger at the same time, hoping this would soon be over. Jack Beaver was the only man that Ned Beaver feared. Jack Beaver was the only man that *everyone* feared.

"Do the math, you jerk!" Jack yelled like a drill sergeant. "We have ten Mexicans coming up here to dig tree holes tomorrow. That means we got thirty holes and thirty trees to tend with." Jack was talking almost nose to nose with Ned. He was foaming at the mouth angry with his incompetent son.

"You know what needs to be done, right?" Jack asked Ned with anger set deep in his eyes. "If you screw this up tomorrow, I promise you, Ned, you'll be number eleven." With that, Jack turned and walked away, leaving his son in the Christmas tree field. "You'll be number eleven!" Jack yelled again as he headed to his pickup.

"I've got this, Dad!" Ned tried to say with a shaky, crackling voice filled with fear. "I've got this." Jack never turned around or acknowledged his son. Ned knew his father was serious about him being number eleven if he messed up. Ned was never going to let that happen.

Chapter 13

"Commander Buck! You here? Commander Buck, you copy?"

Jesse couldn't believe what he was hearing.

"Commander Buck! Your dog is freaking out on me!"

Two things were certain: the first was it'd been a long time since Jesse heard the name "Commander Buck." The second was that Jesse knew this voice. He took off running around to the back of the house where his dog Louie was going nuts, barking in a frenzy!

"Louie, fall back now!" Jesse commanded his faithful companion. Instantly, Louie sat and didn't make a sound. Louie was on standby, with eyes locked on the suspect, waiting for the next command from his owner. Jesse looked for the voice he heard.

"Commander Buck, is that you! Down here!" Jesse ran over to the edge of the deck and leaned over the railing.

"No way! Recon! Recon!! I knew I recognized that voice! What on earth are you doing here? I don't believe it!"

With tears of joy trickling from each eye, Jesse jumped over the railing and nearly into the lake. Recon climbed out of a green fiberglass canoe, and the two embraced with a man hug like no other.

"I heard a crazy man from California moved in, bought a dead man's house, and built a bar on the same dead man's property," Recon said with tears pouring from his eyes, hugging Jesse tightly. "Once I heard that the name of the bar was the Lasso, I knew it was you! I had to check it out!

I knew it was you! I knew it was you!" Several minutes passed while the two lost friends embraced with joy.

"It's damn good to see you, Lieutenant Recon," Jesse said, not letting go. "Damn good to see you!"

The guys made their way on the deck with small talk. Jesse grabbed them a couple of beers from the fridge, and the two sat on the deck overlooking the lake and caught up.

"Recon," Jesse asked with excitement, "how is it you're here, if you don't mind my asking? Why aren't you back home in Texas with family?"

"Well, sir," Lieutenant Recon started, "to be completely honest with you, after our last mission, I went home. Home wasn't the same, sir. Everything changed. It was different, sir." Recon sat up and looked his commander in the eye, fighting back the tears to be strong, like a SEAL. You feel no pain as a SEAL, but you'll always feel your brother's love as a SEAL.

"There was nothing left for me, sir. I felt all alone. I was all alone. I had nothing, sir. So, I remembered our conversation back in the desert. You always said that one day you'll pack up your stuff and put roots in Eureka, Montana. You talked to us guys a thousand times about a bar named the Lasso. You even told us that you'd call it the Lasso because it'd be so cool inside that it'd naturally rope people in!" Recon stated with a chuckle. "So, one day, I did it. I packed my stuff and headed up here, to Eureka."

Jesse sat across from his friend and listened in awe.

"I knew in my heart you'd show up one day," Recon finished.

"Lieutenant," Jesse questioned, "you left your family in Texas to come up here? Why would you do that?"

"You're not getting me, sir," Recon said calmly. "You're the only family I got, sir. When we got out of the desert and I went home to Texas, there was nothing there for me. My girl was with another man, both my folks had passed away. My friends were now all scattered from coast to coast. I was standing in Texas alone. Texas is a big place to be all alone in." Recon continued with sincerity and honesty. Doing everything he could to hold back tears from his eyes, while he continued his story.

"I came up here almost three years ago now, got this job with the forestry service. I live in a log cabin not ten minutes from here. I knew you'd come up here, sir. I knew that one day you'd be up here too. I didn't know where you were, but I knew in my heart that you'd be here. You're the only family I got, sir."

With that, Lieutenant Allen covered his eyes with both of his hands and wept.

"You're the only family I got."

Jesse jumped out of his chair, pulled the lieutenant up by the arm, and the two men hugged.

"I've got you, Chris!" Jesse said. "I've got you, brother!" Both men were shedding tears from their eyes.

"You're back with family, I've got you," Jesse reconfirmed. "I've got you."

Chapter 14

By now, the sun was coming up over the mountains, and the two men were still talking and drinking beer on the deck. They talked about everything from the missions they were on together to the women they loved, the friends they buried, and the men they killed. It's tough being a Navy SEAL. It's a different kind of life. The life only another SEAL can appreciate.

Life as a Navy SEAL consists of missions and targets. Period. You don't leave a man behind, ever. You don't leave an unfinished mission, ever. You do the job that no one else wants to do. You do the job that no one else wants to talk about. You wash the blood off your hands that no one else wants to get on theirs.

Being a Navy SEAL is a job like no other. You are truly part of a group that become your family, that become your brothers. A group that has each other's back at any, and all costs. The pain that one man feels you all feel. You are all at each other's weddings. When you have a child, all of your brothers have a child as well. As a unit, you think as one. You can predict each other's moves and actions. You are seamless. You are flawless. You are a Navy SEAL. There is no better job in the world.

Chapter 15

Lieutenant Chris "Recon" Allen was part of Jesse's SEAL team. Recon was a good-sized man, standing nearly six feet four and looking like a child. He was only a couple of years younger than Jesse but barely looked old enough to buy alcohol. Recon was also ripped. Nothing but muscle from head to toe. Recon shaved his head bald and had dark brown eyes. Not a real great-looking guy, but he was smooth and very charismatic, a real lady killer.

Recon was also a good man. He was a believer like Jesse, a gentleman wherever he went, and a loyal friend. Jesse was glad to cross paths with him again. As the sun continued to rise on this Monday morning, Jesse let Recon talk about his experience over the last three years. For nearly three years, Recon did what he did best—he collected information. He had dirt on everyone in Eureka and even some people as far south as Butte. Recon explained to Jesse that when the day did come and their paths crossed again, he wanted to give Jesse a full report— and he did!

"Jesse, check this out," Recon started. "Pastor Raines, the pastor in town, didn't seem to exist until a few years back. Just kind of wandered into town and started preaching. Absolutely nothing on this guy until 2009, nothing. No record of birth, no education records, no dental records, no police or FBI records—that man's past is nonexistent." Jesse just listened intently while Recon filled him in.

"Desi the realtor is probably the richest woman in the state. She owns more buildings than Donald Trump! Her niece Erin, she doesn't need to work for you, she's rich too. The Beavers, Jack and Ned, there is just something evil about them. Something is just not right with them. I don't know what they have going on yet, but I'll find out."

Recon was excited to tell Jesse everything he learned about the little town while he was there. It was like he had purpose. Recon had names, home addresses, and phone numbers memorized of anyone in town that had more than a pulse. He knew work schedules and school schedules; there wasn't much he didn't know about the people of Eureka.

"Jesse," Recon kept going, "the only person in town that I don't have something on is Georgia-Jean, the ER nurse down at the hospital."

"Hang on right there. Dig deeper on Georgia-Jean and Pastor," Jesse said as if the two were back in the desert. "Find out what you can, especially on Pastor. No one has a vacant past. This guy knew I was a SEAL. It won't be long before he connects the dots with you and me. We need to know what this guy's mojo is."

"I'm on it," Recon said with confidence.

"Georgia-Jean seems to be very knowledgeable. Find a way to pick her brain and get back to me," Jesse finished. "We'll worry about the Beavers later. Let's figure out Pastor and Georgia-Jean first. Come by the Lasso and fill me in sometime this week when you get some info."

With that, the two men stood up, shook hands, and Recon left, jumping over the railing of the deck, disappearing over across the lake to go start his next mission.

Jesse was in no condition to run the Lasso tonight. He decided to call Erin and ask her to take the Lasso to close.

"Erin, it's Jesse," he started when she answered the phone. "I just can't get in today. Will you be okay running it till close tonight?" Jesse hurried to get the question out, feeling a little tipsy from a night of catching up with Recon.

"I've got this, Mr. Buck," Erin answered almost before he could finish asking the question. "Pastor told me when he got here that you may not be in tonight. We're good. I'll see you tomorrow," Erin finished and hung up before Jesse could say a word.

Pastor, wait what? Jesse thought to himself as he wandered through the house toward his bedroom. *Where did that guy come from?* Jesse kept thinking. *I can't figure him out. Recon better come back with some good information on him. He seems like a good guy, but I'd better be careful.* Jesse now pulled the covers over his head to sleep off the night with Recon. *I'll figure it out tomorrow*, was his last thought as he closed his eyes.

Chapter 16

Wednesday night at the Lasso was family movie night. At 6:30 p.m., the projection screens dropped from the ceiling, and everyone could enjoy a family movie while they gathered at the Lasso. The first Wednesday movie night feature was *Star Wars Episode IV*. In Jesse's mind, he was playing it safe with a familiar classic, not sure how big the crowd was going to be—he sure didn't anticipate standing room only.

Jesse was tending bar while the movie was playing and came across a spitfire of a woman. She was a petite little thing, he guessed in her late sixties. She had short brown hair and was dressed very conservatively.

"Well heck, sweetie," she started. "I'm sure it's my turn for a refill." She finished with a smile.

"What's your favorite?" Jesse asked, snatching her glass off the bar.

"Club soda on the rocks," she said with a smile. "Make that a double, on the double. I'm not getting any younger here sitting at your bar." By the time she had finished laughing, Jesse had her drink back in her hand.

"Mr. Buck," the stranger continued, catching Jesse's attention. "If there's something you want to know about me, just ask. You don't have to send that fine young man over to ask a bunch of questions, I'll gladly tell you anything you want to know."

Jesse stopped for a moment, not sure of what to make of the woman's words.

"Let me introduce myself," she continued, reaching across the bar to shake hands. "I'm Georgia-Jean, the ER nurse in town."

"Pleased to meet you, Ms. Jean," Jesse responded, shaking her hand, acting as if he had missed her previous comment.

"Not Ms. Jean," she fired right back. "Georgia-Jean, and you know what I'm talking about." She finished with a laugh and a sip of her club soda.

Jesse hadn't heard anything from Recon and was stunned that the ER nurse knew as much as she did. Recon was a professional, and for some reason, the dots just aren't connected.

"You see, Mr. Buck," Georgia-Jean spoke, "I'm eighty-four years old, and I've seen a thing or two."

Jesse couldn't believe her first comment. She looked incredible for eighty-four years old and as witty as can be, just as sharp as a tack.

"When someone who isn't bleeding comes up and asks you a question, it's pretty easy to connect the dots," she went on. "Now that we're friends," she added, only pausing for another sip of her club soda, "we can communicate freely." Georgia-Jean finished her club soda and shot Jesse a wink, hopping off the barstool and leaving *poof* just like that.

I have got to talk to Recon, Jesse thought. *This is getting weird.*

Family movie night was a huge success. It was so huge that Jesse was thinking about building a mega screen behind the building. People could picnic on the lawn and watch a movie on a jumbo-sized screen when the weather was nice. It wasn't quite warm enough yet, but he certainly gave it a serious thought. There hadn't been a night at the Lasso yet, where maximum capacity wasn't reached for some period of time. Granted, the Lasso had only been open for a week and the newness may still be in the air, but Jesse wasn't complaining. It had been a good week.

Sunday morning came, and Jesse went to the early service at church. Immediately following the service, he headed back home to spend the day with his beloved companion Louie. The two hiked to the other side of the lake where Jesse set a one-cubic-foot block of solid ice on a stump, positioning it just right, making sure one of the sides was facing the house perfectly and headed back. It was a good fifteen-minute walk if you were humping.

Once back at the house, Jesse set up on the deck with his favorite rifle, a bolt-action .300 Winchester Magnum. He carefully took aim on the block of ice through the scope, making minor adjustments to his position and focusing in on his target. When he was finally dialed in, he sat up and put one round into the firing chamber. Jesse resumed his position, breathed in through his nose and out through his mouth, and then gently squeezed the targeting bead up onto the block of ice across the lake. With his second slow, easy breath of air in through his nose and out through his mouth, Jesse squeezed the trigger. Before the crack of the high-powered rifle could echo across the lake, Jesse watched the block of ice explode into a million pieces when the bullet struck it, leaving nothing but water vapor.

"You still got it," Recon said from behind, startling Jesse.

"I knew you were there," Jesse said, trying to play it off.

"Sure, you did Commander."

"Sneaking up on me is a good way to get shot," Jesse said, putting the rifle down on the patio table.

"Didn't think you could be snuck up on," Recon responded with a smile.

"What have you got for me?" Jesse said, changing the subject, not happy that Recon was able to sneak up on him. *Where is Louie when I need him?* he thought to himself.

"Where have you been all week anyway?" Jesse asked before Recon could speak.

"I do have a job, Commander," Recon replied with a little sass. "Forest ranger, remember?"

Jesse just locked eyes with Recon. While he knew Recon was right and he didn't have a leg to stand on, he thought his old friend would have been in touch before now.

"Georgia-Jean is the sweetest, most fun-loving woman in town," Recon started. "Everyone loves her. Been here her whole life. Good Christian woman. Been an ER nurse for sixty years and will do it till she's pushing daisies."

Jesse sat at the table and cleaned his weapon while Recon filled in the blanks.

"She loves what she does and loves everybody in town—even you."

With that, Jesse shot a look up at Recon as if to say "whatever."

"She saw right through you," Jesse added, looking back down at his rifle.

"What are you talking about?" Recon asked. "I told her to come see you!"

"Keep going," Jesse fired back. "What else you got?"

Recon sat at the table and continued briefing Jesse with his findings.

"Pastor is a mystery," Recon started. "The man was either hatched or is an alien. I've got nothing on him. Nothing at all—I even cross checked TSGFs, hoping to find something, and I have nothing."

Jesse stopped wiping down his firearm and looked Recon in the eye as if they were back in the desert, saying, "Top secret government files aren't going to just identify him. We'll have to dig deeper. He's sixty-something years old. He's got a past. Find it."

"Yes, sir," Recon responded with full respect towards Jesse.

"What else?" Jesse asked, continuing with his firearm.

"The Beavers truck in Mexican laborers from all over Utah, Nevada, California, Idaho, anywhere. Pay them $5 an hour to dig holes for Christmas trees. Rumor has it he'll only hire those that are desperate, sort of new-to-the-territory desperate so he doesn't have to pay them much."

"Interesting," Jesse said. "Anything else?"

"One last thing," Recon added. "Your girlfriend's Corvette is registered to a Bernie Crawford out of Ruth, Nevada, population 510."

"Now that is interesting," Jesse said, looking up at Recon. "What do you have on Bernie?" he asked with curiosity.

"Knowing you were going to ask that," Recon replied, "he's retired from GM, modifies Corvettes out of his house for performance enthusiasts. Calls himself BHP, 'Bernie's High Performance.'"

"He's the guy that built the F1-Corvette," Jesse said out loud at the same time as Recon.

"The only Corvette on the planet to outperform all the supercars— McLaren, Bugatti, all of them," Jesse continued. "That guy is a genius at Corvette modifications. He builds his own superchargers by hand and developed his own fuel injection system. A genius. I know who he is, I've followed his work for years. What do you mean 'girlfriend' anyway?" Jesse asked. "How do you even know about her?"

"Haha." Recon laughed with a smile. "It's what I do."

"You scare me sometimes, Recon," Jesse said. "You just love what you do too much." He shot Recon a wink as if to say thank you.

"Recon," Jesse added, "find out the connection between Karma and Bernie."

"Think they're lovers?" Recon asked, poking the bear.

"No," Jesse replied sharply. "I don't think they're lovers, just want to connect the dots."

"I sense a little jealousy," Recon continued to poke.

"C'mon, let's get some dinner," Jesse suggested, not giving in to his buddy's antics.

Chapter 17

Mondays and Tuesdays were tough for Jesse. He kept finding himself staying up late Sunday night with Recon reminiscing about the past and then dragging himself into work Monday morning with little or no sleep. Erin had Mondays and Tuesdays off so Jesse ran the show from open to close with a light staff. Just tough to function with little or no sleep anymore. Other than the 8:00 p.m. rush, Mondays and Tuesdays were slower, steady but slower than the other days of the week. By mid-week business starts to pick up of course for movie night; by 6:00 p.m., a half-hour before the movie even starts, the place is packed.

At 2:30 p.m. on Monday afternoon, the place was nearly empty when Sheriff Rodney walked through the door.

"Afternoon, Mr. Buck!" Sheriff Rodney said with enthusiasm.

"Sheriff Rodney!" Jesse replied, walking toward the sheriff to shake hands. "What do I owe the pleasure today, sir?"

Sheriff Rodney removed his hat and held it by his chest with both hands. "Jesse," the sheriff almost whispers, "I'll be honest here, son." He continued speaking a little softer. "My chili has won first place at the chili contest in the summer rodeo for the last seventeen years straight!"

Jesse looked puzzled and was not sure what the sheriff wanted him to do with this information.

"And you're telling me this because?" Jesse asked slowly with great question in his voice.

Sheriff Rodney looked over both shoulders to make sure no one was within earshot.

"Jesse." Sheriff Rodney was now whispering. "Your chili is so good I came in to get some more of it."

Jesse burst out into laughter and put his arm over the sheriff's shoulders.

"Sheriff," Jesse said, walking the sheriff over to the table by the piano. "Sit here where no one will notice you. I'll get you a bowl of chili—on the house." Jesse turned toward the kitchen.

"Jesse!" Sheriff Rodney chirped. "I can't eat it here; can I get it to go?"

"No problem, Sheriff," Jesse chuckled.

"Actually, Sheriff, that's my recipe," Erin said, walking in unannounced.

"Hey!" Jesse fired back, completely disregarding that it was Erin's day off. "What do you mean that's your recipe?" he asked.

Erin cocked her little frame and placed her hands on her hips and, with as much attitude as she could muster, replied, "I told you I modified it on the very first day I was here."

Jesse pondered this remark while he thought back to that day.

"Modifying it makes it mine," Erin continued. "Doesn't it, Sheriff?" Erin gave the sheriff a wink.

"Slow down, turbo," Jesse piped up, defending himself. "Modifying my recipe doesn't make it yours." He fired back not thinking before he spoke. "That makes it *our* recipe!"

"You said it, Jesse. It's our recipe then," Erin immediately added. She spun around and headed to the kitchen. Jesse stood there for a moment and wondered how he just lost full credit to his ten-year-in-the-making "soon to be world famous" chili recipe.

"I don't care whose recipe it is," the sheriff added. "I'm just trying to get some to-go." Sheriff Rodney and Jesse stood there for a moment, not sure what either one was going to do next, both kind of waiting to see what Erin was going to do.

"Here you go, Sheriff," Erin said, returning in no time. She was carrying a paper bag, holding it with both hands and walking rapidly toward Jesse and Sheriff Rodney.

"This has a large bowl of chili and a couple of pieces of cornbread. I put some napkins and plastic utensils in there for you as well. Is there anything else I can get for you today?" Erin asked, handing the bag off to Sheriff Rodney.

"No, ma'am," Sheriff Rodney said with a big smile.

"Thank you now, and remember, I was never in here."

Just like that, the sheriff slipped out the back door and disappeared, almost ashamed he liked Jesse's chili over his own so much.

"That is my recipe," Jesse started, walking with Erin toward the kitchen. "What are you doing here anyway? It's your day off." Jesse stopped walking and waited for a response from Erin.

"Relax, Jesse," Erin said with that same sass her aunt had. "I'm not staying. I just came by to give you this flyer."

Erin handed Jesse a flyer that had been folded up in her back pocket.

"Aunt Desi wanted me to let you know that there is a showing for this piece of land on Flathead Lake in Kalispell on Sunday. Thought you might be interested." Erin was leaving as swiftly as she showed up, slipping out the back door as if she was never there.

"Hey!" Jesse yelled toward her. "Tell your aunt I'm looking for her!"

"She'll be at the property on Sunday!" Erin yelled back, never stopping or turning around.

Okay, Desi, Jesse thought to himself. *I guess I'll see you Sunday.*

As Erin walked away, Jesse watched her leave. Erin had an amazing body. She was beautiful from head to toe. Smart, sexy, competent, ambitious. Jesse watched the perfect woman for him leave through the door in which she came. Jesse wanted Erin in the worst way, but knew because of their age difference, he could never have her. He needed to get her out of his head.

As Jesse threw himself into his work at the Lasso, Karma kept crossing his mind. He decided that he really was attracted to her, and even though he didn't really know her very well, he liked having her around. There was just something about her blue eyes and her amazing smile. That little bit of "don't mess with me" mixed in with her quick wit and a touch of playful sass.

"I hope I haven't seen the last of her," he mumbled to himself while wiping off the bar.

The rest of the week went by without a hitch. The crowds at the Lasso continued to be large and steady. Wednesday, now dubbed "movie night" by the townspeople, was a huge success for the second week in a row. With this week's showing of *The Empire Strikes Back*, not only was it a sold-out crowd, but this week people showed up in costume! There were a half dozen Darth Vaders wandering around. There was a person in a Wookie costume, better known as Chewbacca, who came in and was there the whole night and left with not a soul knowing who they were. There was some gossip that it might have been someone from another town.

By the end of Wednesday night, people were already talking about watching *Return of the Jedi* next week. Jesse was so inspired by this that he decided to sponsor a costume contest. The rules for this were simple. If you show up next week in a legitimate costume (meaning you couldn't just show up with a lightsaber and call yourself Han Solo), then your bill for the evening would be picked up by the Lasso. After the movie was over, the guests would choose two grand prize winners for best costume. Each winner would get $250 in cash!

When Jesse was finished yelling this out to everyone, the crowd went wild with cheers and whistling. People were standing up and applauding. With all the noise going on, one would have thought this was a winning crowd at the horse races or something.

Hearing the excitement of the people really left Jesse with a warm feeling. *People are connecting*, he thought to himself as he watched everything happen. *The Lasso really is roping people in.*

Chapter 18

Sunday morning was here before Jesse knew it. The sun was shining bright and felt warm on his skin even though there was a hint of a nip in the cool morning air. Jesse was finishing getting ready for church while talking to his dog Louie as if it were a normal conversation.

"Louie, look how beautiful it is outside today!" Louie just lied on the bed with front paws hanging over the edge and cocked his head as if he were listening intently.

"It's such a perfect day outside today, Louie!" Jesse continued. "Do you know what we're going to do today, Louie? Today, we're going to drive the Corvette!" With that, Jesse scratched Louie on the head behind his ears and headed out the door.

Jesse wore a salmon-colored shirt under his black suit, no tie. His feet strutted a freshly polished pair of black cowboy boots. He looked quite dapper today. Jesse walked over to the garage he had built when he got up there and hit the button on the remote control. As the oversized garage door rolled up, the sunlight made its way inside the building, shining on the 2004 Commemorative Edition Z06 Corvette that Jesse loved to drive so much. It was like a ray of sunshine from the heavens above, beaming down on his car.

"Yea, baby," Jesse said, staring at the vehicle for a moment. Then Jesse walked over to his car and got inside. He couldn't get his seatbelt on or the key in the ignition fast enough. Pressing the clutch pedal to the floor, he turned the key and lit the fires. With a sharp crackle from the cold

Borla exhaust, the Corvette roared to life. "Hello Handsome," was the message that displayed on the information center located in the center of the instrument cluster. The smile Jesse was wearing extended from ear to ear. Putting the transmission into first gear, Jesse tiptoed the car out of the garage and headed to church, closing the garage door behind him.

Pastor Raines always delivered a powerful message. His sermons were short but sweet, generally only lasting thirty-five or forty minutes, but the message was solid. Today, Jesse listened to Pastor talk about being alone.

"Even when you are alone in your home with no one else around you, you are not alone. When you feel defeat, you are not alone. When you feel misery, you are not alone. When you are joyous, you are not alone. The fact of the matter is, people, you are never alone because Christ is always with you!"

By now, Pastor's delivery was aggressive and strong. Slamming his hand down on the podium that he stood behind in the front center, he continued.

"Did you hear what I told you! You are never alone! Christ is always with you!" *Slam* went his hand onto the podium.

"Christ is always with you," Pastor said one last time in a normal-talking voice. After a moment of letting it all sink in with the congregation, he finished up with "Can I get an amen?"

The people of the congregation shouted back with a harmonious delivery of "amen!"

It only takes about fifteen minutes for the church parking lot to clear out on a nice Sunday afternoon, and since this was the nicest day of the year so far, no one was wasting a moment. Jesse sat in his car with the windows down and waited for the lot to clear as he saw Pastor walking toward him.

"That's a mighty fine-looking piece of machinery," Pastor said with a grin.

"Thank you, sir," Jesse replied with a smile.

"That car looks fast," Pastor said, eyeing it over. "Real fast. Sounds nice too. Pop your hood for me?"

"Haha," Jesse laughed with a smile. "Stop by for dinner tonight with Recon and me, you can ogle over it then. I'm on my way down to Flathead Lake to look at a piece of property Desi has up for sale."

"I was down there yesterday and looked at it. Nice piece of land— waterfront, secluded, fantastic views. One could build a nice house there, that's for sure. Hey, Jesse," Pastor said, looking him in the eye with a kind of serious look.

"What's up, Pastor?"

"Don't be giving Desi a hard time about not telling you that house you bought was Tim's. You belong there. Let it go."

"Pastor—" Jesse started but was immediately interrupted by Pastor.

"Forgive and forget and let that be the end of it. Now get out of here and go enjoy your day." Pastor turned and walked away. Jesse knew in his heart that Pastor was right, but not knowing upfront that the house he bought was Tim Johnson's still bugged him.

The drive down to the lake was fantastic. Jesse got into the zone and ran through the gears in the Corvette a number of times seeing speeds well into the one forties. The roads were smooth and fast, and the scenery was incredible. By the time he'd gotten to the property, he'd decided Pastor was right and he wouldn't mention anything about the late Tim Johnson being the previous owner of his house.

Pastor was right, Jesse thought to himself. *Let it go and enjoy the day*.

Of course, the property was at the end of a very dusty dirt road. When Jesse finally pulled up next to Desi's Dodge Durango, his Corvette was covered with dust. Desi jumped out of her Durango to greet Jesse.

As Jesse was getting out of his car, Desi wasted no time with her sass.

"Midlife crisis car, Jesse?" she asked with a smile.

"Very funny," he fired right back. "I happen to be a collector."

"Heard that before," Desi said, rolling her eyes. "C'mon, let me show you the lay of the land."

The piece of land for sale was magnificent, twenty-eight acres of a peninsula on Flathead Lake, water on three sides, mostly wooded. The ground was covered with fallen pine needles that made it both quiet and soft to walk on. There was a perfect building site for a large home that overlooked the lake. You could have glass on three sides of your home and see the lake from all of them. The pine trees were tall and healthy. There were a few rolling hills along with some level areas. There was a four-acre meadow that was covered with native grass.

Jesse walked down to the lake's edge and stared at the glass-like surface. You could see the lake's bottom as far out as your eye would reach.

"This is the last large lakefront parcel available on the lake," Desi said, walking up behind him. "If you know anyone who—"

Jesse immediately interrupted with, "I am, Desi. I am interested," Jesse said, turning to look at Desi. "See what the best price you can get this for me would be. The best price. I can't do anything on it yet, but until something better comes up, I want to sit on this."

"What do you mean by best price, Jesse?" Desi asked.

"I mean, $3.8M for this land is too expensive and way overpriced," Jesse stated, slowly walking back toward the vehicles. "I'm thinking the land as is should only be about $1M."

"Ha!" Desi burst into laughter. "Good luck with that!" she said, still chuckling.

"It's only worth what someone is willing to pay," Jesse said. "I'm willing to pay $1M for it."

"We're wasting our time with that offer," Desi told him. "That's an insult."

"How much did the property sell for the last time it was sold?" Jesse asked.

"I don't know, Jesse, I'd have to check," Desi replied, getting a little offended.

"Here are a couple of questions for you," Jesse fired back assertively. "Who owns this, and why are they selling it?"

Desi cocked her head and shot Jesse a snide look, sending the message that it didn't belong to Tim Johnson.

"Really, Buck?" she replied a little offended. "The land belongs to an elderly couple whose kids don't want it. It's too cold up here for them. They have no reason to keep it."

Desi spoke with a sharp tongue and a splash of attitude. She stood there eyeballing Jesse, waiting for some sort of response.

"It's overpriced, Desi," Jesse said calmly. "Tell the sellers you found the perfect buyer, a guy that loves the property, but he can only pay $1M for it. One million dollars in cash. Ensure them that I'm the right man to sell it to, and they'll sell it. Work for me for a change!"

Desi just stood there and watched Jesse walk to his car, get in, and leave. Desi watched the dust-covered Corvette disappear down the dirt road, still trying to wrap her head around their most recent conversation. "He's got to be kidding," she said to herself. "They'll never take a million for this parcel. He's crazy!" Desi shook her head and walked toward the lake. With a little more time to kill at the property, Desi decided to spend it sitting by the water. After all, the weather was much too nice to waste doing anything else.

Chapter 19

Jesse left Kalispell on State Road 424 heading north. It was a pretty drive. It was a road that was cut through a valley with mountains on either side. A nice way to enjoy the day. When Jesse came to Whitefish, Montana, he picked up SR 93 heading north. He was rolling the throttle in second gear when a black Corvette with Nevada tags blew by him in the left-hand lane at a very high rate of speed.

"Karma?" Jesse said out loud to himself. "No way, is that you?" With racecar driver reflexes, Jesse mashed the gas pedal to the floor, launching the Corvette down the highway. Third gear chirped the tires and brought the speedometer into triple digits. Fourth gear, another chirp of the tires, catapulting the Corvette into the one twenties. At nearly 130 miles per hour, he caught the black Corvette and was driving right next to it.

The raven-haired beauty glanced over just enough to recognize who it was. A smile inched across Karma's face as she was delighted to see the only male, she would ever consider to be her man.

"Try to keep up, Buck," she said as she dropped the hammer.

"Game on, sweetheart," Jesse replied, and the race was on. Karma and Jesse piloted their Corvettes up the highway, chasing each other at NASCAR speeds. The two came neck and neck around a corner to find the road blocked by tractor trailers. Jesse was hard on the brakes.

"Rookie," Karma said out loud as she opted to pass on the left-hand shoulder.

"Girl can drive," Jesse thought out loud as he followed her around, passing on the right-hand shoulder.

The truck drivers were laying on their air horns as the Corvettes blew past them and tucked in behind one another, with Karma out front. Every time Jesse tried to pass, she just gave it a little more throttle, not giving him an inch. Weaving in and out of traffic, passing cars like they were standing still, Karma and Jesse were completely focused on the road and each other. Engines revving and hearts pounding, they were driving these Corvettes the way they were made to be driven—fast! Just a few miles shy of Eureka, the two Corvettes passed a Porsche 911 Turbo so fast that the Porsche driver knew he never had a chance.

Karma must have remembered where she was because as she approached the exit to Jesse's house, she backed off the throttle and started slowing down. This put a smile on Jesse's face as he followed right behind. As if she'd been there a thousand times before, Karma led the way right to the house. She pulled up and stopped. Before she could get out, Jesse was parking right next to her. The two jumped out of their cars and ran toward each other, embracing in a hug.

"I've been missing you, Karma," Jesse told her, holding her tight.

"It's good to see you, Buck," Karma said, clinging to him. "It's really good to see you, actually."

Bark, bark, bark was the noise they heard as Louie came running toward them out of nowhere. He was quick with greeting Karma Australian shepherd–style with a tag-like motion with his front paws on her body, almost knocking her off her feet. Karma knelt down and let Louie kiss her cheek as she pet him all over.

"Ah, Louie, you remember me!" Karma said, holding back a tear. "You're such a good puppy, yes you are, yes you are!"

"Apparently, Louie was missing you a little too," Jesse said, watching the two reunite.

"He just knows how sweet I am!" Karma replied, standing up.

"What do you say we get something to drink and catch up a little on the deck?" Jesse asked, holding out his hand, inviting Karma to do the same.

"I would love nothing more," Karma said, wrapping both her arms around his.

As Jesse and Karma walked through the front door, they immediately noticed some commotion on the back porch.

"Who's out there?" Karma asked. She let go of Jesse's arm and cautiously positioned herself to see who was out there and what was going on.

"I don't know," Jesse asked with question. "I didn't see any other cars out front."

"It's Pastor and some other guy," Karma said, a little more relaxed.

"That guy's a friend of mine, he goes by Recon. We go back a ways, it's okay."

"Grab a bottle of wine and bring it out back." Karma nodded her head to Jesse and winked, heading toward the back door.

"I'm on it."

Before Karma could get the back door completely open, Pastor was on his feet, shouting.

"Well, hot damn! Karma's back! Give me some love, darling!" With arms open, he greeted her with a bear hug and a kiss on the cheek.

"Hi, Pastor," Karma said, giving him a hug. "Smells like you boys been out here drinking a while." Pastor was clung so tight to Karma, she had to push him off her. When she finally got free, she had to ask, "Who's this?"

"Hi ma'am, I'm Recon, a friend of Jesse's"

"How you doing, Recon?" Karma walked over to shake hands. "I'm Karma."

"Hi, Karma," Recon replied, getting up to shake hands. "The pleasure's mine."

"So, boys, tell me. What do we owe for the pleasure of your company? what's the occasion?"

"It's Sunday dinner at Buck's house. We were wondering if he was ever going to show up. Now we know why he's late." Pastor and Recon laughed together as they toasted their beers.

"Please sit, fill us in," Pastor said with a hand gesture, inviting Karma to sit at the patio table. Jesse joined the trio on the porch carrying two wine glasses and a bottle of Chardonnay with one hand and half of another bottle in the other.

"How'd you all get here?" Jesse asked. "I didn't see any other vehicles out front."

"Ahh-ha-ha," Pastor and Recon laughed and toasted again.

"We're on a mission," Recon said, laughing like a hyena.

"What's going on with you two clowns?" Jesse asked, a little annoyed. When he was hoping for a quiet evening with Karma, it was obvious that he wasn't going to get one. He'd forgotten all about it being Sunday and Pastor and Recon coming over for dinner, which has become a Sunday ritual.

"We parked the Ranger pickup on the other side of the lake and brought the canoe over," Pastor said, calming down.

"We're really not drunk. Recon just shared a little secret with me that struck us a little funny."

Pastor was starting to laugh again. Recon made eye contact with Pastor and burst into laughter with him.

"Must be some secret," Karma said, rolling her eyes.

"No doubt," Jesse agreed.

"Anything worth sharing?" Karma asked.

"We'll bring you up to speed later," Pastor answered, calming down. "Why don't you two chat a little while Recon and I get dinner ready tonight? Sound good?" Pastor suggested getting up.

"That's a great idea," Recon added, jumping up from his chair.

With Pastor and Recon inside, Karma seized the opportunity to start the conversation.

"Hey, Jesse," Karma asked, leaning toward him, looking him straight in the eye. "Would it be okay if I stayed here with you for a little while? I'll sleep in my own room and I won't be any trouble." Jesse stared into Karma's blue eyes while he pondered the question asked and how to address it.

"You don't have to sleep in your own room if you don't want to," Jesse finally replied softly leaning in to kiss Karma's lips.

"Oh yes I do," Karma said, sitting up straight. "I like you, Buck, but we're not there yet. If this is inconvenient…"

"Stop," Jesse interrupted her right there. "Of course, you can stay here with me as long as you want. I want you here."

"Thank you, Buck," Karma said to him, resting her hand on his and kissing him on the cheek.

The rest of the evening was filled with food, drinks, and laughter. Pastor cooked up some venison steaks on the grill that were amazing, literally melt-in-your-mouth good. Recon whipped together a salad with supplies he brought and they called that a meal.

By the time ten o'clock came, everyone was ready to call it a night. Karma disappeared into her room and locked the door behind her, and Jesse headed to bed, leaving Pastor and Recon on the deck to finish their drinks and find their way out whenever they wanted.

On the way to bed, Jesse stopped at Karma's door and gave it a knock.

"Yes," Karma answered.

"Karma it's me, Jesse, can you open the door for a minute?"

Karma opened the door just enough to stick her head out. "What's up?" she asked in a hurry.

"I was wondering if maybe you'd give me another kiss on my cheek," Jesse asked, pointing to his cheek with a finger. Karma tucked her head back in the room and shut the door without saying a word.

"Guess not," Jesse mumbled to himself with his head down. Just about the time Jesse was two steps away, he heard Karma open the door.

"Come here," she told him softly. "I can do better than that." Karma reached up and put her arms around Jesse's neck and pressed her body firmly against his. He wrapped his arms around her waist and held on to her tightly. Their hearts raced as their lips met. The kiss was slow and passionate.

Jesse started to run his hands down over Karma's behind when she slid her hands onto his chest and gently pushed him away.

"Don't be so eager, Buck," Karma said with a very sexy smile. "Just a kiss will have to do for tonight." Karma savored the moment, checking out Jesse's rugged appeal as she slowly backed into her room.

"Good night, Karma," Jesse said with a sigh and a smile.

"Good night, Buck," Karma said, closing the door behind her.

Safe in her bedroom, Karma locked the door and leaned against it. She put her hand on her chest and felt her racing heart. She closed her eyes and sighed with pleasure.

"That was a really hot kiss," she muttered to herself with a big smile on her face. "Wow!"

At the same time, as Jesse was heading to his bedroom, he too was feeling the intensity of the kiss. *That just might be the woman for me*, he thought to himself, also grinning from ear to ear. *Wow!*

Chapter 20

Tuesday evening was here in no time. Jesse was tending an empty bar at the Lasso when Pastor showed up.

"Sit anywhere you want tonight, Pastor," Jesse said, opening his arms as if to offer him the entire bar.

"I can see I've missed the crowd," Pastor said, sitting at the bar right in front of Jesse.

"The crowd will be here tomorrow night."

"Why, what's tomorrow night?" Karma said, pulling up a stool right next to Pastor.

"You didn't tell her?" Pastor asked Jesse with surprise.

"Tell me what?" Karma insisted.

"Pastor, Karma and I haven't had much of a chance to talk since she's been back—no, I haven't told her."

"Tell me what?" Karma asked again.

"Tomorrow night is *Return of the Jedi* night here, and your man is sponsoring a costume contest!" Pastor said, laughing. Jesse just stood there and nodded his head while looking at Karma.

"Yea, baby!" Recon shouted, entering through the doors like *he* owned the place.

"We're together again!"

"There is no way this wasn't planned," Karma said, sending a wink to Jesse.

"Recon, what are you doing here on a Tuesday?" Jesse asked.

"Pastor told me to meet him for a drink. We tried to go to the Nugget, but their windows are boarded up. The Beaver Dam's parking lot only had two cars in it, and one of those belongs to Ned - ain't stopping there. The only other place in town is the Mountain Oasis, and that was just closed for remodeling. Where else am I supposed to go?"

"What do you mean?" Jesse asked Recon "There *are* three other bars in town."

"Jesse, focus—all the other bars are closed, I just told you that!"

"You want them to go somewhere else?" Karma asked with raised eyebrows.

"No, of course not," Jesse replied, still looking at Recon. "I'm just giving him a hard time for trying!"

"Jesse," Pastor took over, "no one has been to the Nugget since you opened your doors. Jack Beaver shut it down two weeks ago. The Beaver Dam will be closed by the end of the month if business doesn't pick up. Georgia-Jean, the ER nurse, told me that you're putting the hurt on Jack's wallet, and he's none too happy about it."

"How would she know that, and why would she tell you?" Jesse asked.

"Wait," Karma said. "Let me get some drinks for this." She hopped off her stool and walked around the bar.

"Who's drinking what?" Karma asked, pointing around, waiting for shout-outs.

"I'll take a club soda on the rocks," Georgia-Jean said, coming through the door. Pastor was quick to hop down and greet Georgia-Jean with a friendly hug.

"We were just talking about you," he said.

"I figured as much," Georgia-Jean piped up with her spirited self.

"My ears were a-ringing."

"Karma, I'll take a Sierra Nevada," Recon said.

"Ms. Karma, I'd like a double shot of vodka with a shot of Jager on top," Pastor added.

"Wait, what?" Jesse asked.

"On the rocks," Pastor finished.

"What is that?" Jesse asked.

"That's nasty," Karma added.

"It's just a little something we used to drink back in the day," Pastor said, trying to be innocent.

"What day was that?" Recon chimed in, eager to learn anything he could about the man that seemed to appear out of nowhere.

"Jesse, who is this?" Georgia-Jean asked of Karma as she delivered drinks to the bar.

"My name's Rachael, ma'am. Very nice to meet you," Karma said, shaking hands with Georgia-Jean.

"Jesse, I thought you were in love with a woman named Karma," Georgia-Jean questioned, intentionally stirring the pot. Recon and Pastor burst into laughter and pointed at Jesse, waiting for him to say something.

"So," Karma said with her hand on her hip, "you're in love, huh?"

"Georgia-Jean," Jesse said to her, putting his arm around Karma.

"Rachael goes by the nickname Karma."

"I see," Georgia-Jean said, and that's when the light came on.

"You're the one they call Karma?" She looked at Rachael.

"Yes, ma'am," Karma replied with a chuckle.

"Well, Mr. Buck, I'd hold on to her if I were you," Georgia-Jean said with a smile. "I like you already, girl."

She said while looking at Karma. "You take good care of our Jesse now. He's a fine man," she finished with a wink.

"Y'all should know that Karma hasn't left my side in two days. She's been here working her tail off on her own accord. She's an impressive woman."

"Well, you know," Karma said, putting her hand on Georgia-Jean's arm, "the best man for any job is a woman."

"Really?" Jesse commented.

"There isn't anything you can do better than me!" Karma said with laughter and a playful poke in her voice. Pastor, Recon, and Georgia-Jean listened with perked-up ears as they wanted to see where this conversation was heading.

"I can outdrive you," Jesse said.

"Then why didn't you the other night?" Karma asked with as much sass as she could muster. With her hands on her hips and using as much body language as she had, Karma let Jesse have it.

"I beat you back to your house, remember?"

"No, she didn't!" Recon yelled, laughing! Pastor and Georgia-Jean couldn't believe what they just heard and were chuckling uncontrollably. Jesse and Karma stood there laughing and smiling at each other. Jesse finally started to nod his head.

"Yes, she did beat me home the other night," Jesse admitted through the chuckling.

Pastor leaned over into Georgia-Jean's ear and whispered, "Foreplay," while nodding toward Jesse and Karma. The laughter went on for almost a full minute, and Karma gloated with only a smile. Jesse let her have the moment. Karma was impressed that Jesse didn't try to play it off with some comment like "I let her win." For the first time in her life, Karma found herself with a genuine man. Karma stepped forward and put her arms around Jesse.

"You know we're going to have to have another run at it," Jesse said, looking down at Karma, but not letting go.

"Anytime you want, Buck," Karma replied with a smile. She leaned up on her tiptoes and planted a peck on Jesse's lips. "Anytime you want."

Jack Beaver stood outside in the shadows and peered into the Lasso through the window. He watched the tight-knit group of friends laughing and having a great time as they sat at the bar. Boiling over inside with frustration and anger, Jack was nearly foaming at the mouth. *What makes this outsider so great?* he thought to himself as he stared without blinking an eye. *No way this man comes into my town and takes it over. No way.* Jack stepped back from the window and vanished into the night.

By ten thirty, the only two people left in the Lasso were Jesse and Karma. Jesse was already done with the books for the evening and watched across the Lasso at Karma finishing tidying up. Karma moved with a certain grace, elegance, and precision all at the same time. *What's not to love about Karma, Georgia-Jean?* he thought to himself, referring to Georgia-Jean's comment earlier that night.

"Karma!" Jesse yelled across the empty floor. Karma stopped and looked over toward Jesse waiting to see what was what.

"It's going to be a long night tomorrow, what do you say we get outta here? Have a glass of wine by the lake. Good idea?"

"That sounds like a great idea, Mr. Buck," Karma said, walking to the back. "I'll start shutting down and locking up!"

The ride home to the house on the lake started off quiet. The only noise was the purr of the truck's engine coming from under the hood. Jesse reached over and grabbed Karma's hand to hold.

"I like having you here," Jesse said softly, looking over at Karma.

"I like being here with you, Buck," Karma replied with a smile. She leaned over and hugged Jesse's arm and held it close as they drove home in silence, just savoring the moment and enjoying each other. Sometimes silence is more powerful than any words spoken. They pulled down the drive and approached the house.

"Huh, the place looks dark," Jesse said. "Motion lights aren't coming on."

"I think I might have turned them off by mistake when we left this morning," Karma said with an innocent smile. "Sorry."

"No worries," Jesse said, getting out. "I'm sure we'll be fine." Jesse and Karma hopped out of the truck, not expecting anything to be wrong, and headed toward the door in the black Montana night.

"I can't see a thing," Karma said, walking up the front steps. "It sure does get dark out here."

"I know," Jesse added. "I can't tell what key it is."

"Aahhh! I just walked into something," Karma said in a panic. "Oh my gosh, there is something hanging from the rafters! Aahhh! Get it off me! Get it off me!" Karma screamed. "Get it off me!"

"Karma, . . . I got, I got you!" Jesse said, trying to find her in the dark. "Back to the truck!" Jesse hollered. "Run back to the truck now!" Jesse hit the unlock button on the key fob, unlocking the doors and illuminating it like a beacon in the dark. The couple ran to it as if they were being chased by Sasquatch.

Jesse yanked the passenger side door open and grabbed a Colt .45 from the glove box. Karma wrapped her arms around him and clung to him tightly.

"Are you okay?" Jesse asked with a great deal of concern in his voice. "Look at me, let's see—"

"I'm fine, I'm not hurt, but I have wet, sticky stuff on me."

"Come here into the light" Jesse said, pulling Karma around to the headlights of the pickup. "Oh my gosh!" Jesse said. "You're covered in blood!"

"Louie!" Karma said as she started to tear up. "Louie's hanging from the rafters. It's Louie!"

"Louie!" Jesse screamed. "Louie, come!" There was nothing.

"Karma," Jesse said, pulling Karma toward the front door of the truck. "Get in the truck and lock the doors. Call Recon and tell him I said *emergency surveillance.*"

"Where are you going?" Karma said with tears coming from her eyes.

"Louie, come now!" Jesse turned and screamed into the dark woods. "The blood you're covered in is still warm.

Whoever did this might still be here," Jesse said, handing Karma his mobile phone. Jesse racked the slide on his .45, putting a round into the chamber. He pushed the door closed, and Karma locked the doors and was on the phone with Recon in seconds.

"Louie, come!" Jesse continued to holler. Jesse walked around whistling for Louie. There was nothing. Jesse didn't want to leave Karma alone in the truck until Recon showed up. All he could do was wait. He knew Recon wouldn't be long.

"Louie, come now!" Jesse yelled again. Still, there was nothing. Jesse turned to Karma and yelled through the truck glass.

"Call Sheriff Rodney!" Jesse yelled for Louie while scanning the dark in all directions. Karma nodded her head yes and was back on the phone.

"Louie, come now!" Jesse yelled again, hoping it really wasn't his dog hanging from the rafters on the porch.

Jesse ran around the truck and jumped in the driver's side. He immediately fired up the powerful V8 engine and turned on the lights.

"Where are we going?" Karma asked with concern. Jesse slammed it in reverse without saying a word and mashed the accelerator to the floor. Dirt and gravel flew as Jesse backed up fifty feet or so. Then slamming the pickup into drive and turned on the high-beam lights, he spun the vehicle around and circled up behind the back of the shop. He drove slowly and was on full alert.

"We're just looking, Karma," Jesse said, reaching over to hold her hand again. "Whoever did this cut the power to the whole house."

"How do you know?"

"When I was outside yelling for Louie, I looked through the window to the kitchen and the clock to the microwave is off. Everything is off."

"What's going on, Jesse?" Karma asked with fear in her voice.

"I don't know, Karma," Jesse answered. "I'm gonna find out though." He looked Karma straight in the eye as if he was now on a mission. After looping around the shop and seeing nothing, Jesse headed back over to the house and shone his lights directly onto the porch.

"What the hell is that?" Jesse asked, squinting to make out the object hanging from the rafters. "That's not Louie," he continued with caution, unable to be certain at this point what it was.

"There's a knife in its chest," Karma said as her eyes started to tear up again. "Someone skinned Louie."

"It's not Louie," Jesse said, getting out of the truck. "Stay here and lock the doors behind me." The instant Jesse shut the truck door, Karma locked them.

"Louie, come now!" Jesse screamed into the night. With both hands on his pistol, Jesse moved with extreme caution toward the porch. As he got closer, his heart started to pound.

"Louie, come!" he yelled. Jesse looked around and listened intently. He couldn't hear over the truck's engine so he turned to Karma and signaled to her to turn it off. Karma reached over and shut it down but left the headlights burning. Jesse could hear something in the bushes between where he was and the guest cabin.

"Louie, come!" Jesse yelled again. There was nothing. He made his way to the porch, and there hung a dead animal. Hanging from a noose, the remains were beaten, partially skinned, just completely mutilated. He examined the animal slowly; whatever this was, it was not Louie.

A tear of relief came to his eye as he turned to Karma, shaking his head and shouting, "It's not Louie, it's not Louie."

Karma put her hand to her chest and smiled with relief.

"Louie, come!" Jesse yelled into the night one more time. As he walked toward the truck, he could hear sirens coming down the road fast. He pointed down the drive, and Karma jumped out.

"Sheriff's coming," he said to Karma with a head nod.

The flashing lights lit the drive up like Christmas, and in seconds, Sheriff Rodney entered with a skidding halt in a cloud of dust, jumping out of the car with his gun drawn.

"You folks all right? What's the matter, Mr. Buck?"

"Sheriff Rodney," Jesse said, walking toward him. "When we got home, we found this." Jesse brought the sheriff up to speed as they walked toward the porch.

"Louie, come now," Jesse continued to yell periodically.

"That ain't no dog hanging there," Sheriff Rodney said. "That right there's a badger. Or what's left of a badger, I might say." The sheriff spun it around and saw the knife in the dead animal's chest.

"Mr. Buck, you see this?" Sheriff Rodney asked, looking closely at the knife.

"No," Jesse replied. "See what?" Sheriff Rodney pulled the knife from the dead badger and held it down in the light from the vehicles so Jesse could read it.

"You're next" read the inscription engraved on the blade.

"Commander Buck! Perimeter secure," yelled a friendly voice appearing from the darkness. "I've got Louie, he's been shot." Like magic, Recon appeared into the light carrying Louie.

"He's alive, but his paw took a hit. Maybe buckshot?" Recon walked up and gently handed Louie to Jesse. Jesse couldn't hold back the tears as his faithful companion was whimpering in pain, but most certainly alive. Karma ran to them with uncontrollable tears of joy falling from both eyes.

"It looks like his mouth is all bloody," Sheriff Rodney said, taking a peek.

"Can we take him inside?" Karma asked.

"No!" Jesse and Recon both answered in unison.

"Recon, what'd you find?" Jesse commanded.

"Perimeter is secure. Power to the premises has been dug up and cut in two different places. Garage and guest cabin look to be untouched. No signs of forced entry on the main residence, but I don't recommend going in until daylight."

"How did you come up with all that?" Sheriff Rodney asked. "You just got here."

"We called him first," Jesse shot out with a quick glance to the sheriff, still holding Louie and breaking the lines of communication between the sheriff and anyone else.

"Recon, can you watch the perimeter until daybreak?" Jesse asked, looking for a direct response.

"I'm on it," Recon fired back and with an about-face disappeared back into the woods.

"Sheriff, Karma and I need to get cleaned up, and we need to take care of Louie right now. I want to keep this quiet, no paperwork for now. We'll just call it some kids playing a prank. Whoever did this will surface in time, and we'll take care of all the reports then. Would that be okay?" Jesse asked this of the sheriff with the utmost sincerity you could imagine.

"I'm not one to bend the rules, Mr. Buck," Sheriff Rodney said, puffing out his chest. "Since you seem to have your hands full right now, how about I come back tomorrow and get the paperwork taken care of. Sound good?"

"Tell you what, Sheriff, why don't you put this in the parking lot until Sunday? Join us for our Sunday cookout, and we'll do what we need to then. Would that be okay? We really need to go now."

Sheriff Rodney thought about it for a moment or two.

"That'll be just fine, Mr. Buck." And almost with disappointment, he turned and walked toward his car. Halfway to his car, Sheriff Rodney turned around, saying, "I'm here if you need me." He tipped his hat and waved. Moments later, he was gone.

"Karma," Jesse said, leaning over and giving her a peck on the lips. "Are you sure you are okay?"

"I'm fine, Buck, why?"

"Please lock up the truck and follow me," Jesse said, looking down at Louie softly whimpering in his arms.

Karma did what she was asked and immediately shut off the lights and locked up the truck.

"Where are we heading, Buck?"

"To get you and Louie cleaned up," Jesse said, looking into the woods. "Grab ahold of my belt and don't let go." With that, they headed into the darkness.

Chapter 21

Jesse walked along the lake carrying Louie, and Karma followed behind holding on to his belt. Karma was dying to know where they were going, but in her heart, she knew they would be safe and, even more so, she knew Jesse was a good man and trusted where he was taking them. Karma didn't trust too many people, but she trusted him. To her, safety was the most important thing she could have in a relationship. She wanted romance with a hint of lust. Great conversation and lots of fun. Trust, loyalty, and understanding were unspoken must-haves as well, but at the end of the day, she needed to feel safe.

"I feel safe with you, Buck," Karma said, breaking the silence after about fifteen minutes of walking through the dark.

"We're almost there," Jesse replied. "Just a couple of hundred feet ahead." In just a few more minutes, they had arrived.

"What is this place?" Karma asked, not being able to see anything in the pitch-black darkness.

"Karma, will you please hold Louie for a moment while I get things fired up?" Jesse asked, passing Louie to Karma.

"Of course," Karma said with open arms.

"When I bought the property, I scouted the layout of the land," Jesse said, fumbling around in the dark. "This is the very tip of my property, and I thought to myself, it would make a perfect place to get some quiet if I ever wanted to. I never thought it'd be used as a safe house."

With that, Jesse pulled the cord of a generator, and seconds later, the "safe house" came to life.

"I'll fill you in more once we get inside."

Once inside, Jesse turned on some lights and laid a tarp over the table.

"You can lay Louie here," Jesse said, pointing to the table. "Let me get the first aid kit."

"What is this place?" Karma asked, obviously in a trailer.

"This is the trailer I came up here in. I bought it because I didn't know how long I was going to be on the road, and when I found this place, I parked it."

"Are we safe here?" Karma asked.

"Yes, love." Jesse chuckled. "We're safe. Besides, Recon is on patrol, no one can get to us here. Please hold Louie down while I look at his paw." Jesse picked up Louie's paw and examined it thoroughly.

"Shouldn't we take him to a vet?" Karma asked.

"The basics with animals and humans are the same," Jesse answered, focused on Louie. After a few more moments of examining, Jesse stood upright.

"Here's the deal," Jesse said, looking at Karma still covered in badger blood. "The bleeding has stopped, nothing is broken. The lead in Louie's paw won't hurt anything. If we try to pick it out, it'll do more damage than if we just let it sit. If we leave it, his body will grow a callus around it. Let's bandage it for now, he should be fine. We'll give him some Tylenol and some honey with his food, and that should get him through the night."

"How do you know all of this?" Karma asked, trying not to lead off that she was very impressed with the extent of his knowledge.

"Life experience, Karma," Jesse replied, now wrapping Louie's paw in bandages.

"Will you please get the peanut butter, honey and bread out of the pantry and make a ball for Louie? He needs to take his meds when I'm done."

Karma wasted no time making the perfect "medicine ball" for Louie, complete with a Tylenol capsule in the center.

"I know why you want the Tylenol, it's a painkiller. Why the honey?" Karma asked.

"Great question," Jesse replied, still working on Louie's paw. "Honey is a natural antibiotic," Jesse continued. "It's great to use on animals or humans for that matter. It has no side effects, and they eat it like candy!"

"I'm impressed, Buck," Karma said, folding her arms across her chest, smiling and watching. "I am really impressed."

"All right, Louie," Jesse said, picking him up off the table and placing him on the sofa. "You should be good until morning." Louie put his head down on the sofa and closed his eyes. His breaths were heavy and deep, but they were steady.

"What about me?" Karma asked with a smile. "When can I get cleaned up?"

"You shower first, and then I will. We'll sleep here tonight and head back to the house when the sun comes up," Jesse said with a smile. "I have towels in the bathroom and extra sweatpants and clothes hanging up."

Karma headed into the shower. Before she closed the door, she turned and looked back at Jesse. After a brief pause, she ducked into the bathroom and shut the door. *That is a good man*, Karma thought and proceeded to get cleaned up.

When Karma finished with her shower, she found a clean pair of sweat clothes on the bathroom counter. She put them on—a little big, but they did the job. When she left the bathroom, the trailer was quiet.

"Jesse?" Karma whispered. There was no answer, and she found Jesse and Louie lying on the bed up front, both fast asleep. Karma turned off the lights and curled up next to Jesse.

"I really do feel safe with you, Buck," she whispered, giving him a kiss on his cheek. "You are a good man and a decent human being." She draped a leg over Jesse and pressed her body up against his. "I hope none of this havoc tonight is because of me." Karma took a big sigh and closed her eyes. Moments later, she too was fast asleep.

Chapter 22

Wham, wham, wham! was heard on the door.

"Yo, Buck! You gonna sleep the day away?" Recon yelled from outside the trailer door. "Let's go! We're burning daylight!" *Wham, wham, wham!* "Commander Buck! You alive?"

Jesse slowly opened his eyes to the unpleasant sounds that Recon was making outside the door. It was just him and Louie on the bed.

"I'm up! I'm up!" Jesse hollered back with a scratchy voice. "Quit banging on the door! Where's Karma? She with you? Open the door, should be unlocked!"

With that, Recon opened the door and poked his head inside.

"No, Karma's not with me. Don't you guys talk? She left about an hour ago."

"What?" Jesse asked. "Where'd she go?"

"Jesse," Recon fired back defensively, "I didn't interrogate her. She just said she had something to take care of. She got in her car and left. What was I supposed to do?"

Jesse sat on the bed and pet Louie while he pondered where Karma could have run off too.

"You seem awfully alert for being shot in the paw last night," Jesse said, scratching Louie behind the ear.

"Jesse," Recon snapped, "forget about Karma for a moment." He made his way back to the bed where Jesse and Louie were sitting. "I've got something for—"

"Hey!" Jesse interrupted. "Don't tell me to forget about Karma, got it?" Jesse spoke with a stern voice and laser-focused eyes. It's been a while since Recon had seen that look in Jesse's eyes. He knew Jesse was serious.

"Look," Recon continued. "I didn't want to mention this to the sheriff last night, but I also found this." He handed Jesse a dusty pistol.

"It's a Thompson Contender," Recon added. "Check out the barrel."

Jesse examined the barrel. Along the side, it read ".45/.410."

"You think?" Jesse said, looking up at Recon.

"Open it."

Jesse broke the action and cocked the barrel forward on the single-shot revolver.

"Sure enough," Jesse said, pulling out the empty .410 shotgun shell.

"I'd bet money that's the round that ended up in your dog's paw last night," Recon went on.

"Yeah, me too," Jesse added, further examining the pistol. "Looks like the serial numbers have been ground off, no way to trace it without a ballistics check. What are you not telling me about last night, Louie?" Jesse asked, looking over at his dog as if a reply were imminent, scratching him under the chin now.

"We should get you cleaned up, Louie," Jesse said, talking to the dog more than Recon at this point. "You sure do have a lot of blood on your face. You're a mess."

As Jesse stood up, Louie jumped off the bed and headed toward the door, eager to get out.

"He's moving pretty good this morning," Recon noted.

"Yea, fortunately, whoever shot him isn't a very good aim," Jesse said, still pondering the amount of blood on Louie's face.

"Recon, any way you can test a couple of blood samples, see if they match?"

"Of course," Recon replied as if that were a stupid question. "I can say they are samples from an animal and take them to the vet's office that the forestry service uses. Why? What are you thinking?"

"Let's head up to the house. I'll fill you in on the way."

Jesse and Recon locked up the trailer and headed up to the house, and Louie was keeping up on three paws, favoring the injured one.

After an extensive examination, it appeared that no one had entered the home last night and that the only damage done was to the underground power line that led up to the house. Jesse's first priority was getting an electrical contractor on the phone and scheduling a visit. He contacted Erin and let her know that he'd be in later this afternoon, and naturally, she was fine with that.

Jesse stashed the pistol with the knife he had from the night he met Karma. Not exactly sure why he was saving either one at this point, but he wasn't ready to part with them. He didn't like what was going on; now it's gotten personal. You just don't mess with another man's life, and you certainly don't shoot an innocent dog.

With the badger buried, the electrical contractor working, and the overall mess cleaned up off the porch from last night, it was time to get cleaned up and into work. Jesse stripped naked and headed for the shower. The hot water felt great running over his skin. He stood there for a moment and just let the hot water wash away the past. With both hands against the shower wall, Jesse lifted his head and began to pray out loud:

"Dear Lord, oh Heavenly Father, please forgive me of my sins as I forgive those who have sinned against me. Lord, please bring Karma back to me safely. Please bring her back safely, Lord. Amen."

Chapter 23

Return of the Jedi night at the Lasso was a huge success. There were Ewoks and Androids. Darth Vaders and Luke Skywalkers. C3P0s and the mystery Chewbacca turned up again, who turned out to be Pastor wearing some two-foot-tall stilts. It was the biggest *Star Wars* convention you could have in a small town.

People even came in from Idaho and Wyoming just to participate in the fun. The local news channel showed up to document the event. Obi-Wan Kenobi was the reporter. Jesse was dressed as one of the many Han Solos, and Erin was one of only three or four Princess Leias. Their picture was taken standing between Chewbacca and one of the Darth Vaders.

The parking lot was so full that people were parking down the street, and when the restaurant reached maximum capacity, the party moved outside. One Hans and Leia couple showed up in a 1977 Ford LTD station wagon that was disguised as the *Millennium Falcon.* You couldn't have asked for a better evening.

It was time to lock the doors and call it a night. Today was an exceptionally long day. Jesse had hoped that Karma would only be gone a few hours and she would appear at the Lasso this evening. That didn't happen. As Jesse headed home alone in the pickup, the silence was deafening. There was hope that he'd find Karma at the house waiting for him when he got there, but when he pulled into an empty driveway, the hope vanished, and his heart sank a little.

"Please come home, Karma," Jesse mumbled to himself as he parked.

Louie was there to greet him as he got out of the truck. "You sure are resilient, aren't you?" Jesse said to his faithful companion as he bent over to give Louie lots of attention. "C'mon, Louie," Jesse said to Louie, getting him excited. "Let's go inside." Louie bolted toward the front door. His injured paw seemed to be nothing more than an inconvenience at this point, a minor one at that. Other than the bandage and the limp, you'd never know he was injured. Jesse entered through the front door and pushed it closed behind him, locking the deadbolt. When he flipped on the light in the foyer, he found a note lying on the floor that read,

Jesse:

Blood results back. Blood on Louie's face did not match blood from his bandage or blood from badger. Blood on Louie's face was human blood.

Recon

"Well, that tells us a little more about what happened last night, huh, Louie!" Jesse said out loud to Louie. "Come here, Louie, come here, boy!" Jesse knelt down on the floor. Louie came limping over to greet his master with licks and kisses.

"You took a chunk outta somebody last night, didn't you! Good boy, Louie! Good boy!" Jesse said, petting and loving his dog all over.

"You're the best dog ever!" Jesse continued out loud as if he was having a conversation with his dog.

Your day is coming, buddy, Jesse thought to himself about the guy that was here the other night. *Whoever you are, I will find you and we'll settle this*. He knew it wasn't some kid playing a joke, and he didn't want to jump to conclusions as to who it might be. It always seems like the people who do these sorts of things are the ones you'd never think of; then again, don't overlook the obvious.

Chapter 24

Everything seemed to move in slow motion for Jesse when Karma was gone. The days dragged by. His heart even ached a little. He kept finding himself confused. He wanted Erin in the worst way, yet he's talked himself out of her due to her young age. He's trying to focus on Karma, yet she keeps vanishing without a reason. He found himself praying for her safe return a lot. To help keep his mind occupied on other tasks, Jesse let Erin run the Lasso while he worked on completing the apartments upstairs. He figured they would be move-in ready in about two more weeks if he kept his current pace up.

In the meantime, the Hickory Sticks approached Erin and asked her what she thought about a live karaoke night on Thursdays. It took her about two seconds to jump on it. Now, the Hickory Sticks played live music to karaoke on Thursday night and played as a cover band on Friday nights. By the time Erin told Jesse about it, everything was done. Jesse let her have the reins and was fairly interested himself to see how this would turn out. He'd never even heard of live karaoke.

The next day was Thursday, and it was a packed house. The live karaoke was a smashing success. The band knew every song that was asked of them, and thanks to YouTube, all the lyrics were made available as well. Jesse had been bringing Louie to work with him to keep an eye on Louie's healing paw. Louie spent his day limping around the floor getting free food from customers and lots of attention. *If I didn't know any better, I'd say Louie was milking his injured paw for all it's worth*, Jesse thought to himself watching his dog in action.

Saturday night finally rolled around. Jesse and Pastor ran the bar as usual. Pastor was flipping bottles and showing off his hidden talent, and Jesse was pouring beer. Jesse never did understand why Pastor insisted on working for free but loved having him there. He was definitely entertaining to watch and never spilled a drop of alcohol.

Jesse knew one day there would be a favor asked of him and wondered from time to time what that favor might be. Not that it really matters. Part of help is being there for someone when *they* need you, not when you are available.

With everyone gone and the cleaning crew bustling away, Jesse sat at his table by the piano and crunched the numbers not only for the week but for the month as well. June was over. July started on Monday. He paused for a moment to think about everything coming up in July. The rodeo, the chili cook-off, the fireworks. In his mind, he'd imagined spending this time with Karma. The reality was he didn't know where she went or when she'd be back. She was like the wind. *How is it that I haven't gotten her mobile phone number yet?* Jesse thought to himself while sipping on some Johnny Walker Blue Label. *I have got to do that!*

"Louie," Jesse said, looking over at his companion sleeping in the middle of the floor of the Lasso. "What do you say we crash upstairs tonight?" Jesse poured a little more scotch over the melting ice in his glass.

"Seems like a good idea to me," Jesse answered for his pet.

"It's a quarter till three," Jesse mumbled to himself, looking at his phone. "I need to get this finished. The cleaners are already done and I'm still working." Jesse returned focus to the project at hand, eager to not be up all night. Before he could get back into his rhythm again, he looked up thinking he heard someone come through the door. Not seeing anyone, he dropped his head and started crunching numbers again.

Jesse was pounding away on the adding machine when he thought for sure he could hear Karma calling his name, "Buck." He knew he was just tired and imagining things when he heard his name again; this time, it was a little louder.

"Buck."

Jesse looked up just in time to watch Karma hit the floor. Jesse sprang from his chair like he was shot out of a cannon and ran over to where Karma was lying.

"Karma, what happened to you, talk to me?" Karma had blood all over her abdomen and her hands. Her clothes were wet with blood as well.

"Water, I need some water," Karma uttered with a very weak voice.

"I need to get you to the hospital!" Jesse said while reaching under her to pick her up.

"No hospitals," Karma said, holding her hand up. "Just get me some water."

Jesse jumped up and locked the front doors. Then he ran to the bar and got a glass of water and some aprons and ran back to Karma.

"Karma, here, take a sip." Jesse helped her sit up enough for her to drink.

Karma sipped almost the entire glass before saying another word.

"More, I need some more." With lightning speed, Jesse was back with a refill.

"Karma, you're hurt," Jesse told her. "You need some help."

"No doctors, Buck," Karma insisted. "I'll be fine. I just need to lie down and rest."

"Let me take you upstairs," Jesse said as he attempted to pick her up again.

"Stop," Karma said, gasping for air. "Just help me up, I can walk."

Jesse knew she was in a lot of pain. He helped Karma to her feet, and the whole time she covered her abdomen with her left arm.

"Let's get you upstairs," Jesse told her, comforting her.

Jesse helped Karma through the Lasso and upstairs where he had his little crash pad.

"Karma, lie down here," Jesse said, helping her onto the bed.

"Slowly, slowly," Karma said, still holding her abdomen and seemingly in great pain.

"Easy, easy . . ." Jesse comforted her, laying her back.

"Karma," Jesse said, looking at her blood-soaked clothes, "I need to see where this blood is coming from. I need to get this shirt off of you."

"Okay," Jesse moved her arm off her abdomen and tore the blouse open, revealing a deep gash across her entire stomach.

"Oh my gosh! Karma, what happened to you? This is bad, you need stitches now, baby."

Karma grabbed Jesse by the arm and glared at him straight in the eyes.

"No doctors," she said, "and don't call me baby!"

Gasping for air, she lay her head back down.

"Stitch it up," she said. "Just do it."

"What happened to you, Karma? Were you in a car accident?"

"I almost lost a sword fight," Karma replied, breathing very heavily.

"I need more water." Karma demanded, sweating and breathing heavily.

Jesse grabbed her glass and helped her drink some more.

"Karma, you're delirious," Jesse said to her while she was sipping water. "You just told me you almost lost a sword fight."

"That's right," Karma answered again.

"Hang tight, Karma. Let me see what I have to stitch you up with," Jesse said, standing up. "I might have to take you to the hospital."

"No hospitals!" Karma insisted with gusto. "Figure it out, Buck, just hurry."

Jesse disappeared to dig up whatever supplies he could. His first aid kit had bandages and antibiotic cream but no sutures and nothing to use as a substitute. He knew Karma was hurting, and if she was telling the truth about the sword fight, that would make sense about why no hospitals. Hospitals ask questions.

So much for sleep tonight, Jesse thought to himself as he scurried around, frantically gathering supplies.

"Karma, I'm back," Jesse said softly with the means to mend her up.

"What'd you find?" Karma asked with her eyes closed.

"I've got some antibiotic cream and bandages from the first aid kit, clean rags to clean you up with. The only thing I could find to stitch you up with fishing line," Jesse told her, getting everything ready.

"Really, Buck?" Karma asked, opening her eyes to look at him. "Fishing line?"

"Hey, Karma," Jesse fired back, "this is a restaurant, not an emergency room. It's either fishing line or staples."

"Fishing line will be just fine," Karma replied painfully.

"Karma, drink this and try to relax," Jesse said, handing her a drink.

"What is it?"

"It's a shot of Jack Daniels," Jesse said. Karma shot the drink down and handed the glass back to Jesse.

"Better make it a double."

Jesse handed her a second, which went down just like the first.

"Karma, lie back and keep your eyes closed," Jesse told her. "First, I'm going to get you cleaned up then stitched up. I want you to tell me what happened while I do this to keep your mind off what I'm doing."

When Jesse started, Karma just lay there and twitched and gasped for air while he cleaned her up. First, the blood, then the wound. The wound had to be nine inches across and as deep as it could go without hitting any major organs. It was only a flesh wound, but it was certainly a deep one.

"Okay," Jesse said, "I'm going to start stitching now."

Karma nodded her head, and Jesse went to work. The red SpiderWire fishing line was a microfilament that made it very easy to work with.

Never thought I'd be doing this, Jesse thought to himself while he very carefully stitched up Karma, hoping not to cause her any more pain than she was already in.

"I was in Vegas," Karma started talking between gasps of air and twitches of pain. "I have a situation down there that I am dealing with…"

Jesse listened with a keen ear as Karma put into words her latest experience.

"…the situation got a little heated..."

Jesse started to stitch a little faster, thinking that he needed to finish stitching before Karma finished talking.

"I'm listening," Jesse said in a soothing voice, hoping she would continue.

"…Two guys grabbed me and lead me into a back room of the casino I was in…"

"What casino?" Jesse interrupted.

"…The room was filled with swords and knives, collectibles, high-end collectibles…" Karma continued, completely ignoring Jesse's question.

"…I took care of the first two guys…"

I'm sure you did, Jesse thought to himself, remembering the hurt she put on Ned Beaver the night they met.

"…Then a big guy came in with a sword in his hand…"

"Water, Jesse," Karma said, stopping her story. "I need a sip of water."

Jesse stopped immediately and helped Karma with some water. She laid her head back down on the pillow and continued.

"…I grabbed a sword off the wall to defend myself…" Karma paused for a moment and caught her breath before she could continue.

"…I hesitated, and he got me. Then I think he thought I was done, so I got him back…" Karma spoke, still breathing heavily and gasping for air. "…I got him good…" Struggling to breath, Karma managed to continue.

"….I got him right across the face. He'll be scared for life. I got out of the room, left the casino, and drove straight here. I drove here as fast as I could."

"Are you telling me you drove straight here from Las Vegas hurt like this?" Jesse asked, finishing up his stitch job.

"As fast as I could," Karma said again.

"Karma, let's get this blouse off you," Jesse said, helping Karma out of the blood-soaked garment.

"Here are two aspirin." Jesse helped Karma take them with water. "Get some rest. I'm going to go pull your car in the garage. I'll be right back."

"Okay, Buck."

"Louie," Jesse said, now looking at his dog who had been watching the whole time. "Keep an eye on Karma."

Jesse covered Karma with a blanket and kissed her on the forehead. He cleaned up the mess and went downstairs, trying to comprehend what he had just heard.

"What in the world is this woman up to?" Jesse asked himself repeatedly.

When Jesse went out front, he found Karma's Corvette right outside of the door. The driver's side door was open, and the car was still running. The car was noticeably dirty, not the way she kept it. When he looked to get inside, he saw a sword in the passenger's side of the car, validating Karma's story. Jesse looked around to see if anyone was watching—he saw no one.

Jesse quickly moved the vehicle into one of the garage spaces behind the Lasso and closed the garage door behind it. All of a sudden, there was much, much more to this woman that had his attention than he ever dreamed of.

"You're safe with me, Karma," Jesse said to himself as he headed back upstairs to where she was lying.

When he entered the room where Karma was lying, he found her asleep. Louie had jumped up on the bed and was lying next to her. Her hand was resting on Louie's back, and Louie was on full alert, complete with paws hanging over the edge of the mattress as if he were ready to pounce. Louie was certainly protecting Karma from danger, just like Jesse had asked him to.

Jesse turned off the light and went to lie down on the other side of the bed next to Karma. He lied down on his back and reached over to hold Karma's hand.

"It's good to have you home," Jesse said softly with his eyes closed. Karma gave his hand a gentle squeeze as if she were telling him "it's good to be home."

Three whole minutes went by, and Jesse knew he'd never get to sleep. With the sun starting to peek over the mountain tops in the distance, Jesse decided to be productive with his time; after all, Louie had things under control up here. Jesse quietly got out of bed and slipped downstairs to the garage. He spent the next couple of hours cleaning up Karma's Corvette. He wrapped the sword up in some aprons from the Lasso and placed it under the back seat of his pickup out of sight.

He backed Karma's Corvette out of the garage and washed it thoroughly on the inside and out. Two hours later, her Z06 Corvette shone like a new car. Jesse pulled it back into the garage and locked it up. Just before he shut the door, Jesse hit the release on the trunk compartment and found Karma's bag and purse. He grabbed them and put them into his pickup and then proceeded to lock up the Vette.

"She can't leave if I don't give her keys back to her, can she?" Jesse said out loud to himself.

"I heard that, Buck," Karma said, standing at the door that led upstairs to the apartments, gently holding her stomach.

"Karma?" Jesse asked. "What are you doing up?"

"Hey, can we go back to your place?" Karma replied, more as a statement and less like a question. "I'd feel better there, less traffic. Know what I mean?"

"Of course, we can," Jesse told her, walking toward Karma. "How are you feeling?"

"Like I almost lost a sword fight," Karma replied with a half-smile. "I need my bag and my purse out of the car." She said pointing at her Vette.

"I already grabbed them out of the back," Jesse answered.

"Is my car safe sitting there?"

"Absolutely," Jesse answered, opening the pickup door for Karma and helping her in. "Give me a minute and we'll be gone." He closed the pickup door behind her. "I've got to get Louie."

Chapter 25

As promised, just a couple of minutes later, Jesse and
Karma were on their way back to Jesse's house. Jesse took
advantage of the opportunity by reaching over to grab
Karma's hand and hold it. Glad to hold Jesse's hand,
Karma gave a gentle squeeze accompanied with a smile.
Then Jesse broke the silence.

"Karma, I'd really like to know what's going on."
Karma let a big sigh out and stared straight ahead.

"I know you would, Buck. It's kind of complicated, and
I'm not sure you're ready to hear it."

"Karma," Jesse continued in a very gentlemanly,
soothing voice, "I'm ready to listen to whatever it is that
you have to tell me. I'm not ready for you to run off again
not telling me where you are going or *if* you even plan on
coming back."

"Jesse?" Karma started again. "I hope you can forgive
me for leaving like I did. That may not have been one of
my best decisions and I'm sorry."

Jesse listened intently as Karma spoke with a very
sincere tone in her voice.

"I wasn't ready to meet you, Jesse," Karma said,
looking over at him and squeezing his hand a little tighter.
"But now that I have met you, I'm really glad I did. I don't
really feel like talking about everything right now, but I
promise you, if you can give me a little more time, I'll start
sharing. Good enough?"
Jesse looked over at Karma. Her beauty was hypnotizing to
him. He knew in his heart that Karma was a good woman.

This woman had his heart in her hands, and she didn't even know it.

"You know I'm going to hide your car key, don't you?" Jesse asserted with a smile.

"I'm okay with that, Buck," Karma said, clinging to Jesse's arm.

"For a month." He continued, looking straight ahead. Karma held on to Jesse's arm for the rest of the way home. There were no more words spoken on the drive, but the truck was filled with emotion. Jesse and Karma were both very glad to be back with each other.

"Why don't you go inside and lie down for a while?" Jesse said as they were pulling down the drive. "You know you're safe here. It's nice and quiet, go lie down."

"Are you sure you're okay with that?" Karma asked, easing herself out of the front seat of Jesse's pickup.

"Of course, I am, love," he replied without even thinking about what he just said.

"That's much better than baby," Karma said, shooting Jesse a smile over her right shoulder.

"Karma," Jesse said, stopping in his tracks, "today is Sunday."

"Do you want an amen?" Karma asked, not sure what Jesse was getting at.

"Funny. Do you want me to tell Pastor and Recon not to come over for dinner today?" With zero hesitation, Karma fired back.

"No way! They love Sundays at the lake and so do I. Dinner tonight is on—just don't ask me to cook anything!" With that, Karma disappeared into the house, into her room, and shut the door behind her.

"She's a good woman, isn't she?" Jesse said, looking down at Louie. "A good woman."

The afternoon was beautiful. Jesse sat out on the back porch with Louie, and they were taking in the fresh air. An occasional fish would jump out of the water and land with a splash. There were geese along the shore and deer sipping from the other side of the lake. It was truly picturesque, so peaceful, so serene.

"This lake needs a name, doesn't it, Louie?" Jesse said out loud to his faithful companion basking in the warm summertime sun. "We need to come up with a name for it."

"Talk to yourself much, Buck?" Karma asked, stepping outside with a bottle of chardonnay and two wine glasses.

"I wasn't talking to myself; I was having a conversation with Louie about naming the lake," Jesse said, getting up to greet Karma.

"How are you feeling?"

"I needed the sleep," Karma replied, handing the bottle of wine and an opener to Jesse. "I'm really glad to be back here with you, Jesse." She stepped up on her tiptoes to plant a peck on Jesse's cheek.

"Sinners!" Pastor yelled as he stepped around the corner of the house with an unopened bottle of Jack Daniels in his hand, laughing as if he caught them doing something they shouldn't have been doing.

"Now I know why you weren't in church today!"

Jesse and Karma looked at each other and chuckled together.

"We had a long night, Pastor," Jesse said, walking over to shake hands.

"I'll bet you did!" Pastor replied with a smile, a handshake for Jesse, and a hug for Karma.

"Gently," Karma said as she hugged Pastor back. "I have a bit of a tummy ache."

"Pregnant?" Pastor impeded.

"No, it's a little more intense than that, Pastor." Karma tried to explain.

"A little rough on you, was he, darlin'?" Pastor asked, laughing, still insinuating what *he* thought was obvious.

"Hey, Pastor," Karma said with charm and a little attitude. "Jesse doesn't get any of this"—she waved her hands down her beautiful womanly figure— "until he puts a ring on this." She finished up, pointing at her ring finger. "So . . . that'll be enough of that . . . We cool?" Karma stood there with her hands on her hips—what a beautiful woman.

Pastor and Jesse stood there chuckling when they heard Georgia-Jean coming around the corner.

"That's the way to do it, girl! You tell him how it's going to be!"

"Georgia-Jean!" Karma said, walking over to greet her with a hug. "I didn't know you were coming."

"Well, how about that," Georgia-Jean said with her ears perked up and wit about her. "The pastor told me that I shouldn't miss Sundays at the lake with you fine people so I told him I'd love to join you, so here I am!"

"Georgia-Jean, you are always welcome here, and going forward if you're not here on Sundays, we'll think something's wrong," Jesse said, inviting her to the table.

"What can I get you to drink, Georgia-Jean?"

"Young man, you should know me by now. I'll have the same thing—a club soda on the rocks. Toss in a dash of lemon if you have one."

"It's three thirty and Recon's not here yet," Pastor spoke, almost asking if anyone knew where he was. "He's never late."

"I'm not late, I'm right here," Recon said, getting out of his canoe and tying it to one of the deck posts, "and I've got the ice." Recon grabbed a twenty-two-pound bag of ice out of the front of the boat and made his way to the deck.

"Karma's back!" Recon said, running over to greet her with a hug. "So that's why you weren't in church, today Jesse!" Recon yelled across the deck. "You were busy sinning!" Recon and Pastor burst into laughter.

"Don't you mind those two troublemakers now, dear," Georgia-Jean said, looking right at Karma. "They wouldn't know a good thing if it bit them."

"Since when do you go to church anyway, Recon?" Georgia-Jean fired.

"Speaking of bites," Recon replied, changing the subject and handing Pastor two rocks glasses filled with ice. "You haven't by any chance seen anyone come through the ER with a dog bite recently, have you?" Recon asked, looking at Georgia-Jean.

"I haven't, no," Georgia-Jean replied, "but I've been working down at Polson Hospital near Flathead Lake all week while they had some staff out. Why?" The deck got silent. Everyone just kind of looked at each other. It was obvious Georgia-Jean didn't know what had happened yet.

"Recon, debrief Georgia-Jean for us," Jesse commanded. Recon brought Georgia-Jean up to speed in less than thirty seconds, which was perfect. He gave her just enough information to be satisfied without overloading her with details.

"Okay," Jesse yelled out, "whose turn is it to cook?"

"I'll be tonight's chef if I'm still invited," Sheriff Rodney said, coming around the corner and onto the deck.

"Get that man an apron!" Jesse yelled out like a game show host walking over to greet the sheriff.

"Of course, you're still invited, glad you could make it. What can I get you to drink sheriff?"

"You can get me a glass of ice for some of that Jack Daniels I see on the table, and on Sundays, it's Rod. Not 'Sheriff,' not 'Sheriff Rodney.' My friends call me Rod."

"Well, Rod," Recon said, handing over a rocks glass full of ice, "don't burn the steaks!" Everyone chuckled.

"Let's make a toast," Jesse said, holding up his wineglass with one arm and his other around Karma, "to friendship."

"To friendship," everyone said, clinking glasses together followed by the traditional taste.

"You get any more friends, Jesse, we're going to have to get a bigger table," Pastor shouted out.

"Can't have too many friends," Georgia-Jean added.

"A bigger table is easy," Karma continued in the conversation. "Look how big this deck is—we could have six or eight tables out here."

"Then you're going to need a bigger grill," Recon added.

Chapter 26

Rain or shine, every morning started with a walk around the lake. Jesse and Karma held hands while Louie ran ahead. Every morning, they shared a little more about each other's past as well as a little more about each other's present. They would focus their conversation more on what they both liked and what common goals they had and common dreams that they'd like to share with each other rather than talk about what they didn't like. Sort of "if we have enough positives together, the few negatives we have won't matter" train of thought.

Jesse was always eager to hear more about what was going on in Las Vegas than Karma was ready to share. Karma never offered any new details. To date, all he knew was what she had told him the night he stitched her up. Jesse was hoping that if he didn't ask, in time Karma would just start to talk a little more about it.

When the morning walk brought them back to the house, their time together continued with bagels and fruit by the lake accompanied with coffee and juice. The two would eat and talk small talk about things going on in town or ideas they had about the Lasso. With each passing day, Jesse and Karma grew closer and closer together. Every night was finished off with a kiss in the hallway, and the two lovebirds would leave each other and head to their separate rooms for the night. The kisses were slowly getting a little longer and a little hotter.

When things got a little too steamy, Karma was quick to step back and put some distance between them so things wouldn't go too far. It didn't matter how much she wanted to give herself to Jesse; she was bound and determined to wait. The only man that was going to have her would be the man she marries. As far as Karma was concerned, there were far too many women too eager to open their legs for just any man, and that by all means wasn't going to be her. From her wedding night on, her body becomes his to have and to hold; but until then, a simple good night kiss would have to do.

On occasion, Jesse would get a hand slapped when he got a little overzealous. In a playful kind of way, Karma loved knowing that she was wanted and desired by this man that she so desired and wanted. Karma knew in her heart that Jesse wanted all of her. Jesse wanted her mind, her friendship, her love, her trust, her understanding, her loyalty, and of course, her body. The best part was not only did Jesse want that of Karma but Karma also wanted that of Jesse. The couple became inseparable. One was never without the other, and they were always holding hands. This was truly a match made in heaven.

Chapter 27

"What part of 'burn his house down' don't you understand?" Jack said sternly to his incompetent son Ned.

"What part of 'throw a Molotov cocktail through the window and leave' sounds like 'hang a dead animal from the porch and shoot his dog'! you idiot!" *Smack!* Jack landed a hard backhand across Ned's face as the two met out in the middle of the Christmas tree farm.

"Say something!" Jack demanded at the top of his lungs. Ned just stood there, his lip now swollen and bleeding from his father's abuse.

"Here's the best part," Jack continued as he paced back and forth in front of Ned, never taking his eyes off him.

"The man's dog bites you. Not only does it bite your dumb ass, this little dog takes a man-size chunk out of your calf."

"Well, I—"

"Shut up!" Jack halted the words from Ned's mouth before the third one was heard.

"Nope, that's not the best part," Jack said with a combination of anger and sarcasm. "The best part is you shot the dog and dropped the gun you shot it with. That's just AWESOME!" *Smack*, Jack Beaver landed a second even harder backhand across his son's face. Ned looked at his father and spit a bloody tooth out into his own hand. Now trembling with fear and adrenaline, Ned had a look of anger and rage brewing across his face.

"Don't look at me like that," Jack spoke aggressively. "If you'd brush your teeth once in a while, you'd still have your tooth."

Ned eyeballed his father as anger started to boil uncontrollably from within.

"You know, boy?" Jack said with even more sarcasm. "That ain't the best part either."

Ned spit blood onto the ground and wiped off his mouth, listening to his father mock him.

"The best part is when you went to the emergency room to get your calf stitched up and you told the nurse you were bit by a dog!"

Smack, Jack backhanded his son Ned for the last time.

Ned exploded with anger, yelling, "I hate you! You bastard, I hate you!"

Ned shoved his father in the chest with both hands, hoping to bring him down, but barely knocked Jack off his balance. Ned lunged himself at his father again, screaming at the top of his lungs with his little-boy chest all puffed out.

"I wish you would just leave me alone!"

Now taking swings at Jack, Ned was completely out of control, screaming at the top of his lungs.

"I'm gonna turn you into the cops you—"

BANG!

Nothing but silence filled the air.

Jack easily shoved his son back with his left hand and with his right a single gunshot wound to the chest. Ned's lifeless body dropped to the ground at Jack's feet. Jack looked at his dead son lying before him with not a single regret.

"I'll do the same to your whore mother if she ever comes back," Jack said, spitting on his dead son's body.

"Guess what, boy? Now I'm gonna bury you next to one of them Mexicans. I'm gonna cover you with manure and plant a Christmas tree on you. No one in the town will even know you're gone. No one in town will even care! You won't be missed by anyone. I can promise you this, boy." Jack spat again on his son's lifeless body.

"I'll keep burying Mexicans up here until I find the one that your momma ran off with. you hear me, boy!" Jack screamed as he kicked the side of Ned's body.

"Do you think the tail can wag the dog, boy! Go run off and tell the cops now, boy! Go on, Ned! Do it!!" Jack continued to speak to the corpse as if he had something to prove.

"You ain't gonna do nothin', boy. Guess what sucker – game over."

By the time the sun was peeking up from the east, Jack had discarded Ned's body just like he said he would, just like everyone else buried on the tree farm. Jack dug a deep hole about ten feet deep, eight feet long, and three feet or so wide and tossed in the dead body. Then he covered the body with about six feet of horse manure and lime, mixed in with a little bit of soil. The top four feet was just soil that the Christmas trees were planted in. There was one body under every tree. Nobody's the wiser.

To everybody else, Jack just brought a bunch of slave laborers up here digging holes for Christmas trees at $5 per hour—under the table, of course. Everyone thought it was the manure layer that gave the trees their fullness and color. Jack would tell you it was the decomposing body that the trees loved so much. Of course, after he tells you that, you'd be in the next hole. Jack was a very angry man. His high school sweetheart and the mother of his son, Ned, had run off with a guy from Mexico. After twenty years of abuse, she literally went to work at one of Jack's establishments, the Nugget, and at the end of her shift left town with this guy she'd only met a couple of hours before. A Mexican guy. From somewhere in Mexico.

A month later, Jack got some divorce papers in the mail from his pregnant wife, and he lost it. He had been on a rampage ever since. Alcohol didn't help; he's always got a drink in one hand and a gun in the other. He was a time bomb that's ticking away and very unstable. Then a new guy comes to town, and his one business puts the hurt on all three of Jack's—it was like poking the bear. Now with Ned's incompetence out of the way, there was nothing stopping Jack from running Jesse out of town for good or digging him his very own hole.

Chapter 28

July 22–23 was when the Tobacco Valley Rodeo came to the Lincoln County Fairgrounds this year. The rodeo was really a frenzy of bull riding, roping, and barrel racing. It was a two-day pass for nothing but fun. People come from all around to participate and watch. Next to the rodeo was a "kiddie rodeo" for those under twelve. It was a safe place for young ins to "test out their spurs." The Tobacco Valley Rodeo dates back over one hundred years, but in recent times, the Tobacco Valley Chili Cook-Off had been the go-to after the first day of bull riding was over.

It all started about fifteen years ago when Sheriff Rodney gathered the officers together to sell chili dogs to raise money for the sheriff's office. Sheriff Rodney's homemade chili was used to cover the hot dogs to give them a little bit of a "true to Montana" taste. Well, no one could tell you where the hot dogs came from, but the chili became an instant favorite. The following year, one of the deputies from the next county over brought his homemade chili to challenge Sheriff Rodney's, as a sort of sideshow to the chili dog fundraising efforts. The rest is history. The law dogs still hosted a chili dog tent for fund-raising, but the main attraction after day one of bull riding was the chili cook-off.

It cost $250 to enter your chili into the contest. Fifty percent of the proceeds go to the sheriff's office, and the other 50 percent of the proceeds go to the favorite charity of the winner. The winner got a three-foot-tall trophy with the previous winner's names on them. As the trophy stood, to date, there had only been one winner, Sheriff Rodney, every single year. With the rodeo only a couple of weeks away, we'll see if Sheriff Rodney's chili continues to be legendary.

Chapter 29

It was Wednesday, family movie night at the Lasso. This week's family movie night was a double feature. There was a six o'clock movie for families, *Mrs. Doubtfire*, and there was a "summertime fun time" movie at 9:00 p.m., *Smokey and the Bandit*. This was another one of Erin's ideas. Erin believed that in order to keep the crowd coming back, you had to make it new and inviting.

The double feature was the new part. The inviting part was the $100 cash prize for the single best Mrs. Doubtfire impersonator and another $100 cash prize for the best Buford T. Justice impersonator during the second movie. Family movie night was consistently a huge success, drawing sellout crowds. There was even an authentic movie theater popcorn machine that "magically appeared" in the corner. "Free popcorn for everyone" read the handwritten sign taped to the glass.

"C'mon, Frog, let's go! We're gonna be late!" Jesse yelled to Karma as he headed to the front door. "Frog" was the nickname given to Sally Field in the movie *Smokey and the Bandit*. Jesse, who was dressed as a young and handsome Burt Reynolds from back in the day, waited for his date to appear. Moments later, Karma appeared, wearing a pair of tight-fitting faded blue jeans and a navy-blue silk blouse, just like Sally wore in the movie.

"How do I look, Bo?" Karma said, spinning around on her tiptoes.

"My, wow, holy cow, Frog! You look incredible! I'd like to jump you!" Jesse said, walking over to her and grabbing her.

"You're terrible!" Karma said, lightly smacking Jesse's hands as they wandered down over her butt.

"Enough of that, Mr. Buck. Let's go!"

"You make a great Sally Field look-alike, Karma—very nice," Jesse said, walking to the door.

"You make a mighty fine Mr. Bandit yourself there, Buck," Karma said with a wink. Jesse opened the front door.

"After you, love." He let Karma lead the way. Karma took two steps outside and stopped in her tracks. With her mouth opened, jaw dropped, she stood there in awe.

"Are you kidding me, Buck?" Karma asked with delight.

"Pretty, ain't it?" Jesse said, standing next to Karma.

"Where on earth did you find that car?" Karma asked.

"That, Frog," Jesse started, "is *the* 1977 Pontiac Firebird Trans Am that was primarily used in the making of the *Smokey and the Bandit*."

"No way," Karma said, walking around the vehicle.

"Look here, Karma," Jesse said, pointing to the deck lid. "It's autographed by Burt Reynolds, Sally Field, Jerry Reed, and Jackie Gleason, all of them."

"Is this yours Buck?" Karma asked.

"Yes, it's mine," Jesse said with a smile. "It only has 38K miles on it."

"There's not a scratch on this car, Buck. It's factory showroom perfect," Karma added. "I'm impressed."

"Shall we head to the Lasso?" Jesse said, opening the passenger's side door for Karma.

"No way, Buck, give me the keys. I'm driving," Karma said, running to the driver's side and jumping in. Jesse laughed as he got into the car.

"I should have known that was coming," he said, looking over at Karma with a twinkle in his eye. Jesse tossed her the ignition key and jumped into the passenger's side of the black Trans Am.

"Okay, to start this—" Jesse started.

"Really Buck?" Karma said, looking over at him. He immediately stopped talking and let Karma have the reigns as she turned the ignition key.

"I've got this." When the 6.6L 400-cubic-inch V8 roared to life, Karma immediately dumped the clutch in first gear and left tracks 100 feet long down the driveway.

"Yeehaa!" she screamed as the black Trans Am was tearing out of sight. Karma slid the car onto the asphalt at the end of the drive and tacked it up. *Chirp* went the tires as she hit second gear, *chirp* again, as she shifted into third. Jesse looked over at Karma; she was smiling from ear to ear.

"This is a cool car, Buck," Karma said, cruising at about eighty, effortless in the powerful seventies muscle.

"A very cool car."

"Enjoy the drive, Frog," Jesse said with a chuckle.

"Because I'm driving home."

Karma rolled up to the Lasso like *she* owned the place. Karma and Jesse looked at each other and chuckled as they peered through the parking lot, only to see five or six other black Trans Ams.

"Let's park this in the garage in back," Jesse said, motioning Karma toward the back of the building. Jesse reached into the glove compartment and hit the garage door button. As the end door lifted, Karma eased the Trans Am into the garage, parking it right next to her Corvette, then shut it down.

"It's still here," Jesse said, noting the Vette.

"It sure is, Buck. Safe and sound, just like you said."

"Just like you," Jesse answered back with a wink. "You can bring it home tonight if you want." He got out of the car. Karma carefully opened her door so as not to hit either vehicle and slipped out.

"I'd like to ride home with you tonight, Bandit, if that's okay," Karma said with a wink as she made her way over to Jesse.

"That sounds like a hell of a great idea, Ms. Frog," Jesse answered back with a grin. The two embraced each other and shared a kiss before joining the crowd inside.

"I love kissing you, Frog," Jesse said softly, looking into her eyes.

"That's a good thing, Mr. Bandit," Karma answered back, "because I want you to know . . . I really like the way you kiss me!

"Hey, Buck?" Karma held on to his arms.

"Yes, love?" Jesse answered.

"How did you end up with that car?" Karma asked.

"*Smokey and the Bandit* is my all-time favorite movie. I was watching Barrett Jackson's auto auction on TV one day, and it came across the auction block. I doubled the last bidder and bought the car." Karma chuckled and slightly shook her head.

"What are your other favorite movies?" Karma asked with a smile.

"Haha," Jesse chuckled. "Let's get inside—our movie is about to start."

Walking into the Lasso, Karma and Jesse entered holding hands. Once inside, they paused to look around. To kind of evaluate the situation. They chuckled to each other as they noticed dozens of people dressed in costume. Buford T. Justice's peppered the room. There were lots of Frogs and Bandits. There were even two Snowman's, one of which was in full costume and brought the dog Fred, a huge basset hound that looked like it came right out of the movie.

"Look at all of these people having a great time, Buck," Karma said, latching on to Jesse's arm. "You did this. You did all of this."

"The Lasso kind of ropes you in, doesn't it?"

"It sure does".

"I didn't do this alone," Jesse said humbly. "Erin deserves much of the credit. She's been instrumental in all of this."

"Make sure you take care of her".

"He does take care of me," Erin said, walking up behind them dressed as Annette, Snowman's wife from the beginning of the *Smokey and the Bandit* movie. "He gave me a raise today," Erin said with a big smile on her face.

"I did?"

"You sure did, Mr. Buck, and I thank you for it!"

"You deserve it, Erin," Jesse told her. "You've definitely earned it."

"Erin, I love your costume," Karma told Erin as the two walked off into the crowd.

Jesse headed over to the bar to get to work. He looked around and thought about what had become of the Lasso. It had become *the* watering hole in Eureka. He liked owning a place that everyone liked to come to.

Pastor and Recon came in through the front door and sat down at the bar, neither one of them in costume and both of them looking like they were up to something.

"Pastor," Jesse started with assertion, "why don't you ever show up dressed in costume? You know, show some support for your local community?"

"I'll tell you what, Jesse," Pastor started. "You show *Jesus Christ Superstar* one night, and I'll show up in costume." Recon burst into laughter.

"Not funny, Judas," Jesse said to Recon. "What are you two clowns drinking tonight?"

"There he is!" someone yelled from the back. The whole place started cheering as Sheriff Rodney entered the room. He was dressed as a near-perfect look-alike for Sheriff Buford T. Justice—the Texas uniform, the badge, the nameplate, right down to the sunglasses – his costume was perfect. Sheriff Rodney stopped and looked around, perfectly imitating Jackie Gleason's role from the movie. Everyone was taking in his perfect imitation and cheering him on. Karma walked over to him and put her arm through his, saying, "Escort a lady to the bar, Sheriff?"

"Much obliged, ma'am," Sheriff Rodney answered, tipping his hat. The crowd made way while Sheriff Rodney and Karma made their way to the bar to sit down.

"Now, that is a great costume, Sheriff," Jesse said.

"How did you pull that off?" Recon added.

"I have a twin brother who's a Texas sheriff. I was online and found out what tonight's movie was. I asked him to hook me up. I love that movie . . . It's one of my favorites!" Recon, Pastor, and Karma all chuckled, sharing the fun with their "newfound sheriff."

"What do you mean you found out online?" Jesse asked with great question.

"What do you mean, what do I mean?" Sheriff Rodney said as if Jesse had two heads. "On your website?" Sheriff Rodney asked back, questioning Jesse's questioning.

"We have a website?" Jesse asked, still obviously in the dark.

"Your website is awesome!" Sheriff Rodney went on. "It has all the events that you're doing here for the next six months. Here, check this out!"

Sheriff Rodney had now pulled out his smartphone and was showing the group of friends the website for the Lasso as Jesse was scanning the crowd looking for Erin. Spotting her talking with another Annette, he watched for a moment until they made eye contact.

"Website?" Jesse mouthed over to her questioningly.

Erin shot him a wink and a smile and went on about her business. Jesse just smiled and thought for a moment about what a blessing Erin has been.

"Show me what we've got here," Jesse said, turning back to the group and leaning in. A few minutes later, Jesse agreed—the website was really cool.

Family movie night was again a huge success. Sheriff Rodney won best costume with his Sheriff Buford T. Justice attire. Dozens of people dressed in costume, and everyone had a great time. A couple of Bandits having a drag race in their Trans Am's upon leaving the Lasso raised a few eyebrows and brought on a few cheers, but nothing more than that.

Eureka was a nice place with good people. What was interesting was people had started coming from surrounding areas to take part in the festivities that were happening at the Lasso. Old Jack Beaver was none too happy about his failing businesses. Rage and anger continued to flow through his veins as he watched the stranger move into and take over his town.

Chapter 30

The whole group—Karma, Jesse, Georgia-Jean, Sheriff Rodney, even Recon—were sitting in church on Sunday as Rev. Pastor Raines gave a sermon on "life-changing events and the Apostle Paul." Paul was a persecutor of people who believed in Christ and were followers of "the Way."

Paul had set out on a mission when God appeared as a bright light in the sky. Paul was completely blind for three days and was given a message. After three days, Paul's vision was returned to him, and he set forth as a believer from that day forward.

Paul, whose name was Saul in the beginning, went from feared persecutor to the most significant individual in Christianity other than Christ himself. Paul was ultimately beheaded for his faith. While Pastor Raines assured the people sitting before him that there would not be any beheadings of those in the congregation for believing in or having faith, he did want everyone to be cognizant of life changing events that have happened to them or that would happen to them. He wanted them to think about the decisions we make before we make them and how those decisions will impact those around them. It was really a good sermon, one of his best.

After church, there was a small parade of cars that made its way down to Jesse's house by the lake. Jesse and Karma played host while Recon, Pastor, and Rod gathered around the table.

"Where's Georgia-Jean?" Pastor inquired.

"You've got a little thing for the ER nurse, don't you!" Recon shouted out with a kind of "poking the bear" playfulness.

"She's a delightful woman with whom I really enjoy her company," Pastor said, defending himself.

"Georgia-Jean had to run an errand down in Kalispell after church," Jesse said, putting a vegetable platter on the table.

"I asked her if she wouldn't mind taking my truck and picking up something for me on her way back. She should actually be rolling in here any minute."

"You had an eighty-five-year-old woman pick up your laundry?" Pastor fired out at Jesse.

"She's not eighty-five, she's eighty-four, and we both know she'd put most fifty-year-old's to shame. Hell, she doesn't look or act a day over sixty! Besides, it's getting loaded for her and she likes driving my pickup," Jesse thoroughly explained so as *not* to get in trouble.

"Since when does she drive your pickup?" Recon questioned.

"Georgia-Jean takes Jesse's truck when he's working on her car, nosy," Karma piped in while passing out wine glasses.

"Sounds to me like there needs to be an investigation," Rod added.

"Anything to keep you busy, buddy," Jesse added. "By the way, it's not laundry she's picking up, and you all will benefit from it." He pointed to the lot of them.

"I am ready for a club soda on the rocks," Georgia-Jean said, stepping onto the deck. Pastor jumped out of his chair like he was struck by lightning.

"I'll get that for you right away, Georgia-Jean."

"Don't forget the lemon this time, honey!"

"See," Jesse said, getting a hug from Georgia-Jean. "I told you she'd be here any minute. Here, Georgia-Jean, why don't you sit down in Pastor's chair? He's not using it, and it's his week to cook."

"Actually," Rod perked up, "Pastor and I talked, and I'm cooking again this week if you all don't mind."

"Fine by us," Karma replied with everyone nodding and answering yes.

"Truth be known," Rod went on, "I had so much fun last week that I'd like to be designated chef."

Immediate silence filled the air as everyone looked around at one another.

"Karma and I will supply the food," Jesse said, breaking the silence. "We don't care who cooks, do we?" He said looking over at Karma.

"Not at all."

"There it is, baby!" Recon yelled out, standing up from his chair, and pointing at Jesse and Karma. "There it is!"

"There's what?" Rod asked as if Recon was losing it.

"I heard it too," Georgia-Jean said, chuckling.

"What did I miss?" Rod asked, looking around, completely lost in the new conversation.

"Some investigator," Pastor said, looking toward Rod. "I have to say I heard it too."

"You two are in love, you two are in love!" Recon started shouting and dancing. Pastor was quick to jump in. They locked elbows and spun themselves around like drunken sailors, chanting, "You two are in love, you two are in love."

Jesse and Karma stood there chuckling at the scene. When the two instigators stopped dancing and sat down, Rod asked the question, "What did I miss here?"

"Well," Georgia-Jean started, "Jesse said to Karma 'we don't care who cooks.'"

Rod truly looked like a deer in headlights, lost with the connection of the dots.

"So, what?" Rod said, lifting up his hands like it was no big deal.

"They are making decisions together out of mutual respect and love for each other," Georgia-Jean added.

Karma and Jesse put their arms around each other and chuckled while the others discussed how they felt about each other.

"And that means they are in love with each other?" Rod asked with great question.

"Yes!" everyone said in unison.

"Hey, Recon, put a team together and get the things out of the back of the pickup," Jesse commanded.

Recon jumped up laughing. "Oh yes, sir," he responded. "C'mon, Rod, let's do this."

"There is nothing wrong with having a mutual respect for each other," Jesse added to the rest of the group with a stern overtone. "Y'all are quick to jump to conclusions," he added while heading into the house.

"He loves me!" Karma whispered to everyone, nodding her head yes.

"I heard that, Karma!" Jesse yelled from the kitchen. Everyone laughed. Recon and Rod reappeared carrying a new table

"Set it up, guys," Jesse ordered. "Anywhere you want."

"No, not anywhere," Karma said, getting up. "Set it over here so there is room to get around and . . ." Karma helped the guys position the table and then they went out for the chairs.

"What's with the extra table?" Pastor asked. "Is our group growing?"

"There will be two more for dinner tonight," Karma answered.

"See," Georgia-Jean interrupted. "They're even talking for one another."

"That question wasn't addressed to anybody," Jesse said, reentering the conversation.

"Wine's here!" Desi shouted out as she and her niece Erin stepped onto the porch.

"How delightful!" Georgia-Jean shouted, getting up. "Erin, it's so good to see you!"

"We had no idea you two were the 'other two,'" Pastor added. "What's the occasion?"

"Does there need to be an occasion?" Jesse asked.

"Jesse and Karma are celebrating tonight," Desi said with a mischievous grin.

"They are in love—they're getting engaged!" Georgia-Jean yelled out.

"See what you did now?" Jesse said to Desi.

"We are not getting engaged," Karma said to kill that conversation.

"Yet," Recon added.

"So, what's going on?" Rod asked, eager to be kept in the loop.

"Desi and Erin have been good to me, so I have invited them to join us for Sundays at the lake," Jesse added to explain the addition of two.

"Okay, but this case of wine isn't wine, it's champagne," Rod added to the conversation, peeking into the box.

"Now he's investigating!" Pastor shouted.

"Desi, what's up with the champagne?" Jesse questioned.

"I thought we needed to celebrate this afternoon," Desi said, grabbing a bottle.

"If no one is getting engaged, what are we celebrating?" Georgia-Jean asked.

With everybody staring at Desi and waiting for an answer, she looked at Jesse, asking, "You really don't know?"

"I didn't tell him," Karma said with a smile.

Desi locked eyes with Jesse and addressed him with the most serious voice and straight face.

"The sellers accepted your offer for the lot on Flathead Lake." She launched the cork from the first bottle of champagne across the deck and into the lake and let a grin extending from ear to ear cross over her face.

Jesse raised his hands in the air, shouting, "Yes! yes! yes!"

"I can't believe you got that land for that price," Desi added. Everyone stood up and gathered into a group hug congratulating Jesse and Karma.

"Well done, Jesse, well done."

After a healthy serving of dinner and endless champagne the group was settled down and talking about what the plans were for the new property and why it was purchased.

"For the price, it was worth purchasing," Jesse said. "Even just to sit on for now." Desi nodded her approval as the real estate guru that she was.

"Desi," Karma started with question, "Jesse and I have been trying to think of a name for this lake right here. Might you have any suggestions?"

"This lake here?" Desi asked, almost confused. "The lake already has a name."

"Really? What is it?" Georgia-Jean asked. "I've lived here my whole life, and I never knew this lake had a name." Everyone sitting around the table was eager to learn the name of the "no name" lake.

"If you tell me, it's Johnson Lake," Jesse said, locking eyes with Desi.

"No, silly," Desi said. "This is known as 'Lost Lake.'"

"There you go, Karma," Jesse said. "Lost Lake. Kind of suiting, isn't it?"

"I like it," Karma answered.

"Sometimes you have to get lost, to find yourself," Desi added. "I thought I told you that." She looked at Jesse. Jesse chuckled as he shook his head.

"Time for a toast," Pastor said, standing up and raising his glass.

"To friendship at Lost Lake."

"To friendship at Lost Lake," everyone repeated.

"That is actually the perfect name," Karma said smiling at Jesse.

Chapter 31

Pastor, Recon, and Georgia-Jean had all left. Erin and Desi both said they had a great time and would be back next week. It was just Karma, Jesse, and Rod sitting by the lake taking in the evening air.

"Why don't you have a woman in your life, Rod?" Karma asked as she nestled up against Jesse.

"Ha!" Rod answered with a laugh. "The woman question!"

"What's that supposed to mean? You're a good guy, you should have a good girl. That's all I'm saying."

"I actually," Rod started to admit, "have a crush on someone, but I'm a little bit uncomfortable when it comes to talking with women."

"That's bologna," Jesse shot out. "You don't have a problem talking to Karma."

"Be quiet, Jesse," Karma said, giving him a poke with her elbow. "Let him talk."

"Karma's taken. I'm not asking her out. There's nothing to be afraid of when I'm talking to Karma," Rod replied a little defensively.

"You don't like rejection," Karma said in an understanding tone. "None of us do, Rod. You are no different from the rest of us. Maybe that cute little someone is waiting for you to ask her out. Who is she? How do you know her?"

"I'm not ready to go there," Rod said sheepishly, as if he wanted to tell them, but didn't at the same time.

"Rod," Karma said with some assertion in her voice. "You are among friends, who is she?" With a big sigh, Rod started sharing.

"It's the new ER intern that works graveyard at the hospital. Her name is Meo, and she's part Chippewa and her smile makes my heart race."

"She's a little young for you, isn't she, partner?" Jesse asked with a smirk.

"Jesse, stop!" Karma said, nudging him lightly in the ribs. "Rod, have you ever talked to her? Does she know you exist?"

"Oh yes," Rod said, lighting up. "We talk frequently when I'm there, dropping off paperwork or something."

"Then ask her out," Karma said, almost demanding.

"What if she says no?" Rod asked as if he wouldn't know what to do *if* she said no.

Just then, Louie came running up to the porch and jumped into Rod's lap.

"Hey there, little fella," Rod said, scratching Louie behind the ears. "Good to see you're not limping!"

"His paw seems just fine, doesn't it?" Karma said as she watched Rod and Louie bond.

"Yeah, amazing," Jesse answered. "You'd never know, would you."

"You're a tough little fella, aren't ya?" Rod continued, petting Louie all over. Louie was taking full advantage of Rod, and Rod was none the wiser.

"So, are you going to ask Meo on a date, or are you going to wuss out?" Karma questioned Rod, jumping right back into the conversation.

"I just don't have time for women right now, Karma," Rod said sheepishly, never looking up from Louie, still petting him all over vigorously.

"Wussy," Jessie said.

"Men," Karma said, shaking her head. "You're not afraid to die, but you're afraid to ask out a woman. And you tell me women are crazy!" Karma looked up at Jesse and gave him a kiss right on the lips.

"Women are crazy, aren't they, Louie!" Rod added.

Chapter 32

The next morning after Jesse and Karma got to the Lasso, Karma immediately asked for Jesse's keys to go "run some errands." Her first stop—the ER. Upon entering the ER, there was no one around. Not a soul. Not a patient, not a nurse, no one. It was actually, eerily quiet. Then a young woman considerably taller than Karma came around the corner.

"May I help you, ma'am?" the young woman asked. She had long dark brown hair and big soft brown eyes, a stunning young woman. Karma gave her a once-over and tried to determine if this was Meo or not.

"Yes," Karma said very politely in her charming way. "I'm looking for a woman named, Meo. You don't happen to know where I might find her, do you?"

"I'm Meo," the young woman answered, taking off her white medical coat and walking over to a closet. "How may I help you?" Meo was wearing a pair of red jeans with a cream-colored sweater. Karma could see why Sheriff Rodney was attracted to her; she was a very pretty woman, and Karma could already tell that she presented herself very well.

"Meo," Karma said, holding out her hand to shake, "my name is Karma, Rachael. Just call me Karma." Meo and Karma shook hands.

"Nice to meet you, Ms. Rachael . . . Karma," Meo said.

"I know you are on your way out, but would you be interested in having a cup of coffee with me?" Karma asked as the two-headed toward the door.

Meo looked at Karma with question, not sure if she should accept the invite or not.

"I want to talk to you about my friend, Sheriff Rodney," Karma said with a more relaxed voice. Meo lit up like Christmas when Karma mentioned Sheriff Rodney.

"You know Sheriff Rodney?" Meo asked, now smiling and most definitely interested in what Karma had to say.

"He's a good friend of mine," Karma said.

"Yes," Meo answered. "I think a cup of coffee would be just fine. Let me grab my purse and I'll meet you at Café Jax."

"Perfect! See you in ten!"

In less than ten minutes, the two women were sitting at a window table in Café Jax, chatting as if they were long-lost friends who had just reconnected. The two women talked about where they were from and how they ended up here in the little town of Eureka. They talked about their favorite foods and pastimes, what they did like and what they didn't like. They discovered that they really weren't that far apart in age and snickered together with the thought that they were the two best-looking women this side of the Mississippi. Not too many men in Eureka would disagree with them either.

Meo was just about to finish her internship and had been hoping that Georgia-Jean was going to offer her a permanent position there in the ER. She was an only child, the last in her family line, and her parents were on a reservation in northern Minnesota and would never leave. Meo loved the northern states and thought Montana was beautiful, so after school, she put in for her internship in

Eureka. She was the only one who applied, so naturally, she got the position.

"Meo is actually a nickname," Meo told Karma. "It's short for 'Meoquanee,' which actually means 'wears red' in Chippewa." Karma peeked under the table and confirmed Meo's red jeans.

"So, do you like to wear red?" Karma asked with a curious smile.

"It's my favorite color," Meo replied, taking a sip from her latte. "I drive a red Jeep too! So, Karma . . ." Meo sat back in her chair. "What is it about Sheriff Rodney that you wanted to talk about?"

Karma sat back in her seat and looked into Meo's eyes, almost through her eyes and into her soul, kind of sizing her up to see if the two would make a good match.

"Sheriff Rodney would like to get to know you a little better," Karma said with caution. "What do you think about that?" Karma watched across the table as a smile came across Meo's face.

"I think he's a handsome man," Meo started. "I would be very interested in getting to know him better. I guess he has this super-crazy schedule that doesn't permit him to have much fun."

Karma sat in her chair and grinned. She looked like the cat that ate the canary.

"Well, Ms. Meo," Karma said, swirling the coffee around in her cup, "what do your Sunday afternoons look like, are you busy?"

"I work Sundays, but I don't go in until midnight. I'm usually up by two or three in the afternoon," Meo answered, looking curious. "Why?"

Karma wrote Jesse's address down on a napkin and handed it to Meo.

"Why don't you join us this Sunday? Just come over after you get up and get ready, and I'll introduce you properly to Sheriff Rodney. There are a few of us that will be there so the setting is warm and laid-back, you'll like it, you'll have a good time."

Meo glowed with excitement when Karma extended her the invitation. "I'll be there," Meo said with a smile.

"Well, Meo," Karma said, getting up from the table, "it's been a pleasure, but I need to get to the Lasso before Jesse sends out a search party."

"Thank you for a great morning, Karma," Meo said, getting up as well. "I can't wait until Sunday!"

The two women hugged, and Karma bolted out the door in a hurry to get back to the Lasso. Meo's heart raced with the thought of getting to spend some time with this man that she was so attracted to.

"I can't wait until Sunday!" she said to herself as she gathered her things and headed off in her own direction.

Chapter 33

Karma hustled over to the Lasso to get working. She had discovered that she really enjoyed working alongside Jesse. *He is such a gentleman and a kind hearted soul,* Karma thought to herself on the way over. *He has never put any demands on me, and he always makes sure I'm taken care of,* Karma took a minute and smiled to herself as these uncontrollable thoughts raced through her head. She savored the moment before she went inside to get to work, not noticing the near-empty parking lot when she pulled up.

"I told you she'd be back soon," Sheriff Rodney said from the bar, eating a bowl of chili with Jesse.

"Baby, it's almost three o'clock," Jesse said, getting up to give Karma a kiss on the lips.

Karma smacked Jesse on the butt hard, telling him, "Don't call me baby! No kiss for you now!"

"C'mon, love," Jesse fired back at her, following her, "please forgive me and give me a kiss." Karma loved it when Jesse called her 'love'. She stopped and spun around, wearing a playful grin.

"You are *so* forgiven," Karma told him, wrapping her arms around Jesse's neck and giving him a kiss to die for.

"Get a room!" Sheriff Rodney hollered from the bar.

"There's one upstairs," Jesse whispered into Karma's ear, grinding on her a little.

"Get to work, Buck," Karma said, pushing him off, yet throwing him an "I want you as much as you want me" kind of smile.

"Gotta put a ring on that finger if you want to hit that," Pastor yelled from across the room, coming in the door.

"Pastor!" Karma shouted, blushing and laughing at the same time. "You did not just say that!"

"Just telling it how it is, Karma," Pastor said with slurred words and a stagger.

"You been drinking, Pastor?" Jesse said, helping him to the bar. "Why don't you have a seat here, drink some water." He went around the bar to get Pastor some water.

Sheriff Rodney and Jesse made eye contact with each other, thinking this was *way* out of the norm for Pastor Raines. Something had to be wrong.

"Just came in to get some chili," Pastor said again with slightly slurred words and acting a little woozy.

"Pastor," Jesse said with a light slap on the face, "what's going on?"

"Hey, he's all right," Recon said, coming through the door.

"I should have known you'd be involved with this," Jesse said, looking up and acknowledging his buddy. "It's Monday afternoon, Recon, really?"

"He's not drunk, Commander!" Recon said in full defense mode. "I just picked him up from the dentist. He's high on Novocain and nitrous." Jesse and Sheriff Rodney looked at each other and laughed.

"I'll get him some chili," Jesse said, laughing harder and harder the more he thought about it.

"Is he going to be able to eat chili?" Sheriff Rodney asked. "Just coming from the dentist and all?"

"I can eat just fine," Pastor said as he drooled all over himself. "It was just a cavity . . . I can't feel my face, but I can eat just fine."

Recon and Sheriff Rodney couldn't help but laugh at their friend knowing they'd all been there before. Karma walked up to the bar with bowls of chili for everyone and a full round of water.

"What brings you in here this early, Rodney?" Karma asked, hoping she wasn't seen chatting with Meo at the café down the street.

"Hi, Karma," Sheriff Rodney said, sliding a bowl of chili in front of him. "I noticed an out-of-town tow truck hooking up to a pickup behind Jack Beaver's place this morning. Thinking that was kind of suspicious, I went down there to check it out. Turns out it was Ned Beaver's truck, being repossessed. Funny thing is, it looked like his truck has been parked there for a while."

"Okay, who cares about Ned Beaver's truck," Recon asked haphazardly.

"I have to second that," Karma added, remembering the guy from her first night in town.

"It's not the truck that has my curiosity going," Rodney continued between mouthfuls of chili. "It's the fact that no one has seen Ned around for a while."

"Maybe a coyote ate him!" Recon spouted out, laughing at himself.

"It wouldn't be the first time," Sheriff Rodney explained, "but highly unlikely."

"He probably just took off," Jesse said, entering the conversation. "Probably got tired of taking crap from his old man and hit the trail."

"That's very possible," Sheriff Rodney agreed. "But why wouldn't he take off in his truck then?"

That was the question that left the group looking at each other in silence. These were all good questions. Where do you disappear to when everyone in town knows who you are?

"Go ask his old man if he knows what happened," Karma said. "If you have a general concern for the guy, go ask his father."

"I'd really rather not talk to Jack if I can help it," Sheriff Rodney admitted. "That guy is just plain difficult."

"Maybe that's more the reason to give him a visit," Jesse suggested.

"It's a small town," Sheriff Rodney said, getting up and wiping off his mouth with a napkin. "I figure if I wait long enough, someone will know something, and this fire will put itself out. Thanks for the chili, Buck." With that, Sheriff Rodney put on his hat and disappeared out the door.

"That is a good question," Jesse said to the others. "Where is Ned?"

"Who cares where that dirty, lanky, foul-mouthed waste is?" Karma questioned with a fiery tone. "I hope he's gone for good!"

Recon, Pastor, and Jesse just looked at each other in silence. They knew there was no love lost between Karma and Ned, and their silence was secret squirrel for "leave well enough alone."

"Recon," Jesse whispered across the bar, checking over his shoulder, "keep your feelers out about Ned." Recon gave a very modest head nod for yes without making eye contact.

If Sheriff Rodney was concerned, Jesse thought to himself, *then that was reason enough to have a heightened awareness as to anything unusual going on around town.*

Chapter 34

Wednesday morning came with its normal set of daily routines for Jesse and Karma. It started with their walk around the lake with Louie, followed by breakfast for the three of them on the deck. Then it was showers and off to work at the Lasso. It was only ten till ten when Jesse and Karma pulled up to the Lasso. The parking lot was bustling with commotion. A tractor trailer was taking up the middle of the parking lot with a smaller box truck parked on the side. The box truck had "Missoula Party Supply" painted on the side.

"What in the world is going on here, Jesse?" Karma asked with a puzzled look on her face.

"I'm not exactly sure, love," Jesse said, equally as puzzled. "I'm thinking we need to find out in a hurry."

Jesse parked his pickup in front, nearly blocking the door, and he and Karma jumped out.

"Hey, buddy," Jesse yelled over to a guy pushing a dolly with a stack of folding chairs on it. "Hey! I'm talking to you!" The man pushing the folding chairs stopped and pointed a finger to himself, asking, "Me?"

"Yeah, you!" Jesse shouted anxiously. "What are you doing here?"

"Hey, pal, I'm just doing what the lady told me to do," the guy said, taking a couple of steps back from Jesse.

"What lady?" Jesse snarled.

"The hot looking blonde. That one right over there!" the guy said sheepishly, pointing to Erin.

"I'm on it," Karma said, leaving the conversation and rushing over toward Erin to find out what the situation was.

"Tell me what you know," Jesse said to the guy, now several feet back from the chairs. "Relax, buddy, I'm not going to hurt you!" Jesse laughed. "I'm the owner, and you need to tell me what you know now!" The guy raised his hands and took yet another step back.

"I was told to put these chairs and tables in the back underneath the tent."

"What tent!" Jesse demanded.

"The big white tent behind the building," the guy murmured, pointing behind the Lasso. Jesse looked up over the top of the building, and he could see the top of what looked to be an enormous white circus-like tent.

"What the hell?" Jesse said to himself as he started in that direction. Jesse turned around and pointed to the guy saying, "Don't move." He hurried to the back to see what Erin had going on.

When Jesse rounded the corner, he stopped in his tracks. He was completely blown away with what he saw. There was a massive production of people bustling around. The tent was huge, three times the size of the Lasso, maybe four. The entire area had been groomed and graded, nearly completely flat. Bundles of fresh hay were neatly stacked in various locations, Jesse imagined it was from the cut grass that outlined the perimeter of the property. There were two rows of Don Johns porta potties, one on either side.

Tables and chairs were being set up everywhere with a huge wooden dance floor being constructed in the center. There were four of what looked like miniature horse corrals placed near the four corners and who knew what else was going on. Jesse felt his blood pressure start to rise. *Where in the hell is Erin!* he thought as he scanned over all the commotion.

"Everybody stop!" Jesse yelled at the top of his lungs. "Stop everything now!" With the sound of Jesse's booming voice, everyone stopped in their tracks. In seconds, the world surrounding him became completely silent.

"He's freaking out!" Karma said to Erin, grabbing her by the hand, laughing. "We'd better go let him in on this!"

Hearing Jesse's booming command, Karma and Erin raced out the back door of the Lasso. Karma headed straight over to Jesse while Erin made her way over to the workers.

"Jesse, . . . it's okay, you're gonna love this," Karma said with the most soothing voice she could come up with.

"Where is Erin and what is going on here!" Jesse demanded. "I can tell you right now I'm *not* loving any of this!"

"Hey, Buck!" Karma snapped back, grabbing Jesse firmly by the arms. "I'm telling you, relax!"

Jesse was watching Erin put everyone back into motion telling them it's okay and to carry on. The look on Jesse's face was not a happy one.

"Jesse, . . . look at me!" Karma demanded, shaking his arms. "Let her explain what is going on before you say a word, okay? Do that for me, please?"

"This better be good," Jesse said, yanking himself free of Karma's clutches and stepping back. "I can tell you now if it's not, she's done."

Jesse turned around and headed into the Lasso through the back door. He immediately went to the bar and filled a rocks glass with some ice. He turned around and grabbed a bottle of Johnny Walker Black off the shelf. He looked the bottle over and put it back. Jesse looked down and opened a cabinet door, grabbing a new bottle of Johnny Walker Blue. He kicked the door closed and went to sit at his table in the corner by the piano.

This better be good, Jesse thought to himself as he filled the glass to the top with scotch. *This looks expensive*, he thought, taking a sip. *She didn't clear any of this with me. This better be good!*

"Jesse!" Karma yelled, entering the Lasso. "Buck, where are you?" Karma yelled, almost with concern when she turned around and saw Jesse sitting in the corner with his drink.

"Really, Buck?" Karma said, walking over to him in disbelief. "Ten thirty in the morning and all you can do is sit on your butt and have a drink?"

"Don't start with me, Rachael," Jesse said, looking at her with eyes that she'd never seen before. Serious eyes, the kind of look in your eyes when you know things could get very ugly, very fast. Jesse had *never* called Karma by her real first name, so she knew he was really, *really* pissed.

"Jesse," Karma said, sitting down next to him, using her most soothing voice, "look at me." Karma placed her hands on Jesse's knee under the table. "Yes, Erin has some explaining to do. You are right."

Jesse finally looked over at Karma. "Go on," he said, taking another sip of scotch.

179

"Jesse, please don't freak out until she tells you everything, okay?" Karma knew that any explanation needed to come from the source, which in this case was Erin. Jesse wasn't one for secondhand information even if it came from Karma. Unless your name was "Recon," Jesse wanted to hear it from the source. Karma also knew that Jesse was mad because an ordeal this big should have been run by him first, and obviously it wasn't. Erin had truly overstepped her bounds.

"Let me have a sip." Karma said prying the glass of scotch from Jesse's fingers.

"Don't break the glass, Buck," Karma said with a twinkle in her eye, looking over to Jesse as she took a sip.

"I think you're overreacting a bit," Karma said, risking Jesse blowing up on her.

"We'll see," Jesse said, pouring more scotch over the ice. "We'll see."

Karma scooted her chair right up next to Jesse's and laid her hand on his leg. Periodically, she would take a sip of scotch from his glass, hoping he would say something, anything, but the room remained silent. Erin appeared in from the back door and looked around without saying a word.

Seeing Jesse and Karma over in the corner, Erin headed toward the bar. Jesse watched Erin closely, wondering what she was doing. Erin, being the brazen woman she was, just like her aunt Desi, grabbed a rocks glass and filled it with ice. Then she filled a second glass with ice and a third.

Jesse watched Erin walk toward the table with the three glasses in her hand. Jesse then glanced into his glass, checking his own ice level, and came to realize that some fresh ice wouldn't hurt. Erin set the glasses down in the middle of the table and sat in the chair directly across from Jesse and Karma. Without saying a word, Jesse finished his glass of scotch and set it down on the table in front of the only empty seat.

He then pulled two of the ice-filled glasses that Erin brought over in front of him and poured half a glass of scotch into each glass. He slid one of the glasses to Karma and kept the other for himself. Setting the bottle down on the floor out of reach from everyone, Jesse looked up at Erin and waited for her to speak.

Erin eyeballed Jesse for a moment with a slight grin on her face, almost as if to "poke the bear." Jesse was not budging; his poker face was stern, and he wanted some answers. Erin took a deep breath, locked eyes with Jesse, and started to talk.

"I put the annual chili cook-off on our web page," she started.

I forgot all about the website, Jesse thought to himself as Erin kept talking.

"Once word got out that Sheriff Rodney's chili was the only winner ever, people started reserving tables. Last year, there were thirty-three entries raising over eight thousand dollars for the sheriff's department. This year, we already have . . ." Erin stopped talking and pulled out her smartphone to access some information and then continued.

"One hundred seventy-one entries and we've capped the entry list at two hundred."

The stern look on Jesse's face started to soften a little as he crunched the numbers in his head, however, he wasn't convinced that Erin's actions were good enough to keep her on the payroll. Jesse and Karma both took a sip of scotch, Karma with a grin from ear to ear, and Jesse with a look so cold and hard his face could have been made of steel.

"Because the event exploded," Erin continued, "this year's event is going to be a two-day event here at the Lasso the weekend before the rodeo. The winner's chili will be served at the sheriff's chili dog stand during the rodeo. This year's gross receipts for entries will equal fifty thousand dollars. Minus the cost for all the rented equipment, the tent, and everything else leaves forty-two thousand dollars. Fifty percent goes to the house, and fifty percent goes to the sheriff's department. The house makes a twenty-thousand-dollar profit and raises twenty-one thousand dollars for the sheriff's office. However, it would be wise if the house donated fifty percent to a local charity, since after all, it originated as charity fund raiser."

Erin could see that Jesse was doing the math in his head and he was wondering where the missing one thousand dollars was.

"The last thousand dollars goes to the top three winners in the chili contest," Erin continued. "Five hundred, three hundred, and two hundred."

The look on Karma's face gleamed with excitement. It was taking her everything she had to sit there and not say a word. Jesse had been eyeballing Erin this whole time with a steel-like poker face. Without a blink, he reached down and grabbed the bottle of scotch off the floor. He topped off Karma's glass, topped off his glass, and then poured scotch into Erin's glass.

Jesse lifted his glass to the center of the table as if to make a toast but still didn't say a word. Karma and Erin lifted their glasses simultaneously, the three glasses clinked together, and everyone took a sip.

"Since people are already pouring into town for the rodeo," Erin continued, "I figured we'd set up the tent early and capitalize on the larger crowd. I have factored the cost of all the rented equipment into the cost of the chili cook-off, so you aren't paying anything to have the tent and everything set up. I'm projecting gross sales to be 20 to 30 percent higher for the next ten days, and the chili contest alone will net you nine grand."

"Erin," Jesse said, looking across the table with a much softer look on his face, "I'm sorry I yelled at you."

Karma squeezed Jesse's leg, recognizing his apology.

"But you didn't yell at me, Mr. Buck," Erin replied, a little confused.

"Oh yes, I did," Jesse confirmed with a smile, "and I'm sorry. You have never done me wrong, Erin, and I'm grateful for that."

"That's what you hired me for, Mr. Buck, to run the show," Erin stated, hoping to further soothe the situation.

"Erin, in the future—" Jesse started but was swiftly interrupted.

"I've got to get back to work, Mr. Buck, you never know when the boss will be watching!" With that, Erin jumped up from the table, shot the rest of her scotch down, and hurried out the back door.

"Well?" Karma asked with a Cheshire cat-like smile on her face.

"You were right," Jesse admitted.

"Again," Karma added, laughing, planting a kiss on Jesse's cheek.

"You know, Karma," Jesse said, filling his glass one more time, "It would be nice to know what's going on before I walk into it. After all, I am the owner." Jesse sipped from his glass while Karma digested his last comment.

"Buck, can I ask you a question?"

"Of course, you can."

"Would it have been better for Erin to ask permission or forgiveness in this situation?"

Jesse stared at the table. *This feels like a setup*, he thought as he sipped his scotch.

"Fortunately, she didn't have to do either," Jesse finally replied with a smile.

"Nice answer, Buck," Karma commented with a smirk. "Nice save."

Karma got up from the table and started walking away.

"Hey, Karma," Jesse said softly. "Thank you."

"Why are you thanking me?" Karma replied, turning around to look at Jesse.

"For asking me to give Erin a chance to talk before I did," Jesse replied. "Thank you."

"You're welcome, Buck, and thank you!"

"Why are you thanking me? In my mind, I already fired her!"

"For letting Erin speak before you did, for doing that for me. You trusted me, and I thank you for that."

Jesse held up his glass, toasting Karma as she walked away.

I did it because I love you, Jesse thought to himself as he watched Karma head out back, surely to help Erin.

He did it because he loves me, Karma thought to herself as she walked away, grinning from ear to ear.

Chapter 35

Erin's projected numbers for increased sales were modest, to say the least. Wednesday turned out to be the highest-grossing day of sales to date, nearly a one hundred percent increase over the previous Wednesday night. Being family movie night, the movie of choice was *Montana Sky*, fitting for the current schedule of events. Thursday was "live karaoke" where some people should be allowed to sing and others, well, shouldn't be allowed access to the microphone. Friday featured the Hickory Sticks as a cover band, and they always had a following.

Friday afternoon and Saturday was the chili cook-off. Since Erin put this together, Jesse thought it best if he let her run it. It was a mammoth success. Chilies that were too hot were eliminated right off the bat. If it was too hot to taste the flavor, you were done. Surprisingly, that eliminated almost half of the entries and all of Friday. Next to be eliminated were vegetarian chilies. You could hear people in the crowd explaining, "Up here in Montana, we like our meat!" For those chilies that were left, they were judged in five categories: flavor, consistency, ingredients, heat, and temperature. Heat referred to the number of BTUs the chili had, and temperature referred to the right temperature to eat.

Fifty people received a blue ribbon and an "honorable mention" for their entries. Third place went to Sheriff Rodney with a two-hundred-dollar prize. Sheriff Rodney was okay with that since he'd been the reigning champion for so many years, not to mention the competition was much fiercer this year. Second place went to a young woman named Sheila Farnsworth who came out all the way from Billings, Montana with a three-hundred-dollar prize. First place went to Jesse Buck for his chili that had taken northwestern Montana by storm. When the announcer called Jesse up to the front to receive his prize, Erin was quick to intervene.

"Excuse me, excuse me," Erin said, walking up to the front. "I do believe I am entitled to at least some of that prize."

"Why is that?" Jesse questioned.

"The first thing I did to your chili recipe was modify it, don't you remember?" Erin replied with the most innocent look on her face. The crowd chuckled while Jesse recalled the conversation in his head.

"Technically, that's my recipe, Mr. Buck," Erin stated, holding out her right hand with her left hand on her hip.

"Aw, give it to her!" someone yelled from the crowd.

"Let her have it," another voice said. Feeling the pressure from the crowd, Jesse handed the envelope to Erin, having to chuckle. Erin grabbed hold of the envelope, but before Jesse released it, he whispered over to her.

"You are coming over tomorrow, right?"

"Of course," Erin replied with a wink and a smile. "I wouldn't miss it." Jesse released the envelope, and the crowd went wild cheering!

"Erin Barns is the winner of the 2016 Tobacco Valley Chili Cook-Off. Let's hear it for Erin!" The announcer could barely be heard on the microphone over the noise of the crowd.

"Next year, Buck," Karma said, coming up next to Jesse and putting her arms around him. "You'll get her next year."

Chapter 36

Georgia-Jean was the first to show up on Sunday. Pastor and Recon followed, just a few minutes behind. Erin and Desi showed up with another case of wine, which was appreciated by all, and lastly was Sheriff Rodney, or better known as "Rod" when among friends. Since the chili cook-off was just yesterday, Karma decided to have baked potatoes today. After all, it was not like there wasn't plenty of chili to go around. She had all the trimmings prepared for on top. There was sour cream, cheese, onion, celery, Fritos—everything. Jesse made a large batch of rice for those who didn't want a potato and when people started showing up this time, everything was pretty much done.

The group was gathered around the tables with most people drinking wine waiting for the baked potatoes to finish when Karma looked up toward the side of the house. She could see Meo peeking around the corner with her finger to her lips, signaling *not* to mention her arrival.

Karma, not telling anyone beforehand what was going on, signaled to those facing that way via a modest head shake, a wink, or some other clever form of communication. When the coast was clear, she winked at Meo, and Meo tiptoed up behind Rod.

"Guess who?" Meo asked Rod as she reached around and covered his eyes from behind. The table was silent, other than some light chuckling.

"I'm not sure it's a good idea to sneak up on a cop," Recon shouted out.

"I'm not a cop, I'm a sheriff," Rod corrected. The group chuckled.

"C'mon, guess who?" Meo said again, a little more anxious.

"C'mon, Rod, how many women do you have in your life to choose from?" Pastor shouted out.

"Pastor!" Georgia-Jean replied anxiously. "Let the man be! I want to see what happens here!"

"I know who I want this to be, but that would be a dream come true," Rod admitted. "If it's not this person, then I'm afraid I have offended someone."

"What if it is that person?" Meo whispered softly into his ear, still covering his eyes with her hands.

"If this is Meo," Rod admitted, "then I'd have to jump up and hug you with delight!" Rod's heart was pounding while Meo just let him hang there for a moment, not saying a word. Everyone at the table was watching silently, waiting to see what was going to happen next.

"I would love a hug from you," Meo finally answered, breaking the silence. She removed her hands and stepped back so Rod could get up.

"Meo!" Rod said with surprise. "What are you doing here?" Meo wrapped her arms around Rod's neck and pressed her body against his, giving him a big hug. Rod wasted no time wrapping his arms around Meo's waist, pulling her close and holding her tight.

"I was invited for lunch," Meo answered, giving him a peck on the cheek. "Is it okay that I'm here?"

"Are you kidding?" Rod said, pushing her away just far enough to make eye contact. "It's fantastic that you're here!"

The group started whistling and cheering, nearly carrying on like a bunch of heathens.

"Okay, okay you guys, scoot down and make some room for Meo. We'll sit her right next to Rod," Karma instructed.

"So, tell me, Meo, who invited you?" Rod asked, looking directly at Jesse, expecting he had something to do with this.

"Don't look at me, brother. I'm as shocked as you are," Jesse said, defending himself.

"Karma did it," Recon shouted out first. The others were quick to follow, all calling out her name.

"We had coffee together this week, and 'Sundays at the lake' came up," Karma said with a grin. "Thought she'd like to meet some new people." Karma finished by shooting a wink to Rod.

"Meo," Jesse announced, "welcome to Sundays at the lake. From this day forward, you have an open invitation to be here among friends. To drink, to feast, and to enjoy."

"That sounds really nice, Jesse, thank you," Meo replied, looking around the table. "But I have to work Sunday nights so I shouldn't stay here too long."

"Nonsense!" Georgia-Jean spouted out from her chair at the corner of the table. "I took the liberty of rearranging the schedule. You now have Sunday evenings and Thursday evenings off."

"Ah-ha!" Pastor shouted out. "Those are Rod's days off! They'll be sinning together before you know it!" The group burst into laughter.

"Are those really your days off?" Rod asked Meo, looking at her for confirmation.

"No," Meo replied. "Georgia-Jean is just messing with us, right, Georgia?" Meo asked, looking across the table.

"No, ma'am. I only speak the truth or how I see things, and that, Meo, is the truth," Georgia-Jean said with gusto.

"I just want to give you two a little time to figure things out." Meo looked across the table and mouthed a thank-you over to Georgia-Jean.

"You're welcome, darling," Georgia-Jean replied with a warm heart and a smile. "It's the least I can do for our newest ER nurse!"

"What?!" Meo gasped with excitement "Really?!"

"You'll be getting an official job offer this week, that is, if you'd like to join our team up here in small town USA."

"I would love to!" Meo screamed as she jumped up from the table and ran around it to give Georgia-Jean a hug.

"Thank you so much! Thank you, thank you!"

"You're welcome, honey! Everyone seems to love you. You fit in perfectly."

The group of friends cheered wildly, congratulating Meo with her new job offer and what seems to be a new beginning with Rod. After the commotion settled down, the group was curious about the new addition to the circle of friends. After introductions of everybody, Meo shared a little bit during the meal.

People were so intrigued with Meo being half Chippewa that Meo and Rod didn't have much time to talk to each other. Jesse picked up on this, and when dinner was over, he suggested that Rod and Meo take the little rowboat out onto the lake and take in the scenery. Not having to be told twice, Rod grabbed Meo by the hand and headed toward the dock.

"That's a huge rock you have on that hand, Desi," Recon intruded, noticing the large 6.1 carat diamond on Desi's hand.

"When are we going to meet the man that put it there," was the question Jesse wanted to ask since the day they met, just out of curiosity of course, for it was a *big* rock.

"Sorry to let you down, Recon," Desi answered with a deviant smile. "No man put that rock there." The table got quiet, and everyone looked around at each other.

"Okay," Recon answered back as if it were nothing. "I stand corrected. When are we going to meet the *woman* that put that rock there?" There was light chuckling going around the table, and Desi rolled her eyes into the back of her head. Desi got out of her chair and walked over to Recon with her hand extended.

"Pleased to meet you, Recon, I'm Desi, short for Desdemona, a Shakespearian name." They shook hands, and Desi returned to her seat. There was a look of question floating around the table, and finally, Desi just came out with it.

"All the men I have met want either my money or my body or both, so I bought the ring and I wear it to keep the predators away," Desi said with a grin, taking a drink from her wine glass.

"Well, tell it like it is, Desi," Karma said, holding up her glass to toast Desi.

"I'm not trying to be arrogant," Desi said. I work out every day, and I have a lot of money, and let's face it— most men aren't interested in love."

Karma glanced over to Jesse after hearing what Desi just said to find him already looking over at her. Karma knew in her heart that Jesse was a good man and he cared for her greatly. Karma gave a gentle wink to Jesse, acknowledging his stare. A warm smile came across his face. Seeing that smile made Karma's heart beat a little faster and filled her soul with joy.

"Tobacco Valley Rodeo is this week!" Recon shouted out. "Woohoo!"

"You excited there, Tex?" Erin questioned after being silent all night.

"How'd you know I was from Texas?" Recon said, shifting gears.

"Your accent isn't quite East Coast south, and if I had to guess, I'd say Dallas, not San Antonio and certainly not Houston." Laughter filled the air.

"She sure did peg you, didn't she!" Jesse said, laughing in disbelief.

"You told her," Recon fired back, blowing off Jesse's comment.

"No, he didn't," Erin confirmed. "It's your regional dialect. It has Dallas all over it." The group chuckled.

"Yes," Recon said proudly. "I am from Dallas, Texas, and yes, I am excited about the rodeo. Who's with me?"

"The rodeo is a great time," Georgia-Jean said, perking up from her seat, "but I'm more excited about the live karaoke afterward."

"Why is that?" Pastor asked. "You singing for me?" Laughter again filled the air.

"Not exactly," Georgia-Jean said, not giving Pastor much attention. "Erin has a new twist she has added to keep it real, haven't you all heard?"

"I didn't say anything to anyone, Georgia-Jean," Erin offered. "It was more or less just an idea until now."

"What is it?" the others wanted to know.

"So, this week I figured, after you sing the song of your choice, you would then pass the microphone to someone for them to sing next."

Everyone at the table chuckled and agreed that would stir things up a bit.

"Who picks the song?" Jesse asked.

"Whoever is singing gets to pick the song," Erin clarified.

"Who sings first?" Karma asked, waiting for someone to volunteer someone else at the table.

"I already offered to go first," Georgia-Jean said, smiling. "I'll bring tears to your eyes." She chuckled.

"This sounds like a great time," said Jesse. "I don't sing, so don't give me the mic."

"Karma," Recon said, "did you hear that?"

"Sounds like an invitation to me," Desi said, joining in.

"I own the place, I don't have time for that," Jesse said, sipping from his wine glass. "Don't get any ideas." He continued with everyone staring directly at him. "Especially you," he said to Karma with a grin, planting a peck on her lips.

The sun was just going down as everyone was getting ready to leave when Pastor said to Jesse, "What about them?" He pointed out to Rod and Meo, still floating in the middle of the lake.

"They're adults," Jesse said. "They'll find their way in when they're ready."

"Let them be," Karma added.

The good nights were all said, and soon Karma and Jesse were headed off to their separate bedrooms.

"Good night, Jesse."

"Good night, Karma."

Chapter 37

The sun was shining bright when Jesse and Karma met in the kitchen for their morning walk. They greeted each other with a kiss and headed out the back door with Louie.

"Karma," Jesse said softly, giving her a light nudge. "Check this out." Jesse was pointing out to the middle of the lake where Rod and Meo were *still* floating around in the rowboat.

"Unbelievable," Karma said with a grin.

"Should we say something to them?" Jesse asked, not taking his eyes off them.

"No, let them notice us first," Karma said, pulling on Jesse's arm to start walking. Jesse and Karma locked hands and set out for their walk, this time talking about what Rod and Meo *might* have been talking about all night long. By the time Jesse and Karma had walked to the opposite side of the lake, Rod and Meo were paddling toward them. When they were just a few feet from the shore, Rod started to talk.

"We're not in trouble for keeping your boat out all night, are we?" Jesse and Karma chuckled at the question.

"Not at all, my friend. You didn't sink it, why would you be in trouble?" Jesse replied, laughing and smiling.

"Come back to the house and have some breakfast with us," Karma invited. "Tell us how your evening was." Rod and Meo looked at each other for a moment, and then both nodded their heads yes.

"Sure," Meo replied, grinning. "We'd love to."

"It'll be about thirty or forty minutes," Karma instructed. "We'll see you then."

Jesse, Karma, Rod, and Meo ate breakfast out on the patio where just fifteen or sixteen hours earlier they were all enjoying dinner. Rod and Meo were like infomercials about everything they talked about and how their evening together went. What was interesting about listening to them talk was how much they already respected each other. You could hear it in their voices and see it when they looked at each other.

After just one night, they were already overflowing with love for one another. It makes you wonder how some people come together and they just know.

"What do the two of you have planned for the day?" Jesse asked, looking at Rod and Meo.

"We haven't thought that far ahead," Rod answered. "I guess that all depends on whether or not Meo is getting tired of me yet."

"That will never happen," Meo answered leaning in to give Rod a peck on the lips.

"What do you have in mind, Buck?" Karma asked, not sure where this was going.

"It's a beautiful day, and I was going to ask Karma if she'd like to take the boat down to Flathead Lake today and see if we can't fish us up some lake trout for dinner tonight. I was wondering if the two of you would like to join us."

"What boat?" Karma asked, wondering what Jesse was talking about. "That rowboat out there?" She pointed to the rowboat that Rod and Meo had spent all night on. "Not happening, Buck," Karma went on. "We'll never fit in there, not the four of us and certainly not on Flathead Lake! It's huge!" Jesse just stared at Karma, wondering where she was coming from.

"I have a twenty-nine-foot fishing boat in the shop," Jesse said calmly. "I'm sure we'll have plenty of room."

Karma leaned in and latched ahold of Jesse's arm, saying in the sweetest voice, "I haven't been fishing since I was a little girl, Jesse, I'd love to go."

"I don't know, Jesse," Rod said, taking a deep breath. "Being I'm in the coast guard auxiliary, I feel I should check this vessel out before committing to anything."

Jesse, Karma, and Meo all chuckled together as Rod seemed to be the only one that took what he just said halfway serious.

"Meo, what would you like to do?" Jesse asked.

"You heard the sheriff," Meo said, backing up her new man. "Let's go check out this boat."

"I didn't know you had a boat in the shop," Karma said, looking at Jesse as she got up from the table.

"You'll like the shop, Karma," Jesse replied with a smile.

The building was set back from the drive on the left as you approached the house. It was tucked behind some trees and easily missed if you weren't paying attention. As big as it was, Jesse figured it would be better if it were positioned out of the way a little bit. The building, known as the shop, had a pair of sixteen-foot-tall roll-up doors on the left that each measured twelve feet wide. Toward the center of the shop was a half-light steel door that was standard in width and height. Then there were two eight-by-sixteen-foot roll-up doors to the right. Jesse pulled the key out of his pocket and led everyone to the "man door" in the middle. He opened the door and backed up, letting everyone enter before him.

Jesse, being the last one in, reached to the right and turned on all the lights. To the left was the fishing boat, a twenty-nine-foot North River Seahawk OS sitting on a triple-axle easy-loader trailer. The boat was made of a heavy-gauge aluminum, gray in color with forest green paint, matching Jesse's pickup. The boat glistened as it sat there, looking as if it had never been out of the garage.

To the right were three cars perfectly parked, each on their own checkered flag rug. The first car was the 1977 Pontiac Trans Am that Jesse and Karma took out not that long ago. To the right of that was Jesse's 2004 Z06 Corvette, his favorite. To the right of the Corvette was *the* world-famous 1969 Dodge Charger, better known as "the *General Lee*."

"Buck!" Karma shouted with excitement, walking over to the Dodge. "You own a *General Lee*!"

"Not 'a' *General Lee*," Jesse commented. "The, General Lee." Check the deck lid." Jesse said as he pointed toward the car. Rod and Meo didn't know what to think. These cars were immaculate, in absolutely pristine condition.

"Jesse," Meo stated with question in her voice, "where's K.I.T.T.?" Meo was referring to the Trans Am that David Hasselhoff drove in the 1980s series *Knight Rider*. Karma and Rod chuckled at the question being asked and wondered if K.I.T.T. was somewhere to be found.

"I was never a *Knight Rider* fan," Jesse responded. "However, my sister who lives in Utah owns that car. I gave it to her for her birthday a few years back. These are my two icons. The deck lids of both cars are autographed by the actors from the shows. They're the real deal."

"These are definitely cool cars, Jesse," Rod said, more eager to check out the boat. "Are we going fishing in one of these?" Chuckling, Jesse got the hint.

"C'mon, let's go check out the boat. Doesn't matter what you're driving, Buck," Karma said with attitude. "You'll never beat me home!"

"Wow," Meo said with surprise. "What's that all about?" Jesse and Karma chuckled to each other, wondering how much they should tell.

"Just some spirited competition among friends," Jesse answered with a deviant grin.

"Call it what you want, Buck," Karma responded with a wink.

Rod was the first up the ladder and onto the boat. Meo was next, then Karma and Jesse.

"We definitely need to go fishing," Rod said in awe. "Look at this fishing machine!" Rod immediately picked up on the boat's twin second-generation Evinrude E-TEC outboards. Each engine was rated with 300HP at the top and stainless-steel props at the bottom. Jesse just watched as the other three took it all in.

"Go inside," Jesse said, opening the door to the cabin. "This is known as a pilothouse configuration, specifically designed to handle the roughest of seas safely and keep its crew warm and dry inside."

Inside the cabin to the left was a marine head with a dining area ahead of that. To the right was a galley, complete with sink and stove. There were two captain's chairs, one on either side ahead of that and then a V-berth up under the bow. The interior matched the exterior in color, and all the fabric had a fishing-type pattern to it. It was nothing a woman would have picked out, but the boat still had a certain charisma that seemed to be enjoyed by all.

Rod made his way to the captain's chair and looked over the controls. "Radar, GPS—this baby is ready to go."

"I used to take it tuna fishing when I lived in California," Jesse noted. "I'm ready to go today if you all are."

"I'm in," Rod said, not able to get the words out fast enough.

"I'm in," Meo added.

"Most definitely," Karma said last. "After I get a shower."

"It's nine o'clock now," Jesse said, looking at his phone. "Why don't we meet here by eleven, we'll be on the water by noon."

"Perfect," Rod said, already helping Meo out of the boat. "Is that enough time, Meo?" Rod stopped in his tracks and looked up at his new flame.

"Yes, Rod," Meo answered, laughing. "That's plenty of time."

Flathead Lake was absolutely beautiful. It was a warm day, and the water was as smooth as glass. You could see the reflection of the mountains across the lake as far as the eye could see. Sometimes it was hard to tell where the land ended, and the water began. This was truly one of the most beautiful lakes in the country, maybe the world. The first hour or so was spent just cruising around, checking things out.

"I'm ready to go fishing," Rod finally announced, not being too bashful.

"Then it must be time to troll for trout," Jesse said, pulling the throttles back into neutral but leaving the engines idle. Jesse and Rod jumped right on the chore of rigging fishing poles together with trout lures and preparing them for casting. Like two teammates working in harmony, it was instinctive as to what needed to be done, and they each knew how to do it. Rod was obviously no amateur fisherman.

"I've never been fishing before," Meo admitted, watching eagerly as the men worked.

"Really?" Rod asked, looking up at her.

"I've been fishing before," Karma added, "but it was nothing like this. I'd be afraid to ask what this boat cost."

"Then don't," Jesse said, not missing a beat. "You can't put a price on the four of us having a wonderful day on the lake together." Jesse stood up with two fishing poles in each hand and started toward the rod holders.

"I feel fortunate that I get to share this boat with my friends."

With four lines cast out across the back of the boat, Jesse zigged and zagged back and forth over a channel at just barely three miles an hour. After about thirty minutes of intense pole watching, Meo finally broke the silence.

"For some reason, I thought this would be a little more exciting than—" *ZZZZZzzzz!*

She was interrupted by the sound of a screaming fishing real as line was being torn off it. Meo didn't know what to do.

"Fish on!" Rod yelled. He grabbed the dancing fishing pole out of the rod holder and set the hook.

"Meo, . . . here!" Rod yelled with excitement, handing the pole to her. "Keep the tip up and reel it in!"

ZZZZZzzzzz!

"Fish on!" Rod yelled again.

"A twofer?" Jesse shouted, pulling the boat engines into neutral.

"Yeah, baby!" Rod yelled over his shoulder.

"Karma, . . . here!" Rod yelled, handing the second fishing pole to Karma. "Keep the tip up and the line tight!"

"I've got this," Karma said with excitement in her voice.

"Check on Meo," Jesse yelled as he quickly reeled in the other two fishing lines to keep them from getting tangled while Rod helped with the women.

"You're doing great, Meo!" Rod assured her as she was giddy from her first battle with a fish. *ZZZZZzzzzz!* went Karma's reel again.

"It's diving deep!" Karma shouted. "It's running hard!"

"Jesse, . . . get the net!" Rod yelled as Meo nearly had her fish to the surface.

"Right here, Rod," Jesse said, handing the net over.

"Karma, . . . you good?" Jesse shouted, turning to check on her.

"I'm good . . . finish over there!"

"I see it! I see it!" Meo shouted.

"Keep reeling!" Rod instructed her.

"It's fighting me!" Meo said, eager to land her first fish ever.

"A little closer." Rod got the net ready. "A little closer!" Rod was laser focused on Meo's catch and with one gentle swoop of the net he scooped the fish right out of the water. As Jesse opened the live well and pulled the fill plug, Rod unhooked the fish from the lure and lifted it up for Meo to see.

"That's a nice fish!" Rod said, so proud of his girl. "It's close to twenty-eight inches and must be ten pounds!"

ZZZZZzzzzz! went the reel in the background.

"I'm getting tired over here," Karma cried out, looking for some help.

"I'm right here . . . I've got it!" Jesse moved in and took the fishing pole from Karma.

"Holy cow . . . you're not kidding, this thing is a monster!" Jesse shouted as *he* struggled to battle with the fish.

"I'm impressed, Karma," Jesse said, looking over to her. "You handled this fish well."

"I thought it was going to pull me over the side of the boat," Karma admitted, laughing, yet glad she was not holding the fishing pole anymore.

Karma, Rod, and Meo watched Jesse fight the monster fish for nearly an hour when Jesse shouted.

"Rod, . . . take this. Your turn, brother." Jesse handed the fishing pole carefully over to Rod who gladly took a shot at reeling in this potential *trophy* catch.

"I am glad to be done with that," Jesse said in relief.

"I can't believe it's taken this long to reel it in," Meo said, standing next to Rod as he continued the fight.

"It's not in yet," Jesse said with a chuckle.

Another twenty minutes went by while Rod battled the fish.

"Here it is!" Rod cried. "Get the net! Jesse, get the net!"

Karma and Meo darted in different directions to make room for Jesse as he moved next to Rod with an oversized net.

"There it is, there it is! Scoop it up! Scoop it up!" Rod shouted at Jesse.

"I got it! I got it! I got it!" Jesse shouted back. "Bring it around! Just a little closer . . ."

SNAP!

With a powerful thrust of its tail, the monster trout snapped the fishing line and disappeared into the depths of the lake. The silence on the boat was deafening as everyone stared into the water with disbelief of what just happened.

"Well, ladies," Rod said with a giant sigh, "looks like we're going to have to come back." There was a brief moment of sadness on the boat after the fish got away. But at the same time, there was a certain kind of joy that everyone got to experience.

"That must have been a huge fish," Meo said, rubbing Rod's arm.

"I'll come back with you guys . . . any time!" Karma added, leaning into Jesse.

"You don't get them all in the boat," Jesse admitted. "It's excitement like this, that keeps you coming back."

"The one Meo caught will make a nice dinner," Rod suggested.

"That's a great idea," Karma said, looking at Jesse. "Trout on the grill? Perfect end to a perfect day?"

Jesse nodded his head with a smile. "Let's head that way," Jesse said.

"Rod, why don't you take her in while I break down the tackle?"

"I'm on it." Rod darted into the cabin, eager to grab the controls of the twenty-nine-foot "fishing machine" with Meo right behind.

"You all right, Buck?" Karma asked softly, knowing that Jesse was discouraged they lost the fish.

"Yeah, I'm okay," Jesse said in a somber voice. "It's always tough to lose the big ones."

"We'll come back, Buck. We'll catch another one."

"Hang on," Rod yelled over his shoulder as he thrust the throttles all the way forward. The twenty-nine-foot boat launched itself out of the water as the pair of Evinrude E-TECs wound up. Jesse and Karma held on to the grab rail while "Captain Rod" savored the moment. The pair of Evinrude's revved up to full throttle, effortlessly pushing the massive vessel over 50MPH across the glass-like lake. Even at full throttle, the hum from the twin engines was minimal and certainly music to Jesse and Rod's ears.

Karma nudged Jesse, pointing up in the cabin to Meo and Rod. Meo was nearly on Rod's lap, and he was holding on to her tight. He wasn't about to let her go for anything. Jesse and Karma chuckled to each other and then shared a kiss, enjoying a little "self-time" while giving some to Rod and Meo. Karma spun around, backing herself into Jesse, pulling his arms around her. The two of them enjoyed the ride back, taking in the scenery and the closeness they felt for each other.

Chapter 38

Tuesday morning came, and Jesse and Karma finally had the house back to themselves.

"I think we need a lazy day together," Karma suggested during breakfast. "You know, sweats, a blanket, and a good movie or two?" Karma knew Jesse couldn't tell her no. Without saying a word, Jesse just looked up at Karma and smiled.

"Jesse!" Recon shouted, letting himself in through the back door. "I'm glad you're here."

"Recon," Karma said very unenthusiastically, "what are you doing here?" Completely ignoring Karma, Recon sat down on the other side of the table.

"Ned's cell phone has been shut off for nonpayment."

Jesse sat back in his chair and glanced over at Karma, then back at Recon.

"Has Sheriff Rodney talked to Jack yet?" Jesse questioned.

"I don't know," Recon answered, snatching the last piece of bacon off Jesse's plate.

"Who do you think killed him?" Karma asked. Jesse and Recon looked at each other in disbelief.

"Why would you ask that?" Jesse asked Karma, knowing now there was more to her than he knew.

"I'm not an idiot," Karma replied defensively. "Anyone can connect the dots. How did you find out about his cell phone?" Karma asked Recon with a sassy look on her face.

"It's what I do," Recon answered, almost as if being interrogated.

"Stop," Jesse interrupted, looking at both Karma and Recon. "Let's work the problem."

"There is no problem if he's dead," Karma said with a smile.

"Who did Ned fear?" Jesse asked. "Better yet, who are Ned's enemies?"

"Are you kidding me, Buck? Nobody liked that guy. Every man in town has wanted to kill him at one point or another," Karma exploded. "Some girl's father probably got ahold of him and fed him to the wolves!" Jesse and Recon looked at each other.

"We can't rule that out, Commander," Recon agreed. "The guy has a history of abusing women. Someone could have finally evened the score."

Jesse sat there and listened, raising his eyebrows as kind of a possibility. He just knew that something was amiss, and it was obvious that whatever happened to Ned, he wasn't coming back anytime soon, if at all.

"Recon," Jesse said in a very direct tone, "keep doing what you're doing. Keep me posted on regular intervals, and if anything, interesting happens, let me know right away."

With a head nod, Recon jumped up and left out the back door as swiftly as he arrived.

"There's a whole lot of drama going on for one little town," Jesse said, eyeing Karma across the table.

"Little towns have their charm, Buck," Karma replied with a smile.

"Why don't you go pick out a movie while I clean up breakfast?" Jesse suggested. "I'll meet you on the couch in ten." Wearing a smile from ear to ear, Karma didn't hesitate to jump on it.

While Jesse and Karma settled in on the couch to spend some quality time together, Erin was pulling up to the Lasso like she did every morning. She parked right out in front of the restaurant and had her keys in hand to unlock the door long before she got there. Just as she was entering the building, Erin was grabbed from behind and shoved through the door. Once inside, the man spun her around and pinned her to the wall next to the door, holding a massive knife to her throat with one hand and covering her mouth with his other.

The man stank like booze and cigarettes. He was tall and somewhat lanky and overweight at the same time, kind of dirty. His dark-colored cowboy hat was pulled over his face so Erin couldn't get a good look. With the lights still off in the restaurant, it was just dark enough to make it hard to see. His hands were rough, a working man's hands for sure. Erin tried to squirm her way out of his clutches, but it was no use. He was easily overpowering her.

"Be still and listen to me," the man spoke in a very deep, rough voice. Erin stopped squirming and tried to make eye contact.

"Tell your boss if he opens up for business one more time, this place will burn to the ground, and I'll make damn sure he's in it when it happens."

Without another word, the man lowered his knife from Erin's throat and left out the front door. Erin was quick to lock the door as soon as the man was out of sight, and her next move was to call Sheriff Rodney.

Ring . . . ring . . . "You have reached the voicemail of Sheriff Rodney . . ."

"Really, Rod?" Erin said aloud to herself, disconnecting the phone call.

Ring . . . ring . . . Jesse looked at his mobile phone.

"It's Erin," he said, looking up at Karma as he answered. "Hi, Erin, what's up?" Jesse looked straight into Karma's eyes. "Really? Are you okay? Keep trying Sheriff Rodney . . . I'll be right there!"

As Jesse hung up the phone, Karma could tell something was wrong. She jumped off the couch, saying, "Give me a minute, I'll go with you" and ran into her bedroom to get some real clothes on. Jesse grabbed the keys to the pickup and locked the back door. In less than one minute, Karma had on a pair of great-fitting jeans and a button-down flannel shirt. She was stomping her feet on the floor, slipping them into her boots while both hands were putting her hair into a ponytail.

"I'm impressed, Karma," Jesse said with a chuckle. "That was fast!" The couple raced out the door, jumped in the truck, and sped off into town.

Jesse filled Karma in with what had happened on the way. After the debriefing, Jesse handed Karma his mobile phone, telling her, "Text Recon and have him meet us at the Lasso." Karma took the phone and texted four words:

Recon: "Meet at Lasso now".

"Done," she said, handing the phone back to Jesse. Karma looked over at Jesse and saw a look on his face that was "don't mess with me" serious. His focus was intense, almost scary. Karma reached over and laid her hand on his thigh. Jesse glanced over at Karma, acknowledging her gesture.

"This is gonna stop," Jesse said, looking back up to the road. "This is either gonna stop or it's gonna get *really* ugly for someone."

Karma saw a look in Jesse's eyes that she had never seen before. He was most certainly the guy you *didn't* want to mess with.

Maybe I should ask for Jesse's help with my situation in Vegas, Karma thought to herself. She knew that now was not the time to ask, but he just might be willing to help her out for a good cause. *That's a serious question for another day*, Karma kept thinking quietly.

Jesse came flying into the parking lot with a skidding halt right outside the front door, almost hitting Erin's car. Jesse and Karma jumped out of the pickup, not even shutting the doors behind them. Erin was watching for them and unlocked the door as Jesse and Karma ran up. Jesse let Karma enter first and then he looked around to see if he could see anyone around.

"Erin, . . . are you okay?" Karma asked, giving her a hug. For the first time since the incident, Erin's eyes started to water up, and she broke down crying. Jesse came inside and hugged the both of them.

"Where's Sheriff Rodney?" Jesse asked, getting straight down to business.

"I don't know," Erin replied, wiping the tears from her eyes. "I keep getting his voice mail. I've left so many messages that his voice mail is full."

"That's kind of odd," Karma said, looking over to Jesse.

"I think so too," Jesse said, staring at the ground. "He would have heard his phone with that many rings."

"Erin," Jesse said, walking over to her and grabbing her by the arms. "Look at me." Jesse looked directly into her eyes. "Are you hurt or injured at all?"

"No," Erin said, shaking her head. "He didn't hurt me, I'm fine."

"Other than being in shock," Jesse added, giving Erin another hug. "You're safe, it'll be okay." Jesse looked at Karma.

"Let me get you something to drink," Jesse said, letting go of Erin and heading to the kitchen. "Karma," Jesse hollered as he walked away, "call the hospital and ask Meo if she knows where Sheriff Rodney is."

Jesse whipped up a screwdriver for Erin, mixing it fifty-fifty orange juice to vodka and returned from the kitchen.

"What did Meo have to say?" Jesse asked, handing the drink to Erin.

"Meo's not there. She didn't show up for work last night," Karma said with concern.

"Holy cow, Boss," Erin interrupted, shaking her head with surprise. "What are you trying to do, poison me?"

"What did you give her, Buck?" Karma asked, reaching for the glass to taste it for herself.

"I gave her a screwdriver to take the edge off," Jesse answered in innocence as if nothing were wrong.

"Wow, really?" Karma said after taking a sip. "Just taking the edge off?"

"Oh, I'll drink it," Erin said, reaching for her glass from Karma's hands. "I just wasn't ready for it." Jesse and Karma looked at each other and chuckled together.

"She'll be all right," Jesse said, looking at Erin with a confident smile.

Bang, bang, bang, was heard on the front door, and Jesse, Karma, and Erin all looked up together.

"That might be Recon," Jesse said, hurrying over to check it out. As Jesse got closer, he could see it was Recon and someone else. Opening the door, that someone else turned out to be Georgia-Jean.

"Welcome to the party," Jesse said, letting them in.

"What's going on, Buck?" Recon asked with a man hug.

"Come on, I'll let Erin fill you both in," Jesse answered, locking the door behind them.

Erin told everyone what had happened in detail. When she was finished with her story, the questions began to fly.

"Sheriff Rodney has never missed a day of work, ever," Georgia-Jean said with great concern.

"You're sure Meo didn't call in sick last night?" Jesse asked Georgia-Jean.

"Look, Buck, I told you, no one has heard from Meo, and when you call her, it goes right to voicemail." Jesse pulled out his mobile phone and called Sheriff Rodney.

"Who are you calling?" Recon asked.

"Sheriff Rodney. His phone is going straight to voicemail too," Jesse said, disconnecting the call.

"Do you think Sheriff Rodney and Meo are together?" Karma asked.

"Do you think something happened to them?" Recon questioned.

"I don't know what to think," Jesse stated with a serious monotone voice. "We don't have any facts."

"We know, or strongly suspect, it was one of the Beavers who held a knife to Erin's throat this morning, but not exactly sure which one. I would suspect that Rod and Meo are together, which means if something happened to one of them, it happened to both of them. Erin, why don't you take the rest of the week off with pay?" Jesse suggested. "Karma and I can manage this place."

"Jesse," Erin said, taking another sip of her screwdriver. "I'm not letting this guy scare me off. The rodeo is in two days, you need me here. I'll be just fine after another one of those screwdrivers." Everyone chuckled at Erin's screwdriver comment.

That's not a bad idea, Jesse thought to himself. "Recon," Jesse said with a nod of his head, "go whip us up a batch of fifty-fifties." Recon jumped up and did what he was asked without question.

"G-J," Jesse asked Georgia-Jean, "did anyone drive by Meo's house last night to see if her Jeep was there?"

"I don't have the staff to do drive-byes, Jesse," Georgia-Jean answered. "I could do it on my way home. She just lives a few minutes away."

Recon returned with half a dozen screwdrivers, each made with 50 percent orange juice and 50 percent vodka.

"Nice touch," Karma said, pointing to the maraschino cherry on top.

"I can tie that stem into a knot with my tongue," Georgia-Jean admitted, grinning from ear to ear, almost waiting for someone to ask her to do it.

"Do it," Recon said without hesitation, handing Georgia-Jean the cherry from the top of his drink.

"Hey, can we focus here?" Jesse said, taking control of the conversation.

"Recon, after your breakfast," Jesse said, pointing to the drink in his hand, "do drive-bys at Meo's and Sheriff Rodney's. Then you can drop Georgia-Jean off at home. "Georgia?" Jesse interrupted himself and did a double take her way. "Georgia-Jean, are you drinking that screwdriver?"

Everyone turned to see Georgia-Jean looking up from the glass with a straw in her mouth.

"No, sir," Georgia-Jean said after swallowing a mouthful and handing the glass back to Erin. "I'm not drinking, I'm just tasting." Everyone burst into laughter with her response. It was much-needed comic relief from the stressful morning.

"Recon, after you drop off Georgia-Jean, find Jack Beaver. Find Ned Beaver. I want visuals on both those idiots."

"I thought we decided Ned was dead?" Recon questioned, the first time he has ever questioned Jesse since he's known him.

"We think he might be dead," Jesse answered, "but until we have that confirmed, it's just a thought and maybe the wrong one. No assumptions here, we can't make decisions based on assumptions. We need facts. Until further notice, let's meet here at 8:00 a.m. for breakfast and share what we have learned from the day before. Are we good?"

Everyone nodded and agreed with Jesse that they should be meeting regularly. At least until they find Meo and Rod. Whatever was happening in the small town of Eureka was certainly nothing to be overlooked.

"Look, guys," Jesse started, addressing the entire group, "nothing is going to happen with the rodeo in town. There will be too many police and way too many people for something sly to go down. It's not until the rodeo is gone that I think something might happen. Anything else?" Jesse looked around, making eye contact with everyone.

"Yeah," Recon shouted. "What's for breakfast tomorrow?" Everyone chuckled at the light humor.

"Go, Recon. Before I throw something at you."

"Mmmm, mmmm," Georgia-Jean moaned while raising her hand up. "I've got something." Georgia put her fingers to her lips and pulled out the cherry stem—tied into a tiny little knot.

"This is for you, Recon." Everyone was amazed and laughed as Georgia-Jean handed over to Recon the proof of her hidden talent.

The rest of Tuesday was relatively quiet. Not that big of a crowd at the Lasso all day. That was to be expected a day or two before the rodeo got here. People were coming in for the rodeo that day. Wednesday through Sunday, the place should be jumping pretty good. Erin had adjusted the entertainment schedule for live music on Friday and live karaoke on Saturday, thinking the rodeo crowd would prefer the modified schedule due to the daily activities of the rodeo. She had been right with all the other decisions she had made, Jesse figured this was the right one too.

Chapter 39

Wednesday morning, 3:30 a.m.

Unable to sleep, Jesse decided he'd get up and go over to the shop for an early morning workout. When he opened his bedroom door, he was shocked to see Karma in the hallway.

"Where you headed, Buck?" she asked, leaning on the wall.

"Over to the shop for a workout. Care to join me?"

"I'll meet you over there. Let me get changed," Karma answered.

"I'll wait," Jesse replied.

In no time, Karma had changed into a pair of shorts and a sweatshirt to work out in. Jesse couldn't help but admire her legs as she approached him. Karma caught Jesse's ogling over her and smiled. *If you only knew how bad I want you, Jesse*, she thought to herself.

"You like?" Karma asked with a little attitude.

"You bet I do," Jesse replied in a playful tone and a smile.

"You know what it's gonna take to get it," Karma answered back with a wink and a smile.

By the time the workout was over, and Jesse and Karma were both showered and dressed for work, it was still only 5:00 a.m. With no better plan in place, they scooped up Louie and decided to head down to the Lasso to make sure everything was ready for the anticipated rush that was due to hit by this afternoon. Much to their surprise when they pulled up to the Lasso, Erin was already there. Jesse and Karma jumped out of the pickup and let Louie lead the way as they approached the door.

Jesse slipped the key in, unlocking the door and letting Karma and Louie head in.

"Erin!" Jesse hollered as he started turning on all the lights, not thinking to lock the door behind him. "You okay?"

"I was until you just yelled my name!" Erin hollered back, coming out from the kitchen. "You scared the hell out of me! What are you doing here so early anyway?"

"What am I doing here, I own the place, remember? What are you doing here?"

Before Erin could answer, the conversation was interrupted with a "Hey, y'all open for breakfast?"

The three of them turned toward the door to see what was up, and there was a group of six or eight people poking their heads in with a definite cowboy asking the question. Without a doubt, he was here for the rodeo. Jesse glanced down at his phone, and it read 5:35 a.m.

"Yeah, hang on, buddy, I'll be right over," Jesse shouted back to the man. "You two, run to the grocery store and buy up everything you can for breakfast." Jesse handed a large wad of cash over to Karma. "Eggs, sausage, bacon, ground beef, potatoes, onions, pancake batter, syrup, and orange juice—everything you can and get back here right away."

With an immediate task at hand, Karma and Erin bolted for the door.

"We are now," Jesse said to the man heading in that direction. "Welcome to the Lasso".

Jesse cleared a path for the ladies to get out and then opened up the doors for the guests. He was overwhelmed with seeing thirty or forty people out front and more cars pulling in.

"I can have some coffee ready in less than ten minutes, and it's on the house if you can hang for about thirty minutes to place your food order." Holding out his hand for Jesse to shake, Jesse did as if a new friendship was instantly created.

"Y'all hear that? Coffee's on the house!" the cowboy yelled back to the crowd.

"Looks like you better get moving," the cowboy suggested to Jesse.

"Y'all come in and seat yourselves. Coffees on the way," Jesse hollered over his shoulder as he disappeared into the back.

Jesse bolted through the kitchen door and immediately started brewing coffee. As the coffee was brewing, he whipped out his mobile phone and started texting the cavalry.

Recon/Pastor: Guys, I need you at the Lasso now! Come prepared to work!

Karma/Erin: Make two trips if you must; I need to start cooking now!

While the coffee was finishing its brew cycle, Jesse started peeling potatoes as fast as he could.

"Why didn't I think about breakfast this week?" he said to himself aloud as he peeled frantically. "Idiot!"

When the coffee finished, Jesse headed out with a tray of cups. He stopped in his tracks to find the Lasso almost half full. Being a quick thinker and not knowing what else to do, Jesse stepped up onto a table and decided to address the entire crowd.

"Ladies and gentlemen, ladies and gentlemen!" Jesse announced to the crowd, and the crowd quieted down and looked his way.

"Welcome to the Lasso! My name is Jesse, and I'm the owner. I had no intention of being open for breakfast. However, if y'all will bear with me, I promise to make it work today and be superior tomorrow. Sound like a plan?"

The crowd cheered in an uproar, whistling, and screaming, standing, and clapping as if *he* were the rodeo winner himself. Shortly thereafter, the crowd started chanting in unison, "Free coffee, free coffee, free coffee!"

Jesse had to laugh with the spirited group as he made his way around the tables pouring coffee and assured everyone that breakfast would be served soon.

Like magic, Pastor and Recon showed up and fell into place passing out coffee cups and pouring coffee. Jesse relieved himself of coffee duty and headed back to the kitchen to continue peeling potatoes. When he came through the door, he found Karma lighting fires and starting to cook while Erin was unloading groceries.

"Ladies," Jesse started, "we're going buffet-style!"

With head nods from both Karma and Erin, the pace for the day was just set. You couldn't ask for better teamwork. As Karma and Jesse cooked, Recon and Pastor set up the buffet. Erin kept everyone's coffee cup full and promoted the events of the Lasso: family movie night, which was tonight; ladies' night; live music on Friday; and live karaoke on Saturday. Erin's drive, focus, and ambition were impressive. There wasn't a colonel in the military that wouldn't be impressed with Erin and her work ethic. Jesse was blessed to have her on his team.

The buffet was thrown together on a whim and it turned out to be the biggest, baddest breakfast buffet that side of the Mississippi. At $12.99 a plate, all you could eat, there was a revolving door of business. It was nonstop until 11:00 a.m., and the promise was to be open tomorrow at 5:00 a.m.!

Jesse and Erin both had to chuckle because neither of them saw this coming, but the business was always welcomed. You never know in the restaurant business when your "time is up," so to speak. One day you're booming, and the next you're a has-been. Running a restaurant for the duration, through the test of time, is no easy task for anyone.

Wednesday went down as the single highest-grossing day of business the Lasso had seen to date. At one point in time, there was an hour long wait to be seated—even in the tent area. Jesse and Erin had to rethink their game plan for the remainder of the week. They had decided to triple the food and alcohol orders every day for the rest of the week and order back up kegs of beer on top of that, just in case.

Chapter 40

Thursday morning came way too fast. Jesse, Karma, Erin, Pastor, and Recon walked through the door at 4:00 a.m. to start preparing for breakfast. That was a short night's rest since no one left before midnight the night before. Even with the regular staff working longer hours and the additional staff Erin hired without Jesse knowing, they were scrambling to keep up. No one was complaining about the money being made, but everyone wore bags under their eyes like badges of honor. With the Tobacco Valley Rodeo starting that day, the breakfast crowd was sure to be massive.

"Has anyone heard from Sheriff Rodney or Meo yet?" Jesse asked as they were getting their day started. "Recon, how about an update?"

"Oh yea, Jesse, sorry," Recon started, wiping the sleep from his eyes. "Sheriff Rodney and Meo are definitely together. Sheriff Rodney's car is parked outside of Meo's apartment, but there is no sign of Meo's red Jeep anywhere. No accidents have been reported with that kind of vehicle description. As far as the Beaver boys go, they have vanished. Like laundered money—without a trace."

"Looks like the Beavers are hiding something," Jesse said with a calculated look on his face. "I want you on full alert." He eyeballed Recon. "I mean, down in the sand, nothing happens unless you know about it, full alert."

"You got it, Commander," Recon stated. "It's good to be back."

Jesse was uneasy about not knowing where Sheriff Rodney and Meo were. He knew there was a reason for everything, but at this moment in time, the "not knowing" was weighing heavy on his mind. And of all the times for this to happen, it had to be during Rodeo Week.

By nine o'clock in the morning, every cop in Montana was either at the rodeo or looking for Meo's red Jeep Wrangler. Jesse made a few phone calls, and word spread like wildfire. Apparently, Sheriff Rodney's family was very well respected throughout the state and beyond. Hopefully, *that* mystery should be solved soon.

Meanwhile, the breakfast buffet at the Lasso was out of control. Food couldn't be made fast enough, and at $12.99 per plate, business was booming. Erin, being the quick thinker that she was, repeatedly kept dreaming up contests for customers to play, giving them a chance to "eat for free." Interestingly enough, when people weren't at the rodeo, they seemed to be congregating at the Lasso, making it *the* place to meet. The parking lot was full, cars were lined up and down the street. The restaurant was full; the tent out back was full. There were customers everywhere, and better yet, everyone was having a great time.

By the time the doors closed Thursday night, the Lasso had seen its single largest day of revenue to date. It was a staggering three times more than any previous day. Not a single server or bartender made less than five hundred dollars in tips. As everyone left exhausted, they all felt it was well worth the money.

Friday morning, again, came way too early. The sleep-deprived group met one more time at the Lasso to get things fired up for the busy day ahead. Today was a little different because at six o'clock that night, there was to be a "Rodeo Celebration" honoring those who participated in the rodeo for the last two days. It didn't matter if you won or lost; you were being honored with free food and drinks all night. Erin did her due diligence with promoting the "live karaoke" night for Saturday, encouraging people to stay for the weekend and not leave town until after breakfast on Sunday.

Jesse's concerns grew stronger when there were no updates regarding Sheriff Rodney or Meo. There was really nothing he could do about it, which bothered him even more.

Friday turned out to be even busier than Thursday, setting a new record for gross sales at the Lasso. The Hickory Sticks rocked the place well into the night, and for the second time in Lasso history, the crowd drank the place dry. Every last keg was polished off. Jesse and Erin didn't believe that was even possible, but it happened.

After everyone had left, Jesse was looking for Karma so they could leave, he finally found her standing in the garage out back, looking at her Corvette.

"You, okay?" Jesse asked, coming up behind her, wrapping his arms around her, and holding her close.

"Yeah, Buck, I'm fine," Karma said, nestling back against him. "I just miss driving it." Jesse knew then and there that Karma was a true driver.

"Want to bring it home?" Jesse asked softly, kissing Karma on the ear.

"Stop it, Buck," Karma said with a giggle, moving her ear away from Jesse's lips. "Tomorrow. "I'll bring it home tomorrow. Let's get out of here and call it a night."

With that, Jesse and Karma headed home to get some rest. Jesse gave Erin the morning-to-noon shift on Saturday, allowing Jesse and Karma to sleep in.

"Karma!" *Bang, bang, bang.* Jesse shouted her name and banged on her door as he walked past.

"Let's go, . . . we're outta here in ten."

"I'm coming, I'm coming!" Karma shouted back. "A little impatient this morning aren't we, Buck?" she said to herself as she slipped her boots on. Karma took one last glance in the mirror before heading out.

"Girl, . . . you look good!" she said aloud, giving herself a wink.

Karma pulled the front door shut behind her to find Jesse waiting for her in his Corvette.

"What's the occasion?" Karma asked as she jumped into the passenger's side.

"I just miss driving it," Jesse replied with a Cheshire cat like grin.

"Game on, Buck," Karma said, fastening her seat belt. "You know I'm gonna beat you."

"Bwahahaha!" Jesse laughed the most sinister laugh he could muster up. "Bwahahaha!"

"You just can't win, Buck."

Laughing the sinister laugh, Jesse dropped the hammer and popped the clutch, leaving tracks and a trail of dust down the dirt driveway.

Chapter 41

When Jesse and Karma pulled into the Lasso, they couldn't believe their eyes. The place was packed! No one had left town yet. At 11:30 a.m., there was not a single parking spot open, and Jesse ended up parking in the garage next to Karma's Corvette. They couldn't believe the massive crowd. The tent area was full; the restaurant was full. Jesse made a beeline to find Erin and get the scoop while Karma wasted no time slipping into an apron and helped wait on customers.

"Erin," Jesse said loudly, waving to her from across the floor. Erin scurried over and greeted Jesse, grabbing him by the arm.

"What's going on here?" Jesse asked. "The place is packed." Erin pulled Jesse into the kitchen where they could talk and filled him in.

"This is the crowd for the live karaoke contest tonight where you are giving the winner $2,500."

Jesse started laughing. "I am?"

"Yes, you are," Erin stated and kept going. "Jesse, you are also donating an additional $2,500 to the winner's favorite charity."

"Erin!" Jesse said sternly. "Who gave you permission to give away $5,000?" He said eyeballing her.

"Jesse, your net revenue from this weekend will exceed $57,400, you can handle giving away less than 10 percent," Erin stated, storming off out of the kitchen. Jesse thought about it for a minute and raced over to the door.

"Erin, I need to see you now!" Jesse shouted across the restaurant. Embarrassed, Erin swiftly made her way back to the kitchen. Her stern look was almost disrespectful.

"Erin, you need to give me the numbers before you just spout things out," Jesse started. "I am proud of you, and I thank you tremendously. If your math is right, I'll give you a $5,000 bonus as well." Erin started to smile but contained her excitement.

"My math is right, Mr. Buck," she said, eyeballing Jesse before heading out the kitchen door.

"What did you do to her?" Karma said, entering the picture.

"I gave her another bonus," Jesse said, crossing his arms.

"Maybe you should give her a little more," Karma said with a laugh. Jesse just shot Karma a look, in disbelief of what he just heard.

"Cheer up, Buck," Karma added. "You've got me for free!"

"Nice, Karma, nice."

"Sometimes you're a little quick to speak, Buck. Not saying Erin shouldn't ask permission, but you have given her free reign and now you need to honor it. Just saying, Buck."

Jesse knew Karma was right. As he watched her head back out onto the floor, he realized again that Erin had been a major player and contributor to the success of the Lasso. The day was flying by. Erin left at noon as planned, and still, no one had heard from Sheriff Rodney or Meo. There were serious concerns shared with everyone that something serious had happened to the both of them. Jesse pulled Pastor, Georgia-Jean, Recon, and Karma together very discreetly to say a prayer for Rod and Meo, praying for their safe return. Something was certainly amiss.

The bustle of the crowd was fantastic. There were people practicing their karaoke routines in the parking lot hours before it officially started at 5:00 p.m. People were exercising their vocal cords, and many of them were careful not to drink too much so they could have a chance at the prize money. There was a certain magic in the air that let you know tonight was going to be a lot of fun. A few of the local store owners even donated gifts on their own will for the contestants. Jim Foxx, owner of Foxx Camera, donated a palm-sized HD video recorder!

At 6:30 p.m., Jesse and Karma noticed a woman with jet-black hair and a jet-black leather outfit enter through the door. With painted-on black leather pants accentuating every curve, black leather boots, and a black leather jacket, everything was of course accented with metal spikes.

"That's Erin!" Karma shouted, grabbing Jesse's arm with excitement. "She's gonna sing tonight!"

"That's not Erin," Jesse replied, trying to get a better look.

"That is Erin!" Karma insisted.

"Karma, that Joan Jett look-alike that just walked in . . . is certainly not Erin!"

"I'll prove it, Buck."

Karma let go of Jesse's arm and hurried over to see who the Joan Jett wannabe really was. Jesse watched as Karma approached the woman. After a brief moment of laughing and giggling, Karma and the woman locked arms and walked straight toward Jesse. They were laughing and pointing fingers all the way.

"Told you," Karma said, planting a kiss on Jesse's cheek.

"Great costume, Erin," Jesse said, laughing. "You know, Joan Jett was—"

"Stop!" Erin interrupted. "I don't need to hear any more of that comment!"

"I'm surprised you're here tonight after the week you put in," Jesse told Erin in all sincerity. Karma and Erin looked at each other and then back at Jesse.

"Did you really think I was going to miss this?" Erin asked. "This is my baby!"

"Geez, Buck, really?" Karma added. "C'mon, Joan, let me buy you a drink."

Jesse found himself alone, once again and in disbelief with what just happened. *Women*, he thought to himself. He was, however, quite impressed with Erin's costume and she wore it well. Her body was made for sin and the outfit she was wearing made Jesse wish she were hanging on his arm instead of Karma's. She was an impressive Joan Jett look alike, and he wondered if she sang as good as she looked.

At six forty-five, Erin made the announcement informing everyone how tonight was structured with passing the microphone to the next singer. The start time was in fifteen minutes and for people to head out to the tent at the back where the karaoke was going to take place. Jesse was curious to see how this was all going to unfold.

Live karaoke seemed to be an experiment for the band and most people that had showed up to witness it tonight.

Jesse poured a pair of Johnny Walkers, both on the rocks, and headed out the back to the tent. When he found Karma, he handed her one of the scotches. The couple clinked their glasses together and sipped in unison and watched Erin climb up onstage.

Chapter 42

The drummer tapped his drumsticks together to sound out the beat and then started pounding away to the unmistakable tempo of the song *I Hate Myself for Loving You*, a huge Joan Jett and the Blackhearts hit in the late eighties. Erin had her back to the audience, and her leg was keeping time with the drums. The rest of the band was on hold, waiting for Erin to turn them loose. The drummer kept a perfect rhythm as the crowd grew louder with anticipation. Suddenly, the lights dimmed, the band joined in, and Erin spun around with an "Aw" into the mic. The crowd went wild! When Erin got to the chorus, "I hate myself for loving you, / I can't break free from the things that you do, / I wanna walk, but I come back to you that's why I hate myself for loving you!" Most of the crowd joined in and sang it with her.

"Look at her!" Karma said, clinging to Jesse's arm with excitement. "She is getting down up there!"

"She's doing a fantastic job," Jesse admitted. "I never saw this coming."

"Neither did I Buck, neither did I."

"Karma, if I didn't know any better, I'd say she wants to win this tonight."

"Maybe," Karma answered, taking a sip from her scotch. "Maybe."

Erin finished her song with her back to the crowd just like she started. With a stomp of her foot, the band stopped, and the lights came back up. This had been rehearsed a time or two. Erin took a bow on stage and then passed the microphone to a large cowboy-looking fellow who asked the band to play "Ol' Red" by Blake Shelton.

By the time Erin made it to where Jesse and Karma were, three different people had bought her a drink.

"Nicely done, Erin," Jesse said as she approached him and Karma.

"That was very impressive!" Karma said with excitement, giving Erin a great big hug. "What a fantastic way to get things going! I am completely blown away, Erin!"

A couple of contestants performed and did well when Jesse, Karma, and Erin noticed Pastor getting up on stage with the mic in his hand.

"What in the world is that crazy old fool doing up there?" Karma asked the others.

"Look," Jesse said. "He's pointing to someone, watch."

"You never close your eyes anymore when I kiss your lips," Pastor was off and singing.

"Jesse, . . . Karma, . . . look," Erin said, pointing over by the piano.

"He's singing to "Georgia-Jean!" they all said in unison and burst into laughter.

"She's gonna kill him," Jesse said with a smile, not being able to stop laughing.

"He doesn't sound that bad," Karma added. "Look." Karma said as she smacked Jesse in the arm. "He's walking out to her!"

Jesse, Karma, Erin, and the rest of the crowd started singing along when Pastor took Georgia-Jean by the hand and pulled her out on the dance floor. The crowd finished the song as Pastor and Georgia-Jean finished by dance.

"Nicely done, old man!" a stranger yelled from the back of the tent.

"Tomorrow, you're in deep trouble," Georgia-Jean said, looking at Pastor with a smile.

"I can't wait," Pastor replied, planting a kiss right on Georgia-Jean's lips. The crowd roared and cheered as they loved the latest performance.

"You've got to give the microphone to someone now," Georgia-Jean said to Pastor when the song was finished. Pastor scanned the room and then locked eyes with Karma.

"He's heading straight toward you!" Erin said, nudging Karma in the arm.

"Yea he is," Jesse added.

"Don't you dare put me on the spot like that!" Karma shouted to Pastor when he was only a few feet away.

"Your turn, darlin'," Pastor said with a smile, handing the microphone to Karma. "You can't get out of it."

"You're in deep trouble tomorrow," Karma said to Pastor as she slowly got up and made her way toward the stage.

"That's what Georgia-Jean told me," Pastor said with a laugh.

Karma made her way onto the stage and talked to the band. The crowd watched the lead guitarist shake his head no. Karma shrugged her shoulders and started off the stage. The crowd was somewhat displeased with what they saw and started shouting to find out what was going on.

"They don't know my song," Karma spoke into the microphone, pointing to the band. "I can't sing it if they can't play it."

"What's the song?" the crowd demanded.

"Walking after Midnight,'" Karma answered a little sheepishly.

"I've got this," Jesse shouted over the others, jumping out of his chair and hurrying toward the stage.

"I've got this!" he yelled again. Karma looked at Jesse as if he were crazy, wondering what was happening.

"You're singing," Jesse said as he walked past her and up to the piano.

"Drummer!" Jesse yelled over the crowd. "Give me a 4-4 beat!" The drummer immediately delivered what Jesse had asked for. A rather catchy 4-4 tempo filled the air. When Jesse sat down at the piano, the crowd went wild. Jesse lit the keyboard up like he was Jerry Lee Lewis and segued right into "Walking after Midnight."

Karma, was stunned. She had no idea Jesse could play the piano, and certainly not like this. She got her bearings and started to sing.

"I go out walking, after midnight, in the moonlight . . ."

Karma started making it obvious that she was not only singing, but she was singing to Jesse. The guitarist and the bassist joined in after several measures, and the crowd was clapping to the tempo. Jesse's eyes were locked on Karma as she approached him, never once looking at the piano keys.

"Just like we used to do . . ."

"Karma's giving you a run for the money," Pastor said to Erin.

"Look at her go out there."

"This is a duet," Erin replied. "It doesn't count."

"Sure, it counts" Georgia-Jean fired back with a smile.

"We'll see," Erin shrugged off, grudgingly.

Karma was now running her hands through Jesse's hair and doing her best to distract him at the piano while she sang her version of the Patsy Cline favorite. She was wrapping herself around him and was nearly on his lap! How Jesse could keep playing while not missing a note was impressive on its own. A man from the audience reached down and picked up Karma unexpectedly, placing her on top of the piano. Not missing a word, Karma finished the song, singing to Jesse while perched on the rustic looking instrument. When Jesse and Karma finished, the band wrapped up with a crash and the crowd went absolutely wild!

The crowd started chanting, "Karma, Karma, Karma," wanting her to sing another song. Karma was shaking her head no, not wanting the attention from anyone but Jesse. Jesse saw this and got up from the bench and helped Karma down off the top of the piano. Karma passed the microphone off to someone reaching for it, and they made their way back to where they were watching. The crowd cheered Jesse and Karma on for several minutes. Finally, the couple took a bow and pointed toward the next contestant, moving the evening forward.

Erin was the first to give Karma a hug. "Just one of your many talents?" Erin asked with a big smile.

"That was something to watch," Pastor threw in.

"Buck," Karma asked, turning toward Jesse, "why didn't you tell me you could play the piano?"

"Why didn't you tell me you could sing?" Jesse asked back, smiling.

Out of nowhere popped Recon, handing both Jesse and Karma each a double scotch on the rocks.

"That was so much fun to watch!" Recon said with a smile "That was the second-best performance of the evening!" He said shooting Erin a wink. "I love Joan Jett!"

"It was actually really fun to be up there with Buck," Karma said, sipping her scotch with a glow. "I liked singing to you, Buck!" Karma admitted with a playful grin.

"I liked having you sing to me! You have a sexy little singing voice going on there, Karma love."

"That's not even my best asset, Buck."

Pastor, Georgia-Jean, Erin, Recon, Jesse, and Karma watched and chatted while the other performances went on. After about forty-five minutes, the contestants that were competing with each other had all gone once. A few members of the crowd brought a list to Erin, asking her to let the top four performers of the evening perform again, with a different song to help with the judging. This was a twist that Erin couldn't predict, and after getting on stage to see how the rest of the crowd felt about it, they were all in.

"Ladies and gentlemen," Erin announced, taking control of the masses, "I have what is thought to be the top four performances of the night. As I read them off, please give me a yeah or a nay. Sound good?" Erin asked. The crowd responded with overwhelming "yeah." Erin noticed that both her name and Karma's name were on the list and decided to read them off last.

"Steve, who sang 'Ol Red' by Blake Shelton." The crowd cheered a tremendous "yeah."

"Next is Reed who sang 'John Cougar, John Deere, John 3:16' by Keith Urban." The crowd roared another "yeah."

"Third is Erin who sang 'I Hate Myself for Loving You' by Joan Jett." The crowd roared at near deafening levels, whistling, and cheering so loud that Erin's microphone couldn't penetrate the noise.

"The fourth and final—" Before Erin could finish, the crowd started chanting, "Karma, Karma, Karma . . ." Erin paused for a moment and shot Karma a friendly yet competitive smile.

"Looks like we already have a favorite tonight," Erin said.

"Contestants," Erin continued, addressing the crowd, "think about your next song choice. We go live in ten minutes!" Erin stepped down off the stage and headed back over to the group.

"Karma," Erin said, approaching with her hand extended to shake. "Good luck." Karma could clearly see that Erin was a fierce competitor.

"You've got this, Erin." Erin turned and headed toward the ladies' room. When she was out of sight, Karma turned to Jesse, saying, "Let's get out of here, Buck."

"You don't want to stay?" Jesse asked, looking at Karma, surprised that she wanted to go.

"I'm not interested in winning this contest tonight, Jesse. I just wanted to sing to you."

Jesse looked into Karma's eyes. He could tell that she wanted to play. Jesse looked at his drink and finished it with a gulp, setting the glass down on the counter.

"It doesn't matter to me when we leave tonight, Karma." Jesse grinned from ear to ear. "Tonight, I'm going to beat you to the driveway no matter what."

Karma stepped back and put her hands on her hips, surprised to hear such a bold challenge from Jesse and decided to accept.

"If you beat me to the driveway tonight"—Karma stepped into Jesse and pressed her body against his— "I'll be your trophy," she whispered into his ear. Karma planted a kiss right on Jesse's lips and stepped away.

"Game on," he said, grabbing Karma by the hand as he headed to the garage.

"I'll even let you leave the parking lot first," Karma told him to intentionally break his concentration.

Chapter 43

The two Corvettes backed out of the garage and inconspicuously drove through the parking lot. Jesse led the way to the exit as Karma followed only a few feet behind. When the rear tires of Jesse's Corvette hit the asphalt, he dropped the hammer. The back end of his Corvette fishtailed to the left, and smoke filled the back-fender wells as the Goodyear tires left dark black marks on the asphalt, leaving Karma in a cloud of gray tire smoke.

"No way are you getting laid tonight, Buck," Karma said out loud to herself as she followed suit, smoking her own tires as she left the parking lot, hot to run down her lover.

"C'mon, baby," Jesse said aloud as he watched Karma in his rearview mirror. "Show me what you've got."

Jesse led the couple to the highway, and when he slowed just enough to make the turn, Karma ducked to the inside shoulder and drifted her Corvette around him for the pass, just missing the front end of his car.

"No way!" Jesse shouted to himself.

Chuckling to herself, Karma hit her high beams and mashed her foot to the floor, launching her Corvette down the road. The two Corvettes blew past 100 mph and continued to accelerate. Jesse took to the left-hand lane and held pace with Karma, 127 mph on the heads-up display, and accelerating. The two Corvettes closed a third vehicle as if it were not even moving. Neither Jesse nor Karma let off the throttles. Jesse didn't slow down, knowing Karma would have to hit the brakes. Instead, Karma accelerated harder and passed the third vehicle on the right-hand shoulder. The two Corvettes blew by the third vehicle so fast that the driver of the third vehicle swerved from being startled.

"Nice driving, Karma," Jesse said to himself. "The highway is the easy part."

Karma saw the off-ramp up ahead and knew she was closing it fast. Worried that Jesse was going to try to pass her as they turned right at the end of the ramp, Karma knew she was going to have to come in hot. As Karma started to slow, Jesse moved in for the pass.

"Slow down, Rachael, you're not going to make—" Jesse said out loud to himself, backing off the throttle. Karma shifted the transmission from fourth to third, skidding the back tires, putting her Corvette into a perfect four-wheel drift, and mashed the throttle to the floor.

"Not today, Buck." Jesse was stunned.

"You have your car in competitive driving mode," Jesse said to himself. "No more Mr. Nice Guy."

Jesse held down the driver mode button in his Corvette, putting his in competitive driving mode also.

"I'm coming after you, Karma." Jesse knew that there were only about six miles to the house and two places to pass. He was not going to lose this race. The two Corvettes accelerated back into the one thirties. Karma was taking up every inch of road to keep Jesse from passing. Jesse decided to take Karma on the sweeping corner ahead.

She'll never expect that, he thought to himself.

As Karma dipped her Corvette into the apex of the corner, Jesse hit the gas to pass her on the outside—136, 137, 138 mph on the heads-up display. Karma glanced over to see him right next to her. Jesse and Karma made eye contact just for a split second before looking forward finding a herd of deer standing in their way, completely covering the road. With nowhere for either driver to go, the two Corvettes plowed into the herd of deer well into triple-digit speeds.

Chapter 44

Sunday.

Beep. Beep. Beep was all that you could hear in Jesse's hospital room. Pastor sat next to Jesse's bed with his head hung over and his hands folded in continuous prayer, praying that his friends would come through this.

"How bad is he?" Pastor heard a familiar voice, spoken softly from behind him. Looking over his shoulder, Pastor saw Sheriff Rodney and Meo standing in the doorway holding hands. Without saying a word, Pastor got up and walked over to them. As he approached the couple, he opened his arms to embrace them both in a hug.

"I can't believe you're here. We all thought something terrible had happened to you. It's really good to see you both," Pastor said with a heavy voice, holding back tears. After another moment, Pastor released Sheriff Rodney and Meo from the hug and stepped back.

"He has lots of lacerations, many of them deep. He lost a lot of blood. A deer came through the windshield and hit him in the chest cavity, crushing his rib cage. The only thing that saved his life was the airbag; it acted like a cushion between him and the deer. He is alive, but he has two punctured lungs and a concussion. If the swelling in his brain doesn't go down soon, he could lose his eyesight completely."

Rod and Meo listened as Pastor spoke about Jesse's injuries.

"His right arm is broken completely in half just above the wrist. He has glass in his face. He's in bad shape. The doctors are keeping him under until the swelling in his brain goes down, a few days maybe, for pain management more than anything."

"What about Karma?" Meo asked softly.

"Karma has a broken leg," Pastor said without taking his eyes off Jesse. "She also has a few lacerations." Pastor paused for a moment. His lips started to tremble from the emotion he was feeling.

"Karma, is in a coma," Pastor finally managed to get out before pulling his hands to his face and sobbing. "Her heart keeps stopping," Pastor continued. "My deepest fear is that God might be coming for her." Pastor cried uncontrollably.

Meo ran from the room in tears and Rod followed. Pastor, alone in the room with Jesse, sat back down in his chair and continued to cry uncontrollably.

"Not now, God, please not now. Please don't take them now," Pastor prayed.

Chapter 45

Monday

Erin walked into the hospital Monday morning with a very heavy heart. Pastor had reached out to her the night before and told Erin that Jesse and Karma had been involved in a bad accident. Erin demanded details, but Pastor was reserved with sharing any information, knowing in his heart Jesse would want things kept on the quiet side.

"Georgia-Jean," Erin spoke loudly as she caught a glimpse of the town's favorite ER nurse down the hall. Georgia-Jean spun around and waited for Erin to catch up.

"Oh, Erin," Georgia-Jean said, giving her a hug. Erin looked Georgia-Jean in the eye and could see her pain, she could also see the love she has for Jesse that she has been able to keep a secret, until right now.

"How bad is he?" Erin asked softly, not sure she was prepared for the answer.

"You're in love with Jesse, aren't you," Georgia-Jean asked quietly. "I can see it in your eyes, Erin."

"How is he, Georgia-Jean?" Erin struggled, holding back tears. "I really need to know."

"You're secret's safe with me, honey." Georgia-Jean confirmed prior to answering the question. "They both need your prayers, Erin," Georgia-Jean answered, leading Erin down the hall to the rooms that Jesse and Karma were occupying.

Erin slowly walked into Karma's room. When Erin saw Karma lying there on the bed, almost lifeless, tears started streaming from her eyes. She took a deep breath and sat down in the chair next to Karma's bed. Erin reached over and held Karma's hand.

"Karma. It's me, Erin. I know you're in there, Karma."

It was harder for Erin to speak through the tears streaming from her eyes than she thought it was going to be. She took another deep breath and pulled herself together and continued to speak softly.

"Karma, I know you hear me. It's time to wake up, Karma. It's not time for you to go. We've got more singing to do. The crowd loved you, Karma, and we love you too."

Erin stood up and gave Karma a kiss on the forehead.

"I'll see you soon."

Erin wiped the tears from her eyes and walked next door to see Jesse. When she stepped through the door, she stopped dead in her tracks. She gasped and brought her hands up to her mouth when she saw Jesse lying on the hospital bed, as near lifeless as Karma, but looking to be in far worse condition. The bruising on his face, the bandages, his head was so swollen he looked alien. With the machine helping him breathe, Erin couldn't believe her eyes. Feeling light-headed, she turned around to look at something else.

Beep . . . Beep . . . Beep from the heart monitor was all that could be heard next to the sounds of the ventilator.

"Jesse," Erin said, turning slightly, unable to turn around completely and look at him. "I've got the Lasso, Jesse. You take as much time as you need to get better. Just get better. I... I... I need you to come through this, Jesse."

Overwhelmed with emotion, Erin hurried out of the ER, not stopping until she was in her car. She lowered her head and cried into her hands as runaway tears fell from her eyes.

"They were just having fun, this was not supposed to happen to them," Erin said to herself as if she was talking in prayer. "They were just having fun." Erin tried to clean herself up and checked herself in the vanity mirror.

"Perfect," she said, wiping mascara away from her eyes. "I look like a zombie now." Erin headed down the street to the Lasso; she knew it was going to be her baby for a while and she had to pull herself together.

When Erin pulled up to the front door, Sheriff Rodney was there, leaning against the front of his cruiser.

"Good morning, Sheriff, where have you been? We have been worried sick about you and Meo!" Erin said, jumping out of her vehicle.

"Good morning, Erin," Sheriff Rodney answered, tipping his hat. "I understand that someone was harassing you last week?"

"That was last week! Where were you when we needed you!" Erin demanded with a fierce temper.

"Erin, I'm so sorry," Sheriff Rodney said, walking toward her. "First things first, please know that I know about Jesse and Karma, I'm really sorry."

Sheriff Rodney reached out to give Erin a hug. She hugged him back and began to cry again. She just couldn't help it.

"Erin, Erin, it'll be okay, Erin."

Sheriff Rodney tried to do his best to comfort her, but he also knew their beloved friends were clinging on to their lives by a thread.

"It was nothing, Sheriff," Erin replied, pushing Sheriff Rodney away to unlock the door, doing her best to pull herself together.

"A knife to the throat is far more than nothing."

"It's a nightmare that I don't really feel like reliving right now Rodney." Erin stopped and turned around to look at Sheriff Rodney. Her eyes were swollen from crying, and she was fighting back the tears at that moment. Without saying a word, Sheriff Rodney opened his arms again to give Erin another hug. Unable to stop herself, Erin stepped into his arms and started to cry again.

"They were both so full of life," Erin said between tears. "I can't imagine them not pulling through this."

"They're going to pull through this," Sheriff Rodney assured Erin. "Jesse's been through far worse than this, and if I didn't know any better, he's not about to let Karma go either." Erin stepped back from Sheriff Rodney and dried her eyes one more time.

"How's Meo?" Erin asked, changing the subject to get her mind on something else. "We were really worried about you two."

"Meo and I," Sheriff Rodney said with a little hesitation in his voice, "are just fine. We, ah, . . . had a little adventure of our own." Erin could sense there was something Sheriff Rodney wasn't admitting to.

"Are you guys, okay?" Erin asked with concern, not wanting any more sad news.

"Oh yeah." Sheriff Rodney told her, grinning from ear to ear, looking up at Erin. "We got married in Vegas," Sheriff Rodney admitted.

Erin lit up like Christmas. "Get outta here!" she said, grabbing Sheriff Rodney's hand, checking for a ring. "After a week?"

"After three days, actually."

"Rod, are you out of your mind?"

"We are totally in love, what can I say?"

"You're not in love . . . You're in heat!" Erin shook her head in disbelief. "She's twenty-five years younger than you, Rodney!"

"She's only twenty-two years younger than me."

"Really? Who else have you told this to?"

"Well, we told Jesse and Karma yesterday."

"That's not funny, Rodney!" Erin yelled. "Do her parents know?"

"Her parents were there."

"Hey, wait a minute." Sheriff Rodney stopped the conversation in its tracks. "I came here to let you know I'm sorry I wasn't around last week. I came here to let you know that I'll find the rat bastard that did that to you and hold him accountable. If you have a problem with Meo and I getting married, then you have a problem!" By the time Sheriff Rodney was finished, he was almost yelling like a drill sergeant.

"What's all this yelling going on in here!" Recon said with authority as he and Pastor entered through the front door.

"Sheriff Rodney and Meo eloped," Erin said, walking away and back into the kitchen.

"Sinners!" Pastor yelled with a grin.

"Way to go, Rodney!" Recon said, offering Sheriff Rodney a man hug.

"It's not a sin to elope," Rodney replied, rolling his eyes at Pastor.

"Do her parents know?" Pastor asked with a bit of attitude.

"Her parents were there!" Sheriff Rodney replied.

"Then that's not eloping," Recon added as if it were nothing.

"I never said we eloped. Erin said that."

"After three days," Erin said, re-entering from the kitchen, "It's eloping."

"How was the honeymoon?" Pastor asked, grinning.

"How was the sex!" Recon shouted out before Rodney could answer.

"Hey!" Erin shouted. "Enough of that, man talk, while I'm here! If you all are going to be here, you need to get to work! What are you guys doing here anyway!"

"We're here for breakfast," Recon said as if Erin should have already known that.

"You can make your own breakfast," Erin said as if *she* owned the place. Just then the door was heard closing. Meo and Georgia-Jean walked in to join everyone.

"Meo!" Erin shouted. "May I have a word with you in the kitchen, now please!"

"Oh, . . . you're in trouble!" Recon and Pastor both sung out at the same time.

"I'm an adult," Meo said, rolling her eyes. "I can't be in trouble!"

"You certainly are in trouble, girl, get in here!" Erin shouted, yet with a smile at the same time. Erin and Meo disappeared into the kitchen.

"How are you doing this morning, love?" Pastor said, approaching Georgia-Jean with hopes of a hug and a kiss.

"Don't you *love* me?" Georgia-Jean said, pushing Pastor away. "I'm still not happy with you for singling me out at the party the other night! What is the matter with you?"

"Georgia-Jean, did you *not* enjoy that? Did you *not* have a good time dancing with me?"

Georgia-Jean just stood there not saying a word. You could tell she was computing everything that just happened and what Pastor just said. Georgia-Jean was recapping everything that had happened Saturday night.

"Be careful who you call a sinner, Pastor," Georgia-Jean said with hard eyes and a stern smile.

"Bwahahahaha!" Recon and Rodney burst into laughter.

"Called you out, blam!" Recon shouted. Recon and Rodney had tears coming from their eyes as they laughed with all their might, holding their sides and gasping for air.

"Animals," Pastor said, heading over toward the bar to get himself some orange juice.

Georgia-Jean headed back to the kitchen to see what Erin and Meo were talking about and to see what kind of trouble Meo was in.

"If you're making screwdrivers, make three!" Recon shouted after catching his breath.

"You've just gotta love Georgia-Jean," Recon said, sitting down at a table with Rodney.

"She's quite a character," Sheriff Rodney admitted.

"Why did you do it?" Pastor asked, returning to the table with a tray of screwdrivers. "Why did you and Meo run off and get married after three days? Do you know how crazy that looks?"

"Who cares about what other people think, Pastor?" Sheriff Rodney asked. "We got married before the Lord our God. We have committed no sin. We have given no judgment, we are following our hearts and through thick or thin, we're going to make it!" Sheriff Rodney was getting a little huffy and defensive, leaning forward in his chair.

"Is there a problem, Pastor? Do you have a problem, pastor?"

"Easy, Rod," Recon said with a soft, soothing voice, waving his hand to sit back down. "No one has a problem with anything, we're simply curious. It happened so fast; we are all just wanting to know why, that's all. Everyone is a little emotional today. You and Meo disappeared, Erin's knife incident, and now Jesse and Karma have their accident. It's a little stressful around here right now, just relax."

"I love her, that's why," Sheriff Rodney said, eyeballing Pastor.

Recon shot Pastor the "let it go and say a prayer for them" look, hoping to reduce the tension.

"Hope you boys are hungry!" Erin said, entering with a stack of plates and silverware, still talking with a bit of a shaky voice.

"Have we got a breakfast for you!" Georgia-Jean and Meo followed behind, laughing like best friends, each with their hands full of food.

"Pancakes, sausage, Eureka-style country eggs, and biscuits!" The ladies were all smiling and in a great mood.

"What are 'Eureka-style country eggs'?" Recon asked, trying to get a peek of what was in the tray.

"Eggs with everything in them," Georgia-Jean fired back. "We just created them."

"It's a new item for the menu," Erin added.

"Are we going to be open for breakfast now?" Pastor asked as if he had a stake in this claim.

"Our breakfast crowd was good," Erin spoke like a true businesswoman. "As long as I'm in charge and we're making a profit, I'm going to do it."

Pastor got up from where he was sitting and took a step back from the table.

"Before we eat," he started, removing his hat from his head, "I'd like to say a prayer." The room went silent, and Pastor bowed his head. The others followed, and some held hands.

"Dear Lord, oh Heavenly Father. Thank you for bringing us together here today to celebrate life amongst friends and to feast with those we hold close. Lord, today we ask that you lay your healing hand on Jesse and Karma who both rest in the hospital and fight for their lives. Lord, we ask that you give them back to us and help them find each other. We know they have a place up there with you, but, if possible, we would like more time with them down here. In the name of Jesus Christ, our Lord and Savior, thank you, Lord, for hearing our prayers. Amen."

"Amen."

Chapter 46

For days, there was a somber feeling in the air. The group, Pastor, Recon, Erin, Sheriff Rodney, Meo, and Georgia-Jean would continue meeting at the Lasso in the mornings for breakfast. The first thing to talk about was if there were any signs of improvement with Jesse or Karma.

Recon had temporarily moved into Jesse's house and was taking care of Louie. Erin was running a tight ship at the Lasso with a growing crowd for breakfast. Everyone loved her "Eureka-style country eggs." Georgia-Jean was mothering everyone, nothing new there, and Pastor was busy praying.

Once word spread through town about the accident, people were sending gifts for Jesse and Karma by the truckload. There were multiple deliveries every day to the Lasso and the hospital of flowers and cash contributions, gift baskets, and more. Karma even had "a fan" that would come by hoping to get her autograph after hearing her sing karaoke the night of the accident. Even with all the support from the town of Eureka, those closest to Jesse and Karma walked with heavy hearts.

Sunday night, 11:20 p.m., eight days after the accident, Recon showed up at the hospital with Jesse's dog, Louie. The North Country Medical Clinic in Eureka, Montana, was not a busy place, nor was it a very big place as far as hospitals go. When Recon and Louie came marching through the door and headed for Jesse's room, it didn't go unnoticed. A staff member was quick to try to intervene.

"Sir, I'm sorry, but you can't bring that dog in here."

"This is not a dog," Recon replied with a sharp tone. "He's family."

"Sir, sir!"

Meo heard the commotion and was quick to intervein, asking the other staff member to "look the other way." Disgruntled, the staff member did as she was asked. Without another word being spoken from Recon, he marched down the hall to Jesse's room with Louie, leash-less, right by his side.

Upon entering the room, Recon sat in the empty chair next to Jesse's bed and made a hand gesture to Louie instructing him to sit.

"Commander," Recon spoke softly, and with respect. "Commander, it's good to see your breathing on your own now," Recon told him, noticing that the ventilator had been removed. "I brought an old friend with me tonight. If it's okay with you, we're going to stay with you awhile." Recon leaned back in the chair and closed his eyes. Louie jumped up on the hospital bed and lied down next to Jesse, resting his head on Jesse's hand. Both were fast asleep.

Monday morning, 5:27 a.m.

With his left eye still bandaged from the accident, Jesse struggled to open his right eye, the good eye. The room was dim, and his vision was blurry. He could make out a figure sitting in the chair but couldn't clearly identify who it was.

When you don't have your bearings, don't say a word were the first words that went through Jesse's mind. Struggling to focus, Jesse started to check his digits to make sure they were all there. The fingers on his left hand were accounted for. Toes on his left foot wiggled. Toes on the right foot checked out, and when he wiggled the fingers on his right hand, he felt Louie, who woke up and with a single loud bark announcing his presence.

"Louie old boy, where am I?" Jesse asked with a groggy voice, scratching him behind his ear. "Is this a cast on my arm? Karma is that you?" Jesse tried to see, looking at the figure in the chair.

"Karma. Karma," Jesse said with more strength each time.

"Jesse, it's Recon. Good to have you back, Commander."

"Recon, where's Karma?"

"She's in the room next door, Jesse."

"I need to see her," Jesse said, trying to sit up in his bed.

"Nurse! Nurse!" Recon yelled toward the door.

"I need to see her, Recon, now."

"Meo, get in here!" Recon shouted. "Jesse, my friend, rest, don't get up, you're in bad shape, just relax."

"What happened to Karma, Recon, where is she?" Jesse struggled to breathe and move from the pain of his broken ribs. Gasping for air and aching in pain, he continued.

"Tell me what's going on, Recon! That's an order!"

Recon knew that Jesse had just gone into "survival mode." Survival mode for Jesse was you did what he told you to do, and you answered his questions quickly and correctly or you experienced the wrath of Jesse Buck, and it was often swift and severe.

Hearing the shouting, Meo came running into Jesse's room.

"Jesse, you're awake," Meo started with a calm, soothing voice. "You're in the hospital, you've been down for a few days. Give me just a minute, and we'll tell you everything."

"Do you remember the accident, Jesse?" Recon asked, speaking in a soft tone.

"Deer," Jesse murmured, shaking his head back and forth. "The road was covered with deer, there was no place to go. Damn it, Recon, where is Karma! I need to see Karma now!!"

"Karma is right next door, Jesse. Relax, it's early in the morning yet."

"Meo, what's wrong with me, what happened?"

"Jesse, I need you to relax and keep still while I talk with you," Meo explained. "You have deep lacerations to your face; you had a major concussion. Your brain swelled so much that it has caused you to lose your vision in your left eye. We kept you induced in a coma for pain management until the swelling had gone down. Jesse, your rib cage was crushed. Every one of your ribs were broken. Jesse, both of your lungs were punctured. You also have a broken arm. You are going to experience extreme difficulty breathing, you need to settle down. The vision in your left eye should come back over time. We don't believe any permanent damage was done."

Jesse pushed Louie off the bed and started to get up.

"Jesse, you can't get up!" Meo shouted at him. "You're going to hurt yourself."

"I have to see Karma." Yanking the IVs out of his arm, Jesse sat up in bed. "Aahhhh," he moaned from the pain.

"Recon, do something!" Meo shouted.

"Back off, Recon, that's an order."

Recon made eye contact with Meo and shook his head, as if he were telling her not to stop him, to let him go. Recon knew Jesse all too well, and he knew when to stand down.

"Meo, take me to see Karma now," Jesse commanded. "Now!"

Without saying a word, Meo hurried over to Jesse and held out her arm for him to latch on to. Recon stepped back and let them lead the way but followed close behind. When Meo and Jesse entered the room next door and Jesse saw Karma lying on the bed, he immediately started to get teary-eyed.

"What's wrong with her?" Jesse barely got out over his now shaky voice, still trying to give commands.

"Karma also suffered a few lacerations to the face. Nothing too bad, Jesse, they should heal nicely. She has a broken leg, and she also suffers from head trauma."

"How bad?" Jesse asked not taking his eyes off Karma. "What kind of head trauma?"

"Karma wasn't breathing when she was found. She had to be resuscitated. Her heart had stopped several times during the first twenty-four hours, but she seems to have stabilized since then. Jesse," Meo said softly, holding back tears of her own, "Karma hasn't woken up yet. She's in a coma."

"Get out," Jesse commanded, fighting back tears. "All of you . . . get out now!"

Meo and Recon stepped out of the room and pulled the door closed, leaving Jesse alone with Karma.

"I'm sorry, Meo," Recon said, trying to help the situation. With glassy eyes from the tears about to fall from them, all Meo could do was walk away.

"Come on, Louie," Recon said to Jesse's dog who was standing in the hall, not sure of what to make of the situation. "Let's get out of here." With the snap of his fingers, Louie followed Recon down the hall and out the door.

Jesse slowly made his way over to the right-hand side of Karma's bed. Uncontrollable tears were freely flowing from both eyes.

"I'm sorry I did this to you, Rachael. I'm so sorry." Jesse struggled to push Karma over a few inches, making room for him on the bed next to her but managed to do so with great pain. Jesse sat down next to Karma, and after several more pain-filled minutes, Jesse had positioned himself on the bed lying next to her. He picked up Karma's hand in his and kissed it.

"I'm here, Rachel," he whispered to her through his tears. "I'm not going to leave you. I'll be here with you until you decide to wake up."

Jesse kissed Karma's hand one more time and placed it across her stomach. Gently reaching around Karma, he held her while he closed his eyes.

"I'm never going to leave you."

Chapter 47

Tuesday morning

Georgia-Jean and Meo entered the Lasso together, both coming from the hospital. The rest of the group was already there, and Erin was almost finished getting breakfast ready.

"You're just in time today, ladies," Pastor said, getting up and offering his chair to Georgia-Jean.

"Don't get up, Pastor," Georgia-Jean said, rolling her eyes at him. "Meo and I are going to help Erin." Grabbing Meo by the hand, Georgia-Jean dragged her to the kitchen.

Before any real conversation could get started with Rod, Pastor, and Recon, the women returned with breakfast. Everyone took their seats and Pastor said the morning prayer. It was time for the highlights.

"Meo, is Jesse still lying there, you know, next to Karma?" Recon started.

"He hasn't moved."

"He won't eat either," Georgia-Jean added.

"The instant you walk into the room, he screams at you to get out," Meo went on. "We finally just left some food and pain meds on a tray and told him they were there."

"He's praying," Pastor said with confidence. "Doesn't want to be bothered until his prayer is answered. It's called 'passionate prayer.'"

"I've known the commander for a lot of years," Recon answered back with a little attitude. "He ain't praying."

"Can it, boy, you don't know what you're talking about," Pastor said, agitated.

"You can it, Pastor! You think you know him better than I do?"

"Knock it off!" Sheriff Rodney interrupted with a ferocious growl. "Maybe we should all do a little more praying instead of sitting here fighting about it."

"I'm telling you all, Jesse is in there praying with all his might, all his focus, all of his heart, all of his belief. He's praying for Karma, and we should pray too." Pastor extended his hands out on the table offering those beside him to hold hands.

After everyone joined in, Pastor began to pray.

"Bow your heads. Dear Lord, oh Heavenly Father, the life of our friend Rachael is in your hands right now. Lord, we ask you to hear Jesse's prayer, and we ask you to hear our prayer, we ask you, Lord, to give Rachael back to us. Please lay your healing hands and healing power on Jesse and Rachael.

Lord, in Matthew 7:7, it clearly states that if we ask it shall be given to us and, Lord, we are asking you with all of our love, all of our might, all of our belief, all of our faith, Lord, to please bring Rachael out of her coma, to please lay your healing hands on her and Jesse and please do so at once! Lord, we ask you to hear our prayers and answer them today! ask, lord, and you shall receive!

We have asked, Lord, and now we shall receive. In the name of Jesus Christ our Lord and Savior, thank you, God, for hearing our prayers and thank you, God, for answering them. Amen."

"Amen."

"Wow, Pastor," Sheriff Rodney started after the prayer. "Why aren't your Sunday morning sermons as good as that prayer was?" Everyone at the table started to chuckle at Rod's comment.

"Buzz off," Pastor fired back, throwing a piece of bacon at Rod. "There is a lack of Christianity in this country."

"Here we go again, "Sheriff Rodney chimed in. "We've all heard this speech about how there aren't enough Christians in the world."

"Thirty-one-point four percent of the global population is said to be Christian, Sheriff, maybe you should give it a try."

"Pastor, what if when you die you find out that there really *isn't* a higher being or anything like that? What if, Pastor, I'm right and you are wrong? Huh?"

"Sheriff, you are a good man, but don't be so naïve."

Pastor got up from his chair and started talking to the group.

"The reason people deny religion is because it holds them accountable to a higher standard. When you go to church and you are asked to pray and asked to ask for forgiveness of your sins, you are thinking about all the things you shouldn't have done that past week. It holds you accountable. You start to think twice before you do things. We live in a society with zero accountability. Rape, theft, cold-blooded murder, those are all crimes against humanity, and they should be punishable by death, but no one wants to be the bad guy, no one wants to hold anyone accountable. We live in a 'if he can do it and get away with it, so can I' society."

"If the punishment were so swift and so severe that you couldn't imagine doing the crime, there would be no crime or very little crime. But we have taken the power out of the hands of the people who need it and given it to the people who don't deserve it. Guns aren't the problem. Planes aren't the problem. Alcohol isn't the problem. Lack of accountability is the problem. Lack of punishment is the problem. 'Down here' is the problem."

"One day, Sheriff Rodney, one day all of you will have to stand before God and he will ask you, 'Why did you not believe in me? Why did you do the things you did?' I promise you all, one day you will all be held accountable. There are more copies of the Bible on the planet than any other book in history, yet you choose to deny it or choose to believe in something different.

"I'm telling you all, so listen good. Philippians 2:10 reads '*that at the name of Jesus every knee shall bow, in heaven and on the earth and under the earth and every tongue acknowledge that Jesus Christ is Lord, to the glory of God the Father.*' Now I ask you, Rodney, I ask all of you. Would you rather error on the side of 'there is no God' or would you rather error on the side of 'Jesus Christ is your Lord and Savior'? Think about it. Think about it long and hard."

Pastor turned and walked away, leaving his breakfast on the plate, without eating a bite. Everyone was speechless; no one had a single word to say, not even Recon. The words they just heard impacted them all on some level. Breakfast was finished and cleaned up in silence; afterward, everyone went on about their day.

Chapter 48

"Mr. Camper, it's Dennis. We found her. We found Rachael."

"Where is she?"

"She's in a hospital in Montana, she's in a coma."

"Very good, Dennis. Do not let her leave there alive. Do I make myself clear?"

"Crystal."

Chapter 49

Wednesday

Jesse, still lying next to Karma, suddenly had the urge to use the men's room. He carefully sat up in bed. He had to pause a moment for the pain coming from his broken ribs was almost more than he could bear. Once his feet were planted on the floor, he glanced down at his bandages, they were wet with blood, and most definitely needed changing.

Maybe I should let Meo know, he thought to himself, *but not before my trip to the bathroom.*

Jesse didn't have one foot out of the room when he heard a familiar voice.

"Jesse, where do you think you're going, and look at those bandages! They are seeping they're so wet!"

"Let me use the bathroom, Meo, then we can change them," Jesse replied with a soft and crackly voice.

"Do you need some help, Jesse?"

"No, Meo, I've been doing this for years all by myself. I've got it."

"Very funny, Jesse! You must be feeling better."

"Just tired of being here. Meo, what time is it?" Jesse asked, hobbling down the hall in pain.

"It's time for you to quit being so stubborn!"

"Meo, what time is it please?"

"It's three seventeen, Wednesday morning."

Hmmm, Jesse thought to himself. *I must have lost a day somewhere.*

A few moments later, as Jesse made his way back from the men's room, he saw Meo waiting for him in the middle of the hallway.

"In here, mister, now," Meo asserted with a smile. Jesse went to his room, which was still next to Karma's.

"This will be easier if you stay standing," Meo suggested. "Take your robe off."

"I have nothing on but a pair of underwear, Meo."

"Doesn't matter, I've already seen your underwear. Just do it."

Jesse took off the robe and tossed it on the bed while Meo went to work. She carefully cut the bandages off Jesse's abdominal area and dressed the lacerations.

"I'm guessing from these scars this was not your first auto accident?" Meo asked, trying to make conversation more than anything.

"Those scars are from my past life," Jesse answered without admitting anything. As Meo wrapped fresh bandages around Jesse, she noticed nearly a dozen scars all together.

"Looks like that was some kind of crazy life," Meo went on, not knowing anything about Jesse's past. Jesse didn't really like talking about the past, but knowing Meo didn't know anything, he thought that maybe he should tell her something to pacify her.

"Those are war scars, badges of honor. I'm a former Navy SEAL," Jesse admitted with a rather soft baritone voice. Meo slowed her bandage wrapping, pausing for a moment.

"I didn't know, Jesse, I didn't mean to pry."

"You're fine, Meo, you didn't know. It's okay."

"I'll bet you saved a lot of lives. Thank you for being there for us, Jesse."

"I took a lot of lives too."

"Only because you had to," Meo added immediately, wondering how she was going to get out of this conversation, wishing she didn't bring it up. Meo didn't know much about war, except that it was ugly. Being this close to an actual soldier frightened her and comforted her at the same time.

"It's okay, Meo," Jesse said with a calm voice. "I'm done killing people. That job is over."

Meo listened without saying a word. "Okay, you're done. Why don't you lie down in here for a while?" Meo suggested.

"I need to be with Karma," Jesse said, looking at Meo with a stone-cold face. "I promised her I wouldn't leave her." Jesse walked past Meo, and Meo let him go. Arguing with Jesse at three thirty in the morning was not something that she wanted to do.

Through the pain, Jesse managed to climb back on to Karma's bed and lie down next to her. He was much more awake than he wanted to be. He closed his eyes and tried to make himself go back to sleep, but it was no use. He was without a doubt, wide awake.

"Karma," Jesse spoke with a very soft voice, just barely more than a whisper. "It's me, Jesse." Jesse reached down and wrapped his hand around Karma's waist.

"I need you, Karma. I miss you, Karma. I miss your laugh, and I miss your smile." Jesse's eyes started to water up as he now whispered into her ear.

"I miss our good night kisses in the hall every night. I miss our walks every morning. Karma, listen to me! You can't die on me, Karma!" Jesse was now speaking in a loud whisper, doing everything he could to keep the tears from turning into an all-out bawl.

"Please don't die on me, Karma. I never got a chance to tell you that I love you." Jesse laid his head down on the pillow next to Karma's. "I love you, Karma," Jesse whispered.

"I l-love . . . y-y-ou, Buck" were the words Jesse thought he heard in a very weak, dry, groggy voice. Jesse opened his eye and saw Karma lying there silent.

"I'm missing you so bad, Karma, I swear I just heard you tell me you love me," Jesse whispered to himself out loud.

"I . . . d-d-did," Karma barely muttered.

Jesse's eyes opened again, this time fully alert. "Karma, are you awake?" Jesse whispered with tear-filled eyes.

"Wa... t... er," Karma tried to say with a very weak voice. "Water," she finally got out.

Jesse jumped out of bed and got some water from the sink. He gently eased the cup to Karma's lips where she took a very gentle sip.

"When you're done, I'll get Meo," Jesse said excitedly.

Gently shaking her head no, Karma pulled her head away from the cup.

"J-just you," Karma managed to get out. "Ju . . . st you, Buck," Karma said, never opening her eyes. "Just . . . y-you."

After Karma finished the water, Jesse set the cup down. Overwhelmed with emotion, he broke down and cried;

these were happy tears. He lied next to Karma and held her. "Thank you, God," he whispered through his tears. "Thank you so much."

"Jesse, what's the matter?" Karma asked, still struggling to speak.

"I thought I was going to lose you," Jesse answered, wiping tears from his eyes. "I thought you were gonna die".

"Jesse," Karma asked with some concern, talking very slow and weak. "How long have we been here?"

"This will be our eleventh day," Jesse answered softly.

"Jesse, I've got to get out of here!" There was definite concern on Karma's face and in her voice. "They'll find me here. I am not safe here, Jesse! I have got to get out of there now!"

"Whoa, whoa, whoa, Karma, slow down. Nothing is going to happen to you here."

"Jesse, you don't understand. I am not safe here."

"Karma, take it easy. Maybe you need some more rest. Let me get, Meo."

"Jesse, stop!" Karma demanded, looking Jesse in the eye and grabbing his arm. "What part of I am not safe here do you not understand? Get me out of here!"

"Rachael, relax. Nothing is going to happen to you on my shift. Got it! You need to settle down and tell me what's going on."

Still weak and struggling to make words, Karma continued.

"Remember the sword fight I almost lost? Jesse, they'll find me here."

Jesse remembered the sword fight incident all right. He had stitched her up with fishing line.

The seriousness of this situation has just magnified by ten, Jesse thought to himself. He could tell Karma was genuinely concerned, which meant he should be concerned as well.

"Stay here, I'll be right back!"

"Where am I going to go, Buck? My leg's in a cast and I'm tethered to this bed!"

Jesse got out of the bed, mentally disconnecting the pain from his abdomen, and headed over to his room to grab his mobile phone. He needed to call Sheriff Rodney.

"Where are you going, Jesse?" Meo asked, placing her hands on her hips in disbelief that he was up moving around.

"To call your old man," Jesse answered without making eye contact. "Karma's awake."

"Rod's on his way here now, did you say Karma's awake?" Meo asked, hurrying into Karma's room to see her.

"Karma!" Meo shouted.

"Hi, Meo," Karma answered, more concerned about who else might be on their way to see her.

"Welcome back, Karma. How do you feel?"

"I feel weak. Believe it or not, I'm really hungry. I'm thirsty too."

"Okay, we'll get you some food," Meo said, chuckling. "What I meant was, are you hurting? How is your vision? Things like that."

"I don't feel any pain, but I'm not sure about what happened so I don't know what I should be feeling."

"You hit a deer," Jesse said, reentering the room. "You hit me too."

"Do you remember the accident?" Meo asked, checking eyes with Jesse.

Karma looked at Jesse, wondering if she should be answering any questions. Jesse gave a slight head nod, letting Karma know it was okay.

"Jesse and I were driving home, and some deer were in the road. I hit the brakes. I guess I didn't slow down in time," Karma replied, not admitting to quite everything she remembered.

"No, you didn't," Sheriff Rodney said, entering the room. "Good to have you back, Karma."

"Rod, I need to see you in private, now," Jesse said, nodding his head for Sheriff Rodney to follow him. "Karma, we'll be back in a few minutes." Karma nodded her head as Jesse and Sheriff Rodney left the room.

"Take your time, I need to talk to Karma about her condition anyway," Meo added.

While Meo chatted with Karma about the extent of her injuries as well as what had been going on, Jesse and Sheriff Rodney went to the room next door to talk in private.

"Rod, go with me on this, okay?"

"Sure, Jesse, what's this all about?"

"Karma might be in trouble."

"What are you talking about, Jesse? Everyone loves Karma."

"Look, we can't leave her alone, Rod, I'm serious about this. No visitors, no family, no one."

Sheriff Rodney could tell Jesse was serious. He wanted to know more details, but he knew Jesse would only say what he felt he needed to.

"Jesse, you've got to give me a little more to go on than this," Rod said, hoping for a little more detail.

"Absolutely no visitors, Sheriff, for her or me. Only the Sunday crowd, everyone else can wait. If anyone tells you they are a friend or a family member of either one of us, arrest them," Jesse said, holding out his hand for Sheriff Rodney to shake. Shaking his hand, Sheriff Rodney answered with a simple "done."

Jesse and Sheriff Rodney left the room and went back next door to where Karma and Meo were talking.

"So, did Meo bring you up to speed?" Jesse asked, walking up next to Karma's bed.

"We'll let you both catch up a little more," Meo said, grabbing Sheriff Rodney's hand and pulling him toward the door.

"Great to have you back, Karma!" Sheriff Rodney yelled as he was pulled out of the room. Karma and Jesse cracked a small smile.

"It's good to be back, Buck," Karma said as she reached out to hold Jesse's hand.

"Rachael, what's bothering you? I've never seen you this way."

Karma looked down at Jesse's hands and took a big sigh. When she looked up, her eyes were glassy, tearing up. Barely able to hold it together, she began to speak.

"I've never told you about Las Vegas," Karma started, wiping tears away from her eyes. Jesse just sat and listened and was patient with Karma as she pulled herself together.

"Maybe now is not the time, Rachael."

"I really like my name, Rachael," Karma started through a little bit of laughter. "But I have grown so comfortable with you and everyone calling me Karma that it's become a part of me, and when I tell you what I'm about to, I'm afraid . . . I'm afraid . . ."

Karma couldn't hold back the tears anymore. She covered her eyes and wept.

"I'm afraid that . . ."

Jesse leaned toward Karma and held her. She sobbed into his shoulder and wrapped her arms around him and held him tightly, as tightly as they could with her broken leg in cast up to the top of her thigh and his damaged ribs.

"Maybe you should have waited to tell me you love me," Karma said, sobbing.

"Karma . . . shhh . . . Karma . . . it's okay," Jesse said, holding Karma close.

"Jesse, for the first time in my life, I have trusted a man and fallen in love with a man. You should know that I am scared, I am really scared about what the future has waiting for me."

"Karma," Jesse said with his arms wrapped around her. "I don't know what's going on in Las Vegas. I don't know what it is that has you so bothered, but I promise you this, I meant what I said, Karma. I love you. Whatever it is that you need to deal with, we'll deal with it together."

"I love you too, Buck!" Karma said, clinging to him and weeping some more. "Buck, I am not safe here. Meo told me I've been here for ten or eleven days. Buck, you have got to get me out of here. You have got to take me home."

"Karma, wherever we are, where we go, you will never not be safe with me."

Chapter 50

"Sinners! This is not a hotel!" Pastor shouted as he burst through the door into the hospital room where Jesse and Karma were.

"Prayers are answered, Karma. Welcome back!" Pastor said, walking up the other side of the bed, not stopping until he reached in to give Karma a hug and a kiss on the cheek.

"It's good to see you, Pastor," Karma said, smiling.

"Karma," Pastor said, pointing to the door, "I brought you a surprise. C'mon in!" In through the door came Erin, Recon, Desi, Georgia-Jean, and Meo. Everyone was carrying something. The smell of breakfast filled the room.

"What's going on here?" Karma asked with a smile, looking at Jesse for a clue. Jesse shrugged his shoulders and shook his head no, waiting to hear the answer himself.

"Here's what's going on?" Georgia-Jean piped up. "Meo told Sheriff Rodney you were awake this morning. Sheriff Rodney texted Recon with the news. Before anytime at all passed, Erin was preparing food, and we were all told to pick up something from the restaurant and meet here for breakfast."

"We had to do this, we love you, guys," Erin added, with a tear running down her cheek.

In moments, plates were being passed out with all the breakfast favorites from the Lasso: Eureka-style country eggs, Jesse's country potatoes, wild sausage, and tall glasses of orange juice.

"Where is Sheriff Rodney?" Karma asked, looking up toward Meo.

"He'll be back in a moment," Meo said, pointing toward the door. When Meo lifted her hand, the rock that Karma hadn't noticed before suddenly caught Karma's attention.

"Meo!" Karma shouted with excitement. "Are you and Rod engaged?"

"Well, actually . . .," Meo replied softly, with a great big smile. "I'm Mrs. Sheriff Rodney now."

"Huh!" Karma gasped and brought her hands up, covering her mouth. Her eyes were big and she was in complete disbelief. "Let me see that hand, girl!" Karma said, reaching for Meo's hand.

Meo brought her hand over for Karma to see it.

"You're next, Karma," Meo said with a smile and a tear.

"What do you mean I'm next?" Karma said, looking at Jesse.

"I heard Jesse and Karma tell each other that they loved each other this morning," Meo added joyfully.

Everyone in the room started whistling and clapping, cheering on Jesse and Karma.

"Kiss, kiss, kiss, kiss . . .," they chanted, waiting for Jesse and Karma to make good on their love.

Jesse leaned in toward Karma, and just before their lips met, Karma threw her arms around Jesse's neck and gave him the kiss they all wanted to see! The screaming and cheering just got louder.

"Are you going to deny it, Buck?" Karma asked Jesse with an inner glow that was unmistakable. Jesse looked into Karma's eyes and then answered the question.

"No, Rachael, I can't deny it. It's true. I am totally in love with you." Jesse reached down and picked up Karma's hand. "I think Meo might be right," Jesse added with a smile as tears of joy started to run down from his eyes.

"Oh my gosh!" Karma said, forgetting about everyone else in the room. "Jesse, are you serious?"

Jesse turned toward Karma and held her hand in his.

"Rachael, while you were lying here in bed nearly lifeless, my heart ached. For the first time in my life, the thought of losing someone was almost the end of me. I laid next to you, and begged God to bring you back. I promised God that if he did, I'd love you forever. I promised God that whatever lay on our road ahead, I'd never stop loving you and I'd never leave your side. Rachael, it would truly be an honor to give you my last name and be your husband." Karma was now waving her hands over her eyes with uncontrollable tears falling from them.

"Rachael, you are my very best friend. You are my one true love. Rachael Meyer, will you marry me?"

Karma was now crying and laughing at the same time, overwhelmed with emotion, nodding her head yes.

"I would love to marry you, Buck," she said, wrapping her arms around Jesse. The couple embraced in a hug while they cried with joy in each other's arms. Georgia-Jean, Meo, and Erin were all teary-eyed as well.

"What'd I miss?" Sheriff Rodney said, coming back into the room. "Buck, did she say yes?"

"Oh yeah," Meo answered. "She said yes, all right."

"Then I guess you're going to be needing this," Sheriff Rodney said, pulling an engagement ring out of his pocket, handing it to Jesse.

"Karma, may I?" Jesse asked, looking Karma in the eye. Karma held out her hand as she wiped tears away from her eyes with the other. She felt the ring slide onto her finger; it was a perfect fit. When she looked down, she saw the most amazing ring her eyes had ever seen.

"The center stone is 2.2 carats," Jesse told her.

"Both of the side stones are 1.7 carats each. They are set in a high-performance titanium band."

Karma just stared at the ring for a moment and then reached for Jesse, needing another hug.

"It's as amazing as you are, Jesse, I love you, and I'll never leave you either!"

"Should we leave, or are we all going to eat?" Recon asked like he was on a mission.

"We're going to eat!" Karma answered right back. "I'm hungry. I feel like I haven't eaten in a week."

"More like ten or eleven days," Meo said with a smile.

"The two of you might be able to leave as soon as Friday," Georgia-Jean offered. "As long as we can get the doctor's approval. The only thing is, you may need a nurse to come out to the house and check on you for a few days after that. I think I can have it arranged that Meo or I take on that task," Georgia-Jean finished with a wink.

"I need to get back to the Lasso," Erin said, making her way over to Jesse.

"Congratulations, boss," Erin said jealously, giving Jesse a peck on the cheek. "She's definitely the woman for you." As Erin spoke the words, her stomach turned. She knew in her heart and in her mind that she was the right woman for Jesse, not Karma. This engagement was an emotional trainwreck as far as she was concerned. With an aching heart, Erin held steady.

"Thank you for everything, Erin," Jesse said. "I know you've been working hard, and you'll be well paid."

"Forget the money, Buck," Erin said with a smile. "I'm gonna need a vacation!" A chuckle filled the room.

"You've certainly earned one, Erin."

Within fifteen minutes or so, the crowd had left, and Jesse and Karma were alone in the room.

Chapter 51

Jesse got up from the bed and moved over to the chair that was sitting next to it.

"Karma," Jesse said with a rather serious, but genuine tone, "why don't you tell me a little more about what's going on in Las Vegas."

Karma looked down at the ring on her finger. Her heart was filled with love and concern. She remembered the words Jesse just told her and looked up at him.

"You'll love me through anything, Buck?"

"Till the end of time, Rachael," Jesse said, looking her square on. "My heart truly aches for you, and as soon as we can put this behind us, the sooner we can enjoy our honeymoon." Karma smiled and sighed a big sigh.

"This is going to take a while."

"That's okay, love, tell me everything."

Karma started talking. She started back with her parents and their mysterious disappearance when she was a very young woman. She was an only child that lived with her parents not far from the Las Vegas Strip. On an ambitious night, she could walk there with her friends and check out the sights, mostly out-of-towners that had too much to drink or the occasional celebrity; whatever it was, there was always something to look at in Las Vegas.

When her parents disappeared, her uncle Bernie Crawford came down and took care of her while she finished school. Bernie Crawford is a world-renowned speed freak who specializes in high-end Corvette modifications and is still in business today. He's the best on the planet. Her uncle Bernie taught her three things—how to drive, how to work on cars, and how to defend herself with some basic martial arts skills.

So that's where she learned how to drive, Jesse thought to himself as Karma continued to tell her story.

"When I was seventeen, I went out on a date with an older guy. It was summer, August. It was very hot out, and we went to the desert away from the city lights to watch meteors. I was looking up, and the next thing I know, he covered my mouth and nose with a handkerchief. I tried to get away, but I got too weak too fast from what was more than likely chloroform and had passed out before I knew what happened."

"When I woke up, I had been stripped down to my underwear. I was chained in a room, very dazed and confused; everything was a blur. I remember hearing someone say, 'Mr. Camper, this one will pull a premium, she's still a virgin.' I have no idea how long I was in that room. Weeks for sure, maybe months. One day, I started to pray that God would give me the strength to overcome my enemy. God answered my prayers. I started building immunity to whatever they were giving me, and I started getting my strength back.

"Finally, the day came, and I was told that I'd been sold, and it was time to go. While they were moving me, I managed to get out of my bindings. I fought with every ounce of energy I had, I kicked and screamed until I broke free from the men trying to take me. I ran hard and fast, down hallways, and I literally jumped down entire flights of stairs until I slammed into a door hard enough that it opened. I popped out on the Las Vegas Strip, wearing nothing but my underwear and a T-shirt that they had put over me. The T-shirt read "I'll be your Baby" in big letters across the front.

"It was the middle of the day when I ended up on the strip. The sun was bright, and my eyes were having a hard time adjusting. A couple of military guys walking in my direction stopped to see if I needed help, and I told them to get me out of there, not to go to the police. I wasn't sure if the police would believe my story, and I didn't know who I could trust. I was afraid to go home, and I didn't want to go with them, so they brought me to the army recruiting office on the edge of town. There was a female recruiter there, Staff Sergeant Johansen. I'll never forget her, she was beautiful.

"She took me home that night and got me cleaned up. I found out my parents' house had burned to the ground, and I didn't know how to get ahold of my uncle, or even if he was still alive, so in order to be safe, I enlisted into the army. I was gone in three days."

Karma stopped to take a sip of water and wiped a stray tear from her eye.

"Do you need a break?" Jesse asked in a gentleman's voice. Karma shook her head no and kept going.

"After boot camp was over, I called Sergeant Johansen to thank her for everything and see if we could have dinner. It was then that I was told that she was kidnapped, raped, beaten, and left for dead in the desert. When she was finally found by a couple of guys riding dirt bikes, it was too late—she died from her injuries on the way to the hospital." Karma paused again to wipe away more tears. Jesse just listened very intently.

"For the next eleven years, I took every survival course I could in the army. Every martial arts course, every army intelligence course, I used the army as a training ground to prepare myself."

"Prepare yourself for what?" Jesse asked. "Revenge is not the solution."

"This isn't about revenge, Jesse. This is about justice, this is about... karma."

Jesse sat back in his chair and thought for a moment.

"Let me see if I have the nitty-gritty of all this. This Camper guy is trafficking women through Las Vegas, and you want to put an end to his business, right?"

"It's a little bigger than that, Buck. Camper is the *king* of human trafficking in the U.S. Nothing happens without him— no woman is bought or sold without his involvement. His casino is a front, his airline is the primary means of transportation. No one is the wiser, Buck. You shut him down, and you shut down human trafficking in the U.S."

Jesse just sat in his chair and stared at Karma. He was processing everything that she had just told him. Everything was finally making sense.

No wonder she didn't like being called baby, he thought to himself.

"Why do you think they are looking for you here?" Jesse asked.

"Remember the night you stitched me up, the sword fight I almost lost?"

"How could I forget? That was expensive fishing line." Jesse answered, winking his eye at Karma.

"Really, Buck?"

"Well, it was."

Karma rolled her eyes and shook her head. "I crossed paths with the guy that kidnapped me."

"What do you mean you crossed paths with him?" Jesse asked, knowing there was more to the story.

"Okay, I sort of looked him up, and I sort of broke into his apartment, his apartment inside of the Castle X casino. The problem was when he came home, he wasn't alone. He had two other guys with him. I managed to take the two other guys out, but he escaped."

"What's this guy's name?" Jesse asked.

"Rybka, Dennis Rybka."

Knock, knock was heard at the door. "Everybody awake?" asked a man dressed like a doctor entering the room. "You two have quite a story to tell, don't you? Car crash, coma, near-death experience—you two are lucky to be alive."

"Is this going somewhere, Dr. . . . ?" Jesse asked a little defensively.

"I'm Dr. Latimer, Chief of staff for the E.R."

"Dr. Latimer, when will we be able to leave?" Jesse asked, a little stressed. "We can heal in our own home, we don't need to lie here to do it."

"You both have experienced quite a bit of trauma, Mr. Buck. Ms. Meyer was in a coma, and you apparently took a deer to the chest. I'm surprised either one of you are feeling up to leaving so soon. At any rate, Ms. Meyer just woke up from her coma a couple of hours ago. I can't release her until she has been awake for at least forty-eight hours, and it's recommended she stay for seventy-two. She can go home Friday morning. You, however, Mr. Buck, can go home now if you so desire."

"Dr. Latimer, is there any way we can get an early discharge for Ms. Meyer?"

"Mr. Buck, I'm not making any exceptions for you or anyone else. My patients come first, and Ms. Meyer doesn't leave until Friday morning and that's *only* if she is well enough to go. Do you understand me?" Jesse got off the bed and looked Dr.

Latimer in the eye, telling him, "I understand that you can't keep anyone against their will, and if you—"

"Jesse!" Karma interrupted. "Friday morning is fine, let it go." Jesse slowly reclaimed his seat on the bed, sizing up Dr. Latimer the entire time.

"Dr. Latimer, how does everything look?" Karma asked with a soft yet serious voice.

"Actually, I am quite impressed with the improvement both of you have made," Dr. Latimer started. "I really don't see why you *couldn't* leave Friday morning if you want to, Ms. Meyer. Again, Mr. Buck, if you'd be more comfortable at home, you could—"

"I'm not leaving her side," Jesse interrupted.

"Very well," Dr. Latimer said with a sigh. "The only other thing we need is the insurance information for the two of you. We don't seem to have that on file yet."

"We're self-insured," Jesse said immediately. "Just give me the bill for both of us."

"It's an expensive bill, Mr. Buck."

Jesse just stared the doctor in the eye, almost as if he were silently speaking, *Did I stutter*?

"Very well, Mr. Buck," Dr. Latimer finished and left the room in a hurried manner, wanting the conversation with Jesse to be over as soon as possible.

"You could have been a little nicer, Buck," Karma said when the door closed.

"I don't trust anyone right now. I'm ready to be gone," Jesse replied, staring at the door.

"Hey, Buck, what happened to our cars?"

"That, my love," Jesse replied as he turned toward Karma to make eye contact with her, "is a question for Recon, and he'll be here shortly."

Chapter 52

"I'm here now," Recon said, coming through the door, closing it behind him.

"Karma! Glad to see you again! How are you feeling!"

"Not bad, Recon. All things considered, how are you doing?"

"Couldn't be better, Karma, couldn't be better."

"Tell us what you've got, Recon," Jesse said, cutting straight to the point.

"Hey, Commander, relax, I'm getting there."

Jesse didn't like Recon's apparent laissez-faire attitude this morning. However, knowing he was feeling the stress of everything that had come to surface, Jesse decided to maintain composure and hold his tongue.

"Before I tell you that everything has been taken care of, why don't you tell me what happened," Recon fired off at Jesse, expecting to hear the story.

"There's not much to tell," Jesse started. "Karma and I were driving home, and we came around the corner and the road was covered with a herd of deer. There must have been fifty of them. I saw Karma hit the brake so I hit the gas and turned into the herd, hoping to protect Karma from what was about to happen."

Karma sat and wiped tears from her eyes as Jesse recapped his version of the story.

"I went into the herd of deer accelerating and then went sideways. Karma hit my door, and I barely remember the both of us going off the road."

"You drove into the deer to protect me?" Karma asked, crying.

"Absolutely, I did. I love you. I'd do it again."

Karma reached over to Jesse's arm and pulled him toward her. Putting her arms around his neck, she laid a kiss on Jesse that he'd not soon forget.

"I know I picked the right man," Karma told him when the kiss was over.

"Knock it off!" When rolling his eyes at the affectionate couple, Recon noticed the ring on Karma's finger. "Wait . . . he asked you?" Recon continued, getting excited. "You said yes!" He pointed at Karma. Karma nodded her head and wiped the tears of joy away from her eyes.

"First Rod and Meo and now you two! That's awesome! If I could just get Erin's attention!" Recon said, looking at the floor.

Jesse and Karma chuckled at Recon's excitement.

"Keep talking, buddy, we've got a lot of ground to cover here," Jesse insisted.

"Wait, wait, wait a minute. Recon, you've got a thing for Erin?" Karma asked with a smile on her face.

"So, at any rate," Recon continued, completely ignoring the question from Karma. "I wasn't far behind you two. I had left the party at the Lasso and was heading over to the lake behind Buck's house to do some night fishing with Pastor when we rolled up on the accident. I called the hospital directly and had them send an ambulance, not wanting to alert the authorities. Pastor and I pulled you both from the vehicles. First you Karma, then you Jesse."

Jesse and Karma listened intently as Recon shared with them the depths of what he and Pastor encountered the night of the accident. Jesse reached over and held Karma's hand as the story continued.

"The cars are completely destroyed. After the ambulance left with the both of you inside, Pastor and I went to Jesse's place. We picked up his truck and hooked up the flatbed trailer and then we went to clean everything up. We picked up debris for days, Jesse. There still may be some fragments out there. I figured the initial point of impact was where the skid marks started, and they continue until both cars left the road."

"What did they measure?" Jesse asked.

"How fast were you going, Jesse?" Recon asked with a little bit of attitude.

"I have no idea, Recon. I really don't."

"You, Karma?"

"Speed? No. All I can tell you was, I was in the lead."

"Dream on," Jesse fired back, rolling his eyes. "I had you right where I wanted you. You hit me, remember?"

"What is it with you two?" Recon asked, waving his hands. Jesse and Karma just chuckled.

"A vehicle traveling at sixty miles per hour is traveling at eighty-eight feet per second. Based on the law of averages, it would take that vehicle about 160 feet to skid to a stop on dry asphalt. You two clowns were in high-performance vehicles, which would stop faster under normal conditions." Recon started to pace back and forth while he broke down his analysis of the accident.

"Jesse," Recon said from across the room, "Pastor and I measured your skid marks to 347 feet when you left the road. There is only one set of skid marks to measure."

"That's because I was sliding sideways, not skidding," Jesse pointed out. "The slide is going to be longer than a skid because inertia is pushing you. You have no brake resistance slowing you down."

"You two are lucky to be alive."

"Recon!" Jesse commanded. "Where are the vehicles now?"

"The debris from both vehicles has been put in your shop in two separate piles. His and hers."

"How many deer were involved?" Karma asked out of curiosity.

"We think, based on the pieces left in the roadway, y'all killed about a dozen or so deer. There is no way of knowing how many were injured. Coyotes and wolves dragged the carcasses off while Pastor and I were picking up debris from the vehicles."

Jesse got up off the bed and moved toward Recon.

"Hug gently, my ribs hurt," Jesse said, giving Recon a man hug. "I owe you one, Recon."

"Funny thing, Buck, I thought I was done cleaning up your messes."

"Not hardly, Recon. We've got work to do," Jesse replied while looking at Karma, giving her a wink.

"What were you guys racing for anyway?" Recon asked in innocence.

"Sex," Karma said with a smile. "Buck thought he was getting laid that night!"

Chapter 53

Thursday

Jesse and Karma were curled up together in the hospital
bed when they heard a knock on the door. Jesse opened
one eye to evaluate the situation and saw Erin holding
what appeared to be a tray of food.

"Mr. Buck, I brought you and Karma some breakfast,"
Erin said as she carefully opened the door. Behind Erin
followed Georgia-Jean, Meo, Sheriff Rodney, Pastor, and
Recon—the whole crew. Jesse sat up and nudged Karma.

"Karma," Jesse spoke with a whisper.

"Something smells really good in here!" Karma replied
with a groggy voice.

"Erin, looks like you have enough food there . . . for all
of us," Jesse commented.

"I do," Erin replied with a smile. "You told us that
we're all meeting for breakfast until further notice."

Jesse laughed. "I did say that, Erin. You are correct."

"So, what happens now?" Sheriff Rodney asked with a
mouthful of food. "How are you two feeling? Getting out
soon? What's the plan?"

"I'm feeling pretty good, actually," Karma answered
after swallowing a mouthful of orange juice. "I'm getting a
new cast on my leg today, a walking cast!"

"It's still a little tough for me to breathe sometimes,"
Jesse added, "but I'm healing. This cast on my arm is a
little cumbersome, but it is what it is. I think we'll both be

ready to get out of here tomorrow morning. Why, Sheriff? What are you up to?"

"I just want to know where breakfast is tomorrow."

Everyone chuckled with Sheriff Rodney's unexpected reply.

"I've got a great idea," Jesse said, looking over to Karma. "Why don't we have breakfast at the Lasso tomorrow morning after we leave here? How does that sound with everyone?"

The group nodded their heads in unison. "That *is* a good idea, Buck," Karma replied with a wink.

"After the morning rush, you mean," Erin added with a smile. "We're still doing breakfast, Buck, and it doesn't slow down until about 10:00 a.m."

"There's your answer, Rod—10:00 a.m. at the Lasso."

It didn't take long for breakfast to be devoured and for everyone to leave. Around 1:00 p.m., Dr. Latimer came in and took Karma down for X-rays and then to cut her old cast off. Before an hour had passed, Karma was hobbling in through the door on her own two legs, one of which was in a pink walking cast.

"Pink?" Jesse asked with a smile.

"You know it. My favorite color," Karma said, as she concentrated on her movements to the bed.

"I thought your favorite color was black?" Jesse questioned.

"It is on a Corvette. C'mon, Buck, pay attention." Karma paused and shot Jesse a smile that was playful, honest, and inviting all at the same time.

"I'm really looking forward to spending the rest of my life married to you, Rachael," Jesse watched as Karma climbed into bed. "I actually can't imagine life without you anymore."

"You're the only man I trust, Jesse. You make me feel safe. You make me feel wanted. You complete me, Buck, and I love you for it."

"You complete me too, Karma, and I love you for *that*! When do you think you fell in love with me, Karma?" Jesse asked as he reached down to hold her hand.

"I can't say it was any one day, Jesse. I have been falling for you a little more each day. Every day, I fall a little deeper in love with you, even still. You are the only man I have ever loved, and I don't want to know what a broken heart feels like, Jesse, so please don't break it," Karma finished with a runaway tear falling from her eye.

"Your turn, Buck. When did you know you loved me, when did you buy this ring, and how did you know my finger size?"

Jesse smiled with a chuckle. "I happened to find the ring and just by chance, it was the right size."

"You are so full of it!" Karma said, laughing. "Tell me the truth."

"The night I stitched you up, Karma. I don't know what came over me. I knew at that moment in time I never wanted to lose you. While you were sleeping, I sized your finger with a piece of red fishing line and kissed you on the forehead, and I promised you then and there I'd love you forever and I'd never leave your side. I picked out the stones and had the ring made, our initials and the date we met are on the inside."

"The date we met, the first night, at the Lasso?" Karma asked, laughing.

"Yeah," Jesse said, nodding his head. "That's the day."

After a brief pause, Karma looked down at her beautiful ring and started talking with a soft yet serious voice.

"You can't ever stop, Buck." Tears started falling one by one as she spoke with all her heart. "You can't ever stop holding my hand or telling me you love me. You can't ever stop touching me or caring for me. You can't ever leave me, Jesse, you can't do it. You can't ever stop," Karma started to cry softly.

Jesse pulled Karma into his arms and held her close.

"Rachael, your heart is safe with me, Love. I will never leave you, and I will never stop loving you."

"You can't stop calling me Karma either. I love the way it sounds when you say it."

Jesse chuckled and gave Karma a bit of a squeeze. "Don't worry, Karma, that'll never happen. In fact, I don't think anyone will ever stop calling you Karma. Most people around here don't even know what your real name is."

"I think you should lie down next to me," Karma said, scooting over to make room for Jesse. She grabbed his hand and pulled his arm around her. The couple lied close to each other and fell asleep on the hospital bed. The love they shared for each other filled the room with warmth.

Chapter 54

Friday, 7:30 a.m.

Meo opened the door to find Jesse and Karma still curled up next to each other. They had been like that all night; they had not moved.

"Jesse? Karma? Are you awake?" Meo spoke softly so she wouldn't startle them waking them up. "It's time to wake up, you get to go home today."

"I am really comfortable, I don't want to get up," Karma replied, halfway talking into her pillow.

"I'm awake," Jesse said, sitting up. "I am ready to get out of here!"

"Here are a couple of glasses of juice and some meds for pain if you need them. We will start your check-out procedures soon, and you two should be out of here by 10:00 a.m. Oh, . . . Jesse," Meo stated, talking directly to him, pulling keys from her coat pocket, "Recon and Pastor brought your truck down this morning. It's parked out front for you."

"You are so loved," Karma said, looking over to Jesse with a grin across her face.

"Ha!" Jesse answered with a laugh. "They don't want us to be late for breakfast!"

"Neither do I!" Karma fired back. "I'm looking forward to it!"

Before much time had passed, Meo came back in to redress the bandages around Jesse's chest and abdomen followed by the "dos and don'ts" for the next few weeks.

Of course, physical therapy was suggested for both Jesse and Karma, and the last topic was the follow-up visit scheduled for exactly two weeks from today.

The doctors and nurses who took care of Jesse and Karma all came in to say bye to them. Small-town hospitals don't usually get this kind of excitement, so they were glad to have such a nice couple to pamper. Georgia-Jean and Meo walked them to the hospital door where both Jesse and Karma refused more help.

"Your pickup is outside the door and to the right," Meo said after giving Karma a hug good-bye.

"We'll see you in about fifteen minutes at the Lasso," Georgia-Jean added with delight. "What a nice couple."

Jesse and Karma left the hospital holding hands. Just like Meo said, Jesse's pickup was not more than one hundred feet from the door, facing them, parked in a "patient pickup" parking space.

"Hey! Look who came to pick us up!" Jesse said, pointing over to his truck.

"It's Louie!" Karma said excitedly. "Look at him! He sure is happy to see you, Buck!"

"Us, Karma," Jesse said in a very compelling fashion. "Louie is happy to see us! Let me get your door for you." Jesse headed over toward the passenger side of the vehicle.

"Buck!" Karma said, stopping in her tracks. "I can get my own door. You go to your side and take care of Louie before he pops with excitement."

Jesse looked at Karma, and he could tell she was being serious.

"Go on! My hands aren't broken, my leg is. I've got this." Jesse did as he was told and went to the driver's side of the pickup. *Beep-beep* sounded the horn as Jesse hit the key fob, unlocking the doors. Jesse opened his door, and Louie was there to greet him with lots of love. Louie was licking and kissing Jesse's face like a puppy.

"It's good to see you too, old friend," Jesse said as he pet Louie rapidly all over.

Karma watched from the other side of the truck with a smile on her face. "That dog loves you almost as much as I—"

Karma grabbed the hood of the truck with both hands. "Buck," she barely got out of her mouth before she collapsed.

"Karma! Karma!!" Jesse screamed Karma's name, and there was no response. He ran to the other side of the vehicle and found Karma lying on the ground with an arrow from a crossbow protruding from her chest.

"Help! help!" Jesse screamed, not leaving his lover's side. "Don't die on me, Rachael!"

"Help!" Jesse screamed again. "Don't die on me, Rachael, God, don't take her from me!" Jesse carefully picked Rachael up off the ground and started carrying her to the door.

"Meo! somebody, help!" Jesse screamed at the top of his lungs.

Jesse could hear a vehicle tearing off behind him. *Listen, Jesse, listen*, he thought to himself. Jesse paused briefly to hear the vehicle leave. *Distinct exhaust note. High RPMs, lots of power, manual transmission.* He turned around to get a visual, but all he could see was a parking lot filled with smoke coming off the tires.

Dave Bair

"Jesse, what happened!" Meo shouted, coming through the hospital door.

"Get a gurney, Karma's been shot! Now, Meo, move!" Jesse shouted, turning around and hurrying for the door. In an instant, Meo was gone. Georgia-Jean opened the door for Jesse as he came through with Karma in his arms. Meo and a doctor came running down the hall with a gurney.

"You'll have to lay her on her side, she has an arrow through her torso," Jesse exclaimed.

"How did this happen?" Dr. Latimer asked.

"I don't know," Jesse answered, "I was petting the dog and we were talking. The next thing I know, she's on the ground with an arrow through her chest."

"She's got a pulse. It's weak, but it's there," Meo said, walking next to the gurney.

"Mr. Buck, we're going into emergency surgery, you'll have to wait out here," Dr. Latimer said as calmly as he could under the circumstances. "Let's move . . . she's critical," Dr. Latimer shouted.

In an instant, Meo and Dr. Latimer disappeared through the surgery room door, followed by a team of medical professionals hurrying to get to work. Jesse watched as numbness filled his soul. Karma was in danger after all, and he wasn't there to protect her. Jesse fell to his knees in the middle of the hospital hallway and started to cry.

"Why?" Jesse screamed at the top of his lungs, looking up toward the ceiling.

He pulled his hands covered with Karma's blood over his face. A waterfall of tears washed the blood from his hands on to his clothes. Georgia-Jean sat down beside him, also crying, and gave him a hug.

The Lasso

There were no words to be had, just tears.

After a minute or two, Jesse instantly stopped crying.

"Let me up, Georgia-Jean," he said softly, rising to his feet.

"Jesse, are you okay? Where are you going?"

Jesse stood tall in the hospital hallway and wiped the tears from his face. He stood like a stone-cold statue. You could see him calculating what his next course of action was going to be. For the first time since Georgia-Jean knew Jesse, she was afraid of what he might do. Jesse looked over to Georgia-Jean and could see the fear in her eyes. Changing to a softer look on his face, Jesse reached out to give Georgia-Jean a hug.

"It's okay, G-J," Jesse said softly. "I need you to do me a favor."

"Anything, Jesse, name it."

"If anyone calls or tries to seek out information about what is going on with Karma if anyone asks anything, I don't care who they are, tell them a young woman was shot and killed in front of the hospital today."

"Well, Jesse, I can't do that, she's not dead."

"G-J," Jesse said softly, looking Georgia-Jean in the eye, "that was a professional hit on Karma. Someone is watching her; someone is watching us. They need to know she's dead or they'll come back."

Georgia-Jean looked sad; a tear fell from her eye.

"I'm not going to tell a lie for anyone, Jesse, I'm sorry."

Jesse nodded his head and looked down. He understood what Georgia-Jean was saying. He had just asked her to put her integrity aside, which wasn't going to happen. He suddenly felt ashamed for asking her to do what he asked.

299

"You're right, Georgia-Jean," Jesse said with a smile. Georgia-Jean watched Jesse as he turned and walked down the hall. When he got to the operating room, Jesse looked through the little window and then charged through the door. Georgia-Jean panicked and wondered if she should go intervene.

Almost paralyzed with anxiety, Georgia-Jean slowly walked toward the operating room. Her heart was pounding so hard that it almost hurt to breathe. When she was only a few feet away, Jesse came racing out of the operating room, startling Georgia-Jean.

"Oh my gosh, you scared me, Jesse!"

"Georgia-Jean, I'm sorry," Jesse said, giving her a hug, with a relatively concerned voice. "I didn't mean to scare you, and I shouldn't have asked you to lie. That was wrong of me and I'm sorry."

"You are forgiven, Jesse. I have grown to love you and Karma like you both were my own, and I know everything will turn out the way it's supposed to."

"This is what I have to ask of you. No one is to talk to anyone but me about Karma's condition. How is that, better?" Jesse asked, almost apologetic for his earlier request.

"That, Jesse, I can do." Georgia-Jean answered with a look of relief like a huge weight has been lifted off her shoulders.

"Louie is in the truck. I'm going to take him home and get cleaned up. You can rest assured that I will be back in a little bit."

"Okay, Jesse, I'll call you if anything happens."

Chapter 55

"Mr. Camper, this is Dennis."

"Go on."

"I'm calling to let you know the Rachael Meyer issue has been resolved. She was shot and killed at the hospital today."

"Good job, Dennis."

"Mr. Camper, you should know someone else took her out, it wasn't me."

"What?"

"I didn't kill her, sir. Someone else shot her with a crossbow before I could get to her. I watched it with my own eyes, it happened in the parking lot."

"Are you sure she's dead?"

"Mr. Camper, it was a good shot. It dropped her in her tracks, like a deer. I feel confident that problem has been resolved. She's dead, sir."

"Dennis."

"Yes, Mr. Camper?"

"If she's not dead, you will be."

Nothing but deafening silence filled the phone lines. Dennis started to sweat, hoping the next words wouldn't be his last.

"Find out who killed her, pay them twenty-five thousand dollars. Tell them it's the bounty owed for the service they provided. That's half of what I paid you in advance. You pay them since they did your job for you. Tell them we can always use good people. If you have a problem with that, you can go hang yourself."

There was another long pause in the conversation.
"Do you hear me, Dennis?"
"Consider it done, Mr. Camper."

Chapter 56

Jesse got into his pickup and pulled out his mobile phone to send Recon a text. The text read,

Recon: 911—you, Pastor, and Sheriff Rodney, my house ASAP.

As Jesse was heading out of the parking lot, he came across the tire marks that were left by the fleeing vehicle. Jesse pulled over to the side and stopped the truck.

"It's okay, Louie, I'll be right back," Jesse said, giving Louie a scratch on the head before jumping out of the truck. The burnout marks on the asphalt were left by somewhat of a wide tire, which indicates the vehicle that left them has lots of power. Two marks, equally black, meant the vehicle also had a locking rear differential. *Definitely a performance vehicle*, Jesse thought to himself. *Muscle car maybe? No one would waste their time turning off a traction control system on something newer to get away.*

Jesse knelt and put his fingers to the burn marks on the asphalt. No way to tell what brand the tire was at this point, for him anyway. Standing up, Jesse paced the length of the tire marks. "About 135 feet long," he mumbled to himself. "Lots of power. This car has lots of power." He walked back to his truck. After opening the door, he turned to look at the tracks left on the asphalt one more time.

"As God is my witness . . . I will find you . . ."

Jesse jumped into his pickup without finishing the sentence and sped off toward home.

When Jesse came up on the accident site, he slowed down, but didn't stop. *Now is not the time*, he thought to himself and continued to the house. By the time Jesse was out of the shower and dressed in a fresh set of clothes, Recon, Pastor, and Sheriff Rodney were waiting for Jesse in his family room.

"Thank you, guys, for coming," Jesse started.

"What's going on, Commander?" Recon questioned.

"What happened to breakfast?" Rod added.

"Karma has been hunted down and shot," Jesse answered. The room was silent as everyone listened intently to what Jesse was about to say.

"I don't know if she's going to make it," Jesse spoke with tears free-falling from his eyes. He paused for a minute to realize how much he really did love this woman lying, once again, in the hospital.

Taking a deep breath and recovering his composure, Jesse continued with the debriefing.

"When we were leaving this morning, someone shot Karma in the back with a crossbow. It was a good shot—this looks to be a professional hit. I'm not a hundred percent sure, but I can attest to you it was a good shot. A vehicle tore out of the parking lot shortly thereafter, RPMs soaring and smoking tires all the way. I asked the three of you to come over today because I'm going to need a little help figuring out who did this."

"Jesse, I'm a sheriff," Rodney answered back. "I can't consciously let you go on a manhunt and act like some vigilante. I can't have you tearing up a city. Not to mention you're going to get yourself killed!"

Jesse stepped into Sheriff Rodney's personal space, almost standing nose to nose. In a very stern fashion, Jesse told Sheriff Rodney how it was.

"A piece of me, Rod, is dying in the hospital right now!"

"You need to check yourself, Buck," Sheriff Rodney said with a very calm voice, taking a step back away from Jesse, who was obviously emotionally spent. "I'll find this guy for you, Jesse, it's my job, it's what *I* do. Why don't you go back to the hospital? Karma will want you there when she wakes up."

There was silence in the room. No one had the words. Everyone was in disbelief that any of this was going on.

"Recon," Sheriff Rodney said without taking his eyes off Jesse, "why don't you go with him? He needs you right now." Recon answered with a head nod and headed toward the door.

"Go on, Jesse," Pastor added. "Rod and I will take care of Louie and we'll lock up." Jesse left through the front door with Recon close to his heels, neither one of them saying a word.

"Show me the cars," Jesse commanded to Recon as soon as the front door shut behind them. "What made you clean up the mess?"

"I don't really know, Commander. Something inside of me told me I needed to, so I did. Pastor offered to help so I let him. I figured that would have been okay with you."

Jesse and Recon opened the door to the shop. The Trans Am and the Dodge Charger were sitting neatly in place with two piles of Corvette rubbish meticulously stacked between them. The debris piles were not much more than scrap fiberglass, carbon fiber, and aluminum. Both piles were completely unrecognizable as vehicles. In fact, the cars were so destroyed that the only way Jesse knew whose car was whose was by the color of what was left of the fiberglass and composite pieces collected. The piles of debris looked more like they were from a plane crash than a car crash. Jesse shut the door and locked it behind him.

"Recon," Jesse ordered. "Debrief me."

Back inside the house, Pastor and Sheriff Rodney were having a conversation of their own.

"Do you think Jesse is going to turn into some kind of loose cannon?" Sheriff Rodney asked while Pastor was putting some fresh food and water out for Louie.

"I think he's under a lot of stress, Rodney. I think we should just give him some space and do some praying for both Karma and Jesse."

"I can't look the other way if Jesse breaks the law," Sheriff Rodney said as he watched through the window as Jesse and Recon left in Jesse's pickup.

"I don't think Jesse is asking anyone to look the other way, Sheriff. I think Jesse is trying to make sense of it all. He has some valid concerns for Karma's safety."

"Well, Pastor, you can't pray for someone if you don't know who needs praying for. I can't protect anyone if I don't know who needs protecting."

"What do you mean Sheriff?"

Sheriff Rodney turned away from the window to look at Pastor. "How do I know that Jesse isn't the real target? All I'm saying is that I don't really have enough information to work with yet."

"Jesse was standing on the other side of the truck, Sheriff, don't overcomplicate this!"

"I suppose you're right, Pastor. But you have to remember, sometimes big things happen in little towns."

Sheriff Rodney pacified Pastor to get out of the conversation. The two men locked up the house and went on in their own directions.

"Something is just not adding up," Sheriff Rodney said to himself on his way back to the office. "Jesse isn't telling me everything. Or is he? He did tell me that Karma felt unsafe. Who wants to harm Karma?" The thoughts going through Sheriff Rodney's head combined with the unanswered questions were enough to make a man crazy.

"Forget what I told Pastor. This kind of crap isn't *supposed* to happen in a small town!"

Chapter 57

Georgia-Jean was at the administration desk doing paperwork when she noticed Jesse coming down the hall.

"That was quick, Jesse," she said, surprised to see him so fast.

"Any word on Karma?" Jesse asked, walking toward the surgery room across the hall from where Georgia-Jean was sitting.

"Nothing yet I'm afraid. However, if you told the doctor the same thing you told me, then you may know before I do."

"I'll be sure to keep you in the loop," Jesse said, looking over his shoulder.

Jesse, again without permission, let himself into the operating room and closed the door behind him. After a few moments, he came back out and left. Not saying a word to Georgia-Jean, he headed up the hall toward the hospital exit.

"Jesse? Where are you going?"

Without stopping or turning around, Jesse answered the question, shouting over his shoulder.

"To go buy a casket."

"Huh? Jesse?"

Georgia-Jean was so shocked at what she just heard that she went numb. Knowing she wouldn't be able to hold herself together, she grabbed her purse and left the hospital. The only reason she came in today was to see Jesse and Karma off, and now she needed some alone time to just go cry. Georgia-Jean felt her heart pound, aching for Jesse, and the apparent loss of Karma.

She hurried out the door, almost running to her car. She couldn't get inside the car fast enough. As soon as she got the door shut, her emotions got the best of her and she started to cry uncontrollably. Georgia-Jean felt so bad for Jesse and everything that was going on.

"Pull yourself together, Georgia," she said out loud to herself, wiping tears away from her eyes. Georgia-Jean started her car, and just when she was about to put it into reverse, she noticed a piece of paper under her windshield wiper blade.

"What in the world is that?" she said out loud to herself. "That can't be a ticket."

Georgia-Jean stepped out of her car and looked around; there was no one in sight. She pulled the paper out from under the windshield wiper; it was just an ordinary sheet of notebook paper folded in half. Georgia opened it to find a note written to her. The note read,

Georgia-Jean,

Please don't cry, it'll be okay. I need you to trust me.

Jesse

"What does this mean, Jesse!" Georgia-Jean said out loud, in disbelief with what she just read. "This note doesn't make sense, Jesse! Do you think you're God?"

Frustrated and very upset, she got into her car, tore up the note, and threw it on the floor.

"If I were a drinking woman, I swear I'd be pouring one right now!" Georgia-Jean tore out of the hospital parking lot and made a dash for home.

Chapter 58

Saturday

Recon picked up a copy of the local newspaper the *Eureka Times Standard* on his way over to Jesse's. Jesse was waiting in the driveway when Recon pulled up.

"Did you bring your shovel?" Jesse shouted.

Recon nodded his head.

"Did you bring the paper?"

Recon waved the paper in the air and tossed it over to Jesse. Snatching it out of the air with one hand, Jesse opened it up to the obituaries. He saw what he needed to see and folded the paper up.

"C'mon, let's start digging," Jesse said as Recon approached with a shovel in hand.

"Where are we doing this?" Recon asked. "How are you going to dig with that cast on your arm?"

"Up on the top of that crest overlooking the lake," Jesse answered as he walked in that direction, ignoring the cast question.

"Isn't that where you'd want to be buried?"

"I won't care, Jesse, I'll be dead."

Jesse just shook his head. The rest of the day was spent shoveling in silence. There were no words to be said. The hole got wider and deeper as the two former SEALs worked next to each other just like they had done so many times before.

"I never thought we'd be doing this again, Commander," Recon said, hoping to break the silence with some sort of conversation. Jesse stopped digging for a moment and stabbed his shovel into the pile of dirt next to the hole.

"Thanks for being here, Recon. I know this whole thing is kind of awkward."

"Like I've said before, Commander, you're the only family I've got. I'm here for you whether you need me or not."

"I appreciate it, thank you."

"I can handle this part, Jesse. It's the part after this that I'm wondering about."

"You and me both, my friend," Jesse said with a sigh. "You and me both."

"You're staying for dinner, aren't you?" Jesse asked as he began to shovel again.

"I'm not doing this for free," Recon responded with a smile. "Besides, after the week you've had, I certainly can't let you eat alone."

"He wasn't going to eat alone," Pastor said, walking up to the crest. "He invited me over as well."

"Jesse," Pastor asked for confirmation. "Are you sure about this?"

"Pastor, I know God didn't put you on this earth to question my decisions, so why are you?"

"I'm just telling you that most people go about this sort of thing in a different fashion."

"I'm not most people," Jesse fired back.

There is certainly no arguing that Recon thought to himself while he continued to shovel the rocky soil into a pile.

"Well, the pizza's here," Pastor said as he turned and started walking toward the house. "I'll get some paper plates and napkins out."

"C'mon, let's go eat," Jesse said, planting his shovel in the soil. "We've got some details to work out."

Chapter 59

Jack Beaver was sitting in his office at the Christmas tree farm when his nephew, sitting at the entrance in a small booth, tripped the alert button on a hand-held radio.

"Uncle Jack, you copy?"

"Yes, Damon, what is it?"

"There is a gentleman on his way up to see you. Said he was here to pay you."

"Why didn't you stop him at the gate?"

"He's armed, Uncle Jack, I'm not."

Jack Beaver stood up and looked out the window. He could see a late model Ford GT, graphite in color, coming down the dirt road at a good clip, kicking up a massive cloud of dust, heading right for the office. Jack reached down and opened his desk drawer. He pulled out a Glock .45 and jacked a round into the firing chamber. Slipping the pistol into his pants behind his belt so it could be easily seen, Jack stepped out the front door and waited for the visitor.

The Ford GT came to a skidding halt just a few feet from Jack Beaver. When the dust cleared, a well-dressed man wearing a dark gray suit exited the car.

"You Jack Beaver?"

"Who are you and what the hell do you want?"

"My instructions are to converse only with Jack Beaver, the man who shot and killed the young lady the other day. Is that you?"

Jack was shocked. He didn't know he'd been seen. *If this clown saw him, who else could have seen him?* he wondered to himself. Jack pulled the Glock out from behind his belt and held it by his side, clenching it firmly in his hand.

"If you don't tell me what you want, you'll be next."

Without flinching or breaking a sweat, the man continued talking.

"Sir, my name is Dennis, Dennis Rybka. I am here to pay you a bounty on the job you completed. You saved me some trouble and you deserve to be paid."

"What exactly are your instructions, Mr. Rybka?" Jack demanded with an angry, stern voice. Jack realized immediately, since Mr. Rybka had instructions, he was a hired assassin, certainly not the police. Jack, continued to tightly clench the grip of his Glock, ready to do with him like he did with his son if he had to, as he continued to size the stranger up. With eyes locked on the target, he awaited the answer.

"My exact instructions, sir, were to find Ms. Meyer and not let her leave the hospital alive. I was in the parking lot when you took her out. No one else was around. When I was leaving the hospital, I saw you running with your crossbow. I followed you. My instructions then changed. My new instructions were to find you and pay you for doing my job, Mr. Beaver. I am here to pay you."

"Show me the money, Mr. Rybka," Jack said, pulling a bead on the man wearing the suit. "Move slowly or I'll bury you."

Dennis Rybka popped the hood on the Ford GT, not at all threatened by Jack Beaver, and lifted a black satchel out. Holding the satchel flat and opening it toward him, Dennis showed Jack Beaver the inside. Twenty-five thousand dollars in fifties and hundreds. The two men locked eyes; no words were said. Jack Beaver glanced down and saw the satchel full of money, stacks of dead presidents neatly piled together.

Jack Beaver walked backward to the office door and opened it, never taking his eyes off Dennis Rybka. Lowering his pistol, Jack finally broke the silence.

"Maybe you should step into my office for a moment, Mr. Rybka."

Dennis Rybka closed the satchel first and then the hood to the car and headed for the office door being held open by Jack.

"Thank you, Mr. Beaver."

Once inside, Jack closed the door and locked it behind him.

"Have a seat," he said to Dennis as he walked around the other side of a metal desk and sat down. Jack laid his Glock on the desk right in front of him and pointed it at Dennis Rybka, and then the conversation started.

"You have five minutes."

Dennis Rybka picked up the satchel and set it on the desk, placing it right on top of Jack's Glock.

"Mr. Beaver," Dennis started with a cocky attitude and fearless demeanor. "I am not intimidated by you at all, and honestly, sir, if I wanted to kill you and your nephew at the gate, you'd both already be dead."

Jack Beaver jumped up out of his chair and shoved the satchel off the Glock, but before he could get it drawn, the laser from Dennis Rybka's .40 caliber Desert Eagle was showing a dot on Jack Beaver's chest. Jack paused to reconsider his actions.

"I don't have time for your games, Mr. Beaver," Dennis said, placing his pistol on the desk directly in front of him, with it pointed at Jack. "Nod your head if you would like to hear what I have to say."

Jack nodded his head yes, instructing Dennis to talk as he reclaimed his seat.

"You did us a huge favor by resolving us of Ms. Meyer. The money in the satchel is yours. If there is anything we can do for you as a token of our appreciation, please let us know and we will consider it. Furthermore, we are interested in keeping our alliance open in the event we may further need your services or assistance."

"There's a problem in town, new guy, who's tampering with my businesses. I want him eliminated. Can you help me?"

"Give me all the details and I'll make a phone call. Does this 'problem' have a name?"

"Buck, Jesse Buck. I know where he lives."

After a brief three- or four-minute conversation between Dennis and Jack, as promised, Dennis made a phone call.

"I think we can help you with your problem, Mr. Beaver," Dennis asserted, hanging up the phone. "According to the obituary in this morning's paper, Ms. Meyer is to be buried during a private funeral on Monday. We'll want to strike after that."

"I'm fine with that. We can watch this girl being put into the ground, I know where she's being buried, and we can watch it from a safe distance across the lake."

"How do you know this, Mr. Beaver?"

"I just know. Why don't you watch with me? Watch it with your own two eyes."

"I will plan on doing just that, Jack." Dennis got up from his chair and headed for the door. Before opening it to leave, he turned to ask Jack Beaver one more question.

"Why Ms. Meyer, Mr. Beaver, what was your beef with her?"

"I could give two damns about that broad," Jack Beaver said as if she were just trash that washed up on the beach. "It's Buck I want dead. I just didn't have a clean shot on him, so I shot her out of spite."

"Well, Jack, nice shot," Dennis said, opening the door. "I'll meet you here at 7:00 a.m. Monday morning."

Chapter 60

Sunday

Sunday at the lake today was simple with Jesse, Recon, and Pastor. There was an uneasy tension in the air that everyone felt. Jesse was angry, focused, and very short-tempered. Recon was rather impartial, and Pastor was going with the flow. Conversation was nonexistent while the three men put together lunch. BLTs and potato salad were a simple menu but tasty on a solemn day. After lunch was prepared, the three friends sat at Jesse's dining room table and waited for Pastor to finish saying grace before they dove in.

"Pastor," Jesse said with a mouthful of potato salad and a very nonchalant voice, "is there anything you would like to share with Recon and me about your past?"

Pastor looked across the table at Jesse, wondering what he was getting at. *He would only ask that if he knew something*, he thought to himself while he chewed slowly.

"Jesse, why don't you enlighten me with what you think you know about my past."

"Recon, do it."

"Pastor Raines, a.k.a. Thomas A. Cary, born and raised in Oakland, CA, only son of Elizabeth and Thomas Arthur Sr. You grew up going to Catholic school, did some time in juvie when you were thirteen for lighting a neighbor's cat on fire. At fifteen, you were emancipated and joined the military—"

"Just what are you getting at, Jesse?" Pastor shouted, slamming his fist down on the table, interrupting Recon. "Do you think I did this? Huh?"

"You are a CIA GHOST, are you not?" Jesse asked Pastor very calmly, eyeballing him, already knowing the answer.

Pastor was shocked with the discovery. A GHOST agent was never to be found out. GHOST agents were super-untraceable.

Jesse had connections somewhere. It's no secret that the CIA is the backbone for government tasks that, well, shouldn't be made public. CIA GHOST's are so classified and so secret, that not even the director of the CIA knows about them. There is only a head GHOST agent, known only as the Kaiser, a single recruiter and the agents themselves. "GHOST" was an acronym for Government-Hired Operative for Strategic Tasks. There were only ever fifty GHOST agents in the entire world at any given time. Most of which are killed in the line of duty and forgotten about.

Those who survive are never really retired; they just go into deep hiding. CIA GHOST agents are paid absurd sums of money and kept on retainer. GHOSTs were kept on call for life. In the rare event that you are "relieved from command," the U.S. government would gladly pick up the tab for your living expenses in some exotic location like Monaco for "services rendered" under a completely GHOST-like identity—completely untraceable.

CIA GHOST agents or GHOSTs as they were known by the few who knew them were highly trained and very intelligent individuals. All GHOSTs were former Navy

SEALs, Army Green Berets, or on occasion a lone Air Force Ranger who would sneak into the group. The group was tight, elite, and the very best of the very best.

"I am a GHOST, Jesse, that is correct. How did you find out?" Pastor didn't waste any time admitting this for he knew if Jesse knew his identity, he knew a lot, and it was pointless to lie.

"My job is to discover things, Pastor. To find things out. My job, Pastor, is to know more than everyone else, and I am the very best at what I do."

"You're smarter than you look, Recon," Pastor spouted out without looking at him.

"Pastor, this isn't about you," Jesse said, taking over the conversation. "I have a feeling we're being watched, and whoever wanted Karma wants one or more of us as well. All three of us have pasts here, we've all made enemies all over the world. This is a conversation we need to have."

"You can think what you want. No one is after me, Jesse, and I like it that way."

"Look, Pastor, tomorrow at the burial, just keep your eyes open. In the upcoming weeks, keep your attention focused. No one knows who you really are, but Recon and I and we are not going to give up your identity. We might need your help. As a brother, I am asking you to help us."

Pastor sat and thought for a moment. He knew in his heart that Jesse was "good people." He knew in his heart that he couldn't turn his back on a brother that has been committed to the same causes he had. He knew that Jesse could be right, and this just *might* be something other than what it seems. Regardless of where this was going, Pastor knew what he had to do.

Pastor stood up and looked Jesse in the eye. "I guess we never really are retired, are we, Commander?"

Jesse stood up and gave Pastor a man hug.

"Let's do this!" Recon shouted out. "Whoo!"

Pastor and Recon left about an hour later after some conversation was had about tomorrow and things to come. When they were out the door and it was locked behind them, Jesse sat down in his favorite black leather recliner to catch his breath. His faithful companion Louie was quick to jump up on his lap like he did frequently when he was a puppy.

"It's been a while since you jumped up on my lap, old fella. You doing, okay?" Jesse asked Louie as he scratched his pet and rubbed him behind his ears.

"You miss Karma, don't you? I do too, Louie, I miss her too." Jesse laid his head back and closed his eyes. In seconds, Jesse and Louie were both fast asleep in the chair almost as if they were comforting each other in Karma's absence.

Chapter 61

Monday

Chime . . . chime . . . chime . . . chime . . . chime . . . The clock on the wall chimed its way to five o'clock. Jesse opened his eyes and decided it was five in the morning with rays of sunshine on their way. Louie was still lying with Jesse, and knowing he had to get up, Jesse thought for sure Louie would have to go out.

"Louie," Jesse said, giving his companion a pet. "C'mon, boy, let's go out." Louie wasn't moving.

"Louie?" Jesse laid his hand on Louie's side; he wasn't breathing.

"Oh, Louie . . .," Jesse said out loud as his eyes started to tear. "No . . ."

Jesse pet Louie with long slow strokes the length of his body before holding him up to his chest to give him one last hug.

"You were the best dog ever, Louie. You were the best."

Jesse got up out of the chair, and with Louie in his arms, he headed outside. He carried Louie with love and care as he walked up to the crest where there was an empty hole for the ceremony later that day. Jesse carefully placed Louie on the ground and began to dig a smaller grave right next to the one he and Recon dug for Karma just the day before.

After the hole was dug, Jesse left to get Louie's towel, the towel that was used to dry him off after baths or wipe his feet with after walks in the rain. The towel that the two of them used to play tug-of-war with; it was Louie's favorite towel. Jesse carefully wrapped Louie up and gently placed him in the smaller hole. Louie was put to rest wearing his collar and his red bandana.

"So long, old friend. No fences, no leashes. Run free. You will be missed by many. I'll see you at the Rainbow Bridge," Jesse said as he pulled dirt over his beloved pet's body.

"Out here kind of early, aren't you, Commander?" Recon said as he approached Jesse on the crest.

"Louie died last night. He curled up with me in the chair and closed his eyes one last time. I just buried him."

"Oh, man, Jesse," Recon said, feeling the grief of his best friend. "I don't have the words."

"There aren't any words to be had right now, Recon, there just aren't any."

After the hole was filled, Jesse dropped the shovel and headed toward the house. Recon followed a few feet behind. The rays of sunlight seemed awfully bright for a day that felt so gloomy.

Perched on the other side of the lake were Jack Beaver and Dennis Rybka, both dressed in camouflage and lying low to the ground, watching, waiting to see what unfolds.

"I'm positive this is where my problem lives," Jack said to Dennis in almost a whisper. "I'm also positive that's where he's going to bury the woman, on the crest where that mound of dirt is."

"We can't take him out today, Mr. Beaver. Possibly tomorrow or Wednesday for sure."

"That'll be just fine, Dennis. I want the girl eliminated as well."

Dennis looked at Jack Beaver as if he were an idiot. They were sitting, watching, waiting for "the girl" to be buried. *Surely this clown can't be serious. What girl would this be?* Dennis thought with as much sarcasm as he could.

"Aren't we here to watch her go into the ground?"

"Not this girl, you fool! Erin, the girl who runs the restaurant for this guy! Get rid of her! Take her out too!"

"Mr. Beaver, I am not up here to be your personal mercenary. Take caution with how you talk to me."

"You'll do as I tell you you'll do, or I'll bury you under one of my pine trees myself! Take out Jesse and the broad and then you can go back to your pathetic little life wherever you came from!"

"Mr. Beaver, shut your mouth or your next words will be your last."

Jack Beaver grabbed a knife out of his boot, and without warning, he sprang on to Dennis' back. Jack grabbed Dennis' forehead with one hand and sliced Dennis Rybka's throat with the other. It happened so fast Dennis had no time to react. Gasping for air and suffocating in his own blood, Dennis squirmed for a few moments, grabbing his throat with both hands, but the wound was deep and precise. All he could do was die.

"My last words, huh? You're not worth burying underneath a pine tree. You can lie here dead, you pathetic little weasel. Looks like I have a new job and a new Ford GT. Thanks for your time and your help, loser!"

Jack got off Dennis Rybka's body and searched it for anything he could find. Car keys, cell phone, cash, and wallet were among the things he collected. Jack covered

Dennis Rybka's body with leaves and natural debris that were lying on the floor of the woods as if this was protocol.

"The wolves will get to you before anyone finds you!" Jack said to the lifeless corpse. Just as Jack was looking away, he noticed Dennis' boots. They were top quality, very rare American alligator skin, chocolate in color, typically retailing for around $13,000 a pair. His boots looked to be brand new.

"If your boots fit, I'll take them too!"

After slipping on Dennis' boots, Jack resumed position, lying on the ground with binoculars in hand, watching across the lake. He was determined to witness the burial, then he would have some credibility when Dennis' boss called. He would have the obituary; he would witness the funeral, and he could approach "the man" with the details of what he'd like to happen to Mr. Buck and the bimbo he had running his business. *I should have cut her throat when I had the chance*, Jack thought to himself while he lied on the ground watching across the lake.

Chapter 62

"Recon!" Jesse hollered, handing him the keys to his truck. "You need to get moving in order to get back here by 1:00 p.m. Everything has been taken care of and paid for, just hook up and go. Hurry back here, don't be late!"

"Commander, I've got this," Recon said, giving Jesse a man hug. Jesse watched as Recon headed out in a hurry. Before the cloud of dust Recon left while tearing out of the driveway had settled, Pastor was pulling in. Jesse watched as Pastor parked a mint condition 1966 Cadillac Hearse on the crest not far from the empty grave. He wasted no time heading toward Jesse.

"Here a little early, aren't you, Pastor?"

"I got a text from Recon. I heard about Louie, so I came to check on you."

"Yeah. It's been a bit of a tough morning, thanks for coming."

"Today isn't going to get any easier, Jesse. Regardless of what tomorrow brings, today is just gonna be a bad day."

"Today already has been tough, Pastor, there's no mistake in that. The rest is just going through the motions."

"I'm not sure I follow your train of thought there, Jesse, but I'll tell you what, you can explain it while I whip us up some breakfast."

Jesse and Pastor went inside and prepared breakfast. Pastor cut up the ingredients while Jesse put it all together. In no time at all, the duo had created a couple of sausage omelets with cheese, onion, pepper, and mushrooms, and were sitting down ready to eat.

"Let me say grace this morning," Pastor insisted.

"Don't pray for me today, Pastor, I'm fine."

"What do you mean, Jesse?"

"Maybe you'd better pray for the people I'm after," Jesse said with a cold soul. "I promise you, Pastor, this is gonna get ugly."

Pastor looked at Jesse sitting across from him. After a moment, a slight smirk started to spread across Jesse's face, almost like a child who had just gotten away with something. As Pastor read Jesse's mind, a sinister little grin crept across his own face, almost approving of the manhunt that Jesse was obviously plotting in his head.

"I think I'll take care of the praying, Jesse."

Breakfast was silent, nothing spoken between Jesse and Pastor. Pastor couldn't help but notice how quiet Jesse's house was without Karma and Louie. The noise would surely return in time, but today there was a quiet that was deafening, almost an eerie experience altogether. Very much like the calm before the storm, and Pastor was afraid that any storm brewing in Jesse's head could rage at epic proportions. Whoever was behind this just picked a fight with the wrong man. Words of wisdom: Don't mess with a Navy SEAL.

Navy SEALs don't know how to lose. They don't know defeat. They are masters of discipline and control, built on a mindset of courage and muscle. SEALs are resourceful creatures that are designed to fight, built to win, and bread to survive. There is nothing but victory. Now someone had completely crossed the line. Pastor knew that Jesse needed to be prayed for, but he really feared the life or lives of the responsible parties. Whoever is responsible for wreaking havoc in Jesse's life would be held accountable on earth *and* in heaven.

"Pastor!" Jesse shouted. "Did I lose you? Not hearing me? You busy praying?" Pastor looked up at Jesse and came back to his senses.

"Sorry, Jesse, I was lost in wonderland for a moment."

"Come out of the rabbit hole, Pastor, I need you. I need you to focus. Rod is going to be here soon; we need to get an omelet ready for him."

"Too late. He's about to walk through the door right now," Pastor said, seeing Rodney approach the front door through the window.

Sheriff Rodney walked right in and greeted Pastor and Jesse.

"You holding up okay, Buck?"

"Yeah," Jesse replied with a somber voice. "I didn't get your omelet made."

"That's just fine, Jesse. I'd prefer to do it myself."

"Help yourself, you know where everything is. I'm heading back to get showered and cleaned up."

"I gave Recon the stuff you asked me to!" Sheriff Rodney hollered down the hall as Jesse was walking away.

Without saying a word, Jesse went into his bedroom and shut the door behind him. When Pastor and Rod heard the door to Jesse's bedroom shut, they looked at each other. Pastor shrugged his shoulders, and Rod shook his head.

Rodney proceeded to make his omelet in silence, cutting up anything he could find in the refrigerator to put in: tomatoes, lunch meat, cheese, olives, some of this and a little of that. He even added some kielbasa that was more than likely left over from the last time everyone gathered here after church.

"Putting that kielbasa in your omelet might be a bad idea, Rod," Pastor shouted out as a suggestion.

"A little mold on your food won't hurt you, Pastor," Rodney replied while looking over his shoulder and shooting Pastor a wink.

"Maybe not, but a little food rot will."

"Not worried, Pastor. Penicillin's made from mold."

"Well, you'd better add some sugar to it then."

"Why is that?"

"Never mind Rod. I sure do hope Meo does most of the cooking at your house."

"Speaking of Meo, she's bringing a tray of hors d'oeuvres for everyone to nibble on after, well you know, after."

"After what, Rod?" Pastor poked at his friend who was more focused on his omelet.

"Hey, I don't do these things well, okay? Quit being a jerk, go save somebody!"

"Maybe the soul I'm trying to save is yours, Rodney."

"Okay, you're just creeping me out now. I don't need to be saved, just be quiet while I do my thing over here!"

Pastor chuckled at his friend's reaction. "You sure are easy, Rod. Meo *did* marry a big teddy bear, didn't she?"

"Don't let him get to you, Rod," Jesse said, reentering the room. "There's something wrong with that guy." Jesse shot Pastor a wink, letting him know his comment was all in good fun.

"Hey, Rod," Jesse said as he looked over at the ingredients cut up on the counter. "I wouldn't use that kielbasa if I were you."

Pastor and Rodney chuckled together when they heard Jesse's comment.

"We're already past that, Jesse," Rod answered.

"Thanks for meeting up with Recon this morning, Rodney, I really appreciate that."

"Yeah, huh, about that—"

"Stop!" Jesse interrupted. "Not another word about that to anyone, got it?"

"Got it."

"No one, Rodney, not your wife, not Georgia-Jean, not anyone."

"Not a word."

"Let's just get . . . I just want today to be over. Then we'll figure out the rest tomorrow or Wednesday."

Jesse took a deep breath and looked at the floor. He knew his temper was short and he needed to stay focused to get through the day. The last thing he wanted to do was to take out his frustrations on everyone, especially his friends.

"Look, guys, just give me some space right now. After the burial, we'll have some munchies that Meo is bringing and anyone that wants to stay for dinner can.

Chapter 63

By the time twelve o'clock came, everyone was at Jesse's house. Meo brought Georgia-Jean, Desi, and Erin in her bright red Jeep. Rod and Pastor were of course already there, and Recon showed up just after twelve. He was the only one *not* dressed in black. It really was a bright sunny day outside. You always picture funerals to be held on gloomy days in the damp cold; today, it was exceptionally bright. There was not a single cloud in the sky, and the temperature was warm, but not too hot. It was the perfect day for a celebration, not a funeral.

The time had come to put the casket in the ground. It was simple, nothing flashy. It almost resembled a pine box more than that of a high-dollar casket that you would find today. Karma would have wanted it that way. Jesse and Recon handled the top or head end while Rod and Pastor handled the bottom. The men placed the casket down into the hole next to the grave that Jesse filled over Louie just hours before. Not a single word had been spoken, and everyone was in tears.

After the coffin was in place, Jesse and Rod pulled the ropes out from underneath it and tossed them aside. Jesse placed some sunglasses over his eyes and stood alone with his head down. After a brief moment, he nodded for Pastor to go ahead and deliver the eulogy.

"Dear Lord, oh Heavenly Father, we lift up to you Rachael 'Karma' Meyer on this day . . ."

From across the lake, Jack Beaver was watching everything through his binoculars.

"One down, two to go," he mumbled to himself, still lying in the dirt. "Too bad you're not alive to watch this, Rybka, you might have actually enjoyed it!" Jack spoke out loud to the corpse lying to his right. "Yup, Rybka, you remind me of my son, Ned. Neither of you were the sharpest tools in the shed. I had to kill him too. Like you, his superego was a little too big for his britches.

Haha. The both of you were idiots! As soon as they start pulling the dirt over her, I'm leaving you here for the wolves."

". . . In the name of the Father, the Son, and the Holy Spirit, amen."

"Thank you, Pastor," Jesse said softly. "Why don't you and Rod take the women inside and Recon and I will finish up out here."

"I'll help," Rod added. "Meo, why don't you and the other ladies go inside, we'll be there soon."

Meo nodded her head and walked with the other women and Pastor inside to Jesse's house. Jesse, Recon, and Sheriff Rodney all started pulling dirt into the grave on top of Karma's casket. No words were spoken. Tears fell from all six eyes of the three men filling the hole. From across the lake, Jack was watching intently.

"Well, well, that's good enough for me. See ya, Rybka."

Jack Beaver pulled himself from the earth's floor and headed out. He'd seen enough. It was time to start planning.

When the three men were finished filling in the grave, there was a perfect mound, clearly identifying the burial site from anywhere on the property and certainly from across the lake. The final touch was a cross that Jesse made from pressure-treated wood that he covered with a black tar-like paint. He set the cross at the head of the grave and asked Recon and Rodney to give him a minute. Jesse knelt next to the grave and started to speak out loud.

"Karma, I keep telling myself this isn't real, yet I'm kneeling next to your grave. My heart is aching for you. I want to feel you in my arms again so bad. I promise you, love, we will find the man responsible for this and he will be held accountable. I love you."

Jesse got up and dusted himself off while he headed toward the house. When he was just a few feet from the door, his phone rang from his pocket; he had forgotten he had it on him. Thinking everyone that needed to reach him was already at his house, he pulled the phone from his pocket out of curiosity to see who it was. A 7-0-3 phone number was being displayed. *That's a northern Virginia number*, he thought to himself. *I'd better take this call.*

"Hello, this is Jesse."

"Mr. Buck, my name is Bobby Morgan, I am your father's lawyer."

"Yes, I know who you are, Mr. Morgan, how can I help you?"

"I'm afraid I have some bad news for you, Mr. Buck. Your father passed away on Friday. As I'm sure you know, I am the executor of his estate. You need to come home, son."

"Mr. Morgan, I'll see you in the morning."

Made in the USA
Middletown, DE
29 March 2022

63196220R10198